Things were always dangerous in a blizzard, but this was beyond the normal—something strange was definitely going on...

Jon went to the window again. "We really have to go now, Gregory. The snow is sticking, and the wind is picking up."

Jon and Gregory left Gifford smoking his pipe by the hearth and cautiously drove home. They lived in an old farmhouse on Yona Road with a white standard poodle named Renoir, a long-haired black cat named Felix, and a short-haired calico named Felicia. After making sure that their outdoor animals Vincent Van Goat and Sassyass were warm enough in the barn, Jon and Gregory settled down by the living room picture window to watch the blizzard. Near one o'clock Jon's cell phone rang.

"I wanted to make sure you all got home safely," Gifford said. "I just heard a big tree limb crack in Lottie's yard across the road. The night is noisy."

"We're fine, Giff. Thanks. We're eating popcorn, drinking tea, and watching the storm."

"Just a moment, Jon. Well, I'll be! I'm looking out my window now, and I see that Lottie has company. She'll have them all night if they don't leave soon."

"Did you call Fairfield, Giff?...Hello. Are you there, Giff?...Hello?"

Jon lost the cell connection.

On a cold winter evening in the small mountain town of Witherston, Georgia, antique dealer Hempton Fairfield auctions off rare Cherokee artifacts, Appalachian antiques, and a young African Grey parrot. Late that night, a blizzard stops traffic for a three-mile stretch of the Witherston Highway, prohibiting anyone's arrival or departure and stranding an eighteen-wheel semi full of chickens. The next morning two bodies are discovered in the snow, the chickens are running free, and the parrot is missing, leaving a number of unanswered questions. What happened? Where's the parrot? How did the chickens escape the stranded truck? Who rightfully owns the remnants of the thousand-year-old Cherokee civilization? Who killed the two men? *And*, most importantly, how many more bodies will turn up before the killer is caught?

KUDOS for *Fairfield's Auction*

In *Fairfield's Auction* by Betty Jean Craige, we are taken back to Witherston, Georgia, and the fun and crazy people in this small town in the Georgia mountains. This time, newcomer to the town, Hempton Fairfield, is an antiquities dealer auctioning off Cherokee artifacts, and the local Cherokees take exception. Two young Native American men create a scene at the auction, which results in their being arrested. After all the artifacts are auctioned off, Fairfield auctions an eighteen-month-old African Grey Parrot named Doolittle. Later that night someone steals the parrot and holds it for ransom. Mev, the town's detective, her husband Paco, and their two twin fifteen-year-old sons, attempt to track down the kidnappers and rescue Doolittle. Then the bodies start turning up and the team has a much different job than they expected, especially when they start examining the provenances on some of the artifacts sold at the auction. Like the first book in the series, this one is a fun read, with a strong plot full of twists and turns, charming characters, and delightful humor. ~ *Taylor Jones, Reviewer*

Fairfield's Auction by Betty Jean Craige is the second book in the *Witherston Murder Mystery* series, and like its predecessor, it's a cute, clever, and fun cozy mystery. A new arrival to Witherston, Hempton Fairfield, an antique dealer, holds an auction to sell Cherokee and Native American artifacts, which offends some of the local Native American residents. Later that night, one of the buyers, a man who bought a Cherokee blowgun is murdered. As the bodies pile up and the provenances of the things sold at auction come into question, the resulting investigation uncovers some deep dark secrets. Add in an eighteen-wheeler full of chickens, a few animal activists, an abused and talkative African Grey parrot who knows too much, and some weird and wacky characters, and you have a combination that's hard to beat. *Fairfield's Auction* is full of plot twists, colorful characters, and hilarious situations, mixed in with a few profound points on White Man's greed and abuse of their Native American neighbors making it both a thought-provoking and delightful read. ~ *Regan Murphy, Reviewer*

ACKNOWLEDGMENTS

I want to thank some dear friends for their help in this murder mystery. By brainstorming with me while I figured out the plot, listening politely while I read aloud to them my own words, reading the manuscript critically, and giving me their frank opinions, Susan Tate, Margaret Anderson, and Valerie Greenberg made writing this novel a whole, whole lot of fun. Margaret and Valerie read the manuscript in what I thought was its final form and let me know I still had some perfecting to do. Susan taught me a lot about the history of her home state and inspired me to set my mystery in north Georgia, a part of the country I hold dear to my heart. Valerie told me about chickens.

I thank my oldest friend, Sue Moore Manning, whose artistic ability I've admired since we were in first grade, for creating the drawing "Doolittle in the Chicken Truck."

I thank Holly Marie Stasco, a talented young graphic artist educated at the University of Georgia, for creating the maps of Witherston and North Georgia.

I thank the two young men who posed for the photos of Jaime Arroyo and Waya Gunter. They asked me not to name them.

In the early stages, I had many questions about transferring money, banking, and web security, questions which Pat Allen, Chuck Murphy, and John Rudy answered for me. Andrew Wills, a former student of mine who is now an attorney in Washington, DC, gave me the idea for the ransom payment. Thank you, Pat, Chuck, John, and Andrew.

I thank Terry Kay for inspiring me to write fiction.

I thank my African Grey parrot Cosmo for inspiring me to put a parrot in this mystery.

Finally, I thank my friends at Black Opal Books—Lauri, Faith, and Jack—for their confidence in me and their appreciation of my stories.

FAIRFIELD'S AUCTION

A Witherston Murder Mystery

Betty Jean Craige

A Black Opal Books Publication

GENRE: COZY MYSTERY/WOMEN'S FICTION

This is a work of fiction. Names, places, characters and incidents are either the product of the author's imagination or are used fictitiously, and any resemblance to any actual persons, living or dead, businesses, organizations, events or locales is entirely coincidental. All trademarks, service marks, registered trademarks, and registered service marks are the property of their respective owners and are used herein for identification purposes only. The publisher does not have any control over or assume any responsibility for author or third-party websites or their contents.

FAIRFIELD'S AUCTION ~ A Witherston Murder Mystery

Print ISBN: 978-1-626944-09-1

First Publication: FEBRUARY 2016

Published by Black Opal Books **http://www.blackopalbooks.com**

FAIRFIELD'S AUCTION

A Witherston Murder Mystery

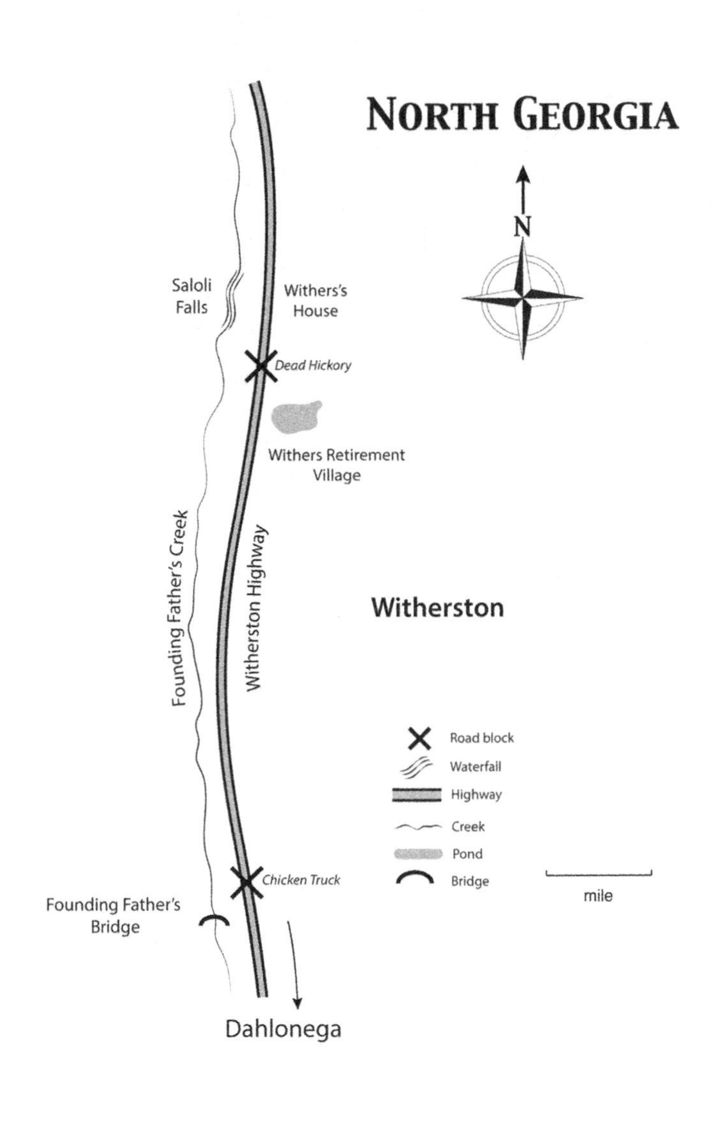
NORTH GEORGIA
N
Saloli
Falls
Withers's
House
Dead Hickory
Withers Retirement
Village
Founding Father's Creek
Witherston Highway
Witherston
Road block
Waterfall
Highway
Creek
Pond
Bridge
mile
Chicken Truck
Founding Father's
Bridge
Dahlonega

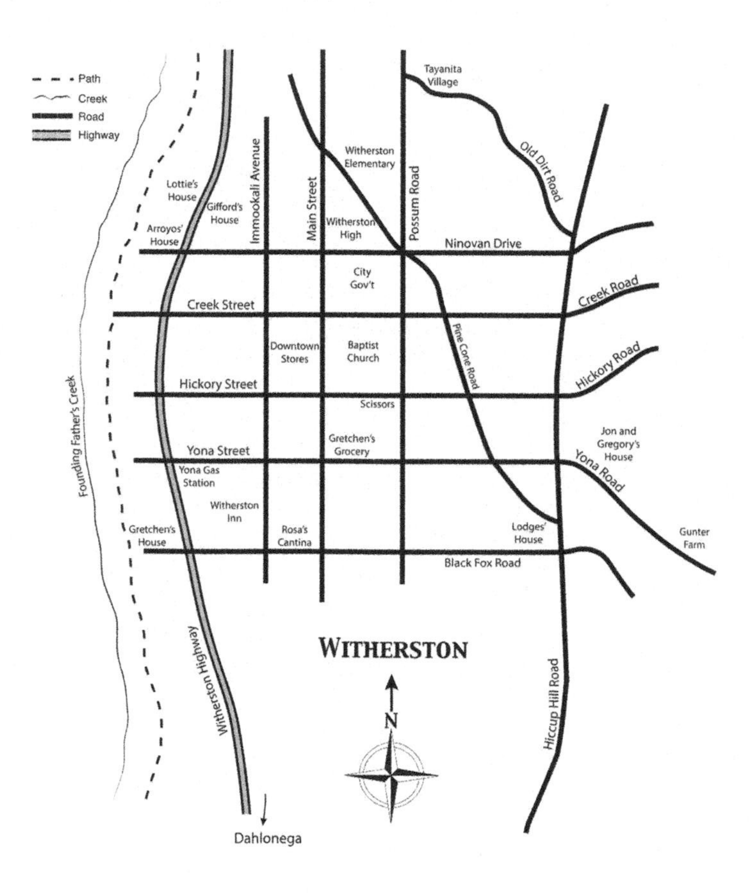
Path
Creek
Road
Highway
Tayanita Village
Old Dirt Road
Witherston Elementary
Witherston High
Possum Road
Main Street
Immookali Avenue
Lottie's House
Gifford's House
Arroyos' House
Ninovan Drive
City Gov't
Creek Street
Creek Road
Downtown Stores
Baptist Church
Pine Cone Road
Hickory Street
Hickory Road
Scissors
Founding Father's Creek
Jon and Gregory's House
Gretchen's Grocery
Yona Street
Yona Road
Yona Gas Station
Witherston Inn
Gretchen's House
Rosa's Cantina
Lodges' House
Gunter Farm
Black Fox Road
WITHERSTON
Witherston Highway
Hiccup Hill Road
N
Dahlonega

PROLOGUE

In Witherston, Georgia, a cell phone rang. A young man picked it up and read the text.

~ *Alpha, iMessage, Monday, November 30, 10:44 p.m. I have work for you. Do you want to earn $12,000 a year or more for 12 nighttime jobs?*

~ Who are you?

~ *Call me Alpha. I will call you Six.*

~ Why did you text me?

~ *I think you will like the work I offer you. By the way, I know where you live.*

~ What's the deal?

~ *The work is illegal. Does that bother you?*

~ Does it involve killing?

~ *No.*

~ OK, but no violence.

~ *No violence. Your first job, which is a test, is to kidnap a pet. When I give you an address, you kidnap the pet, send me a photo of it by instant message, leave a ransom note—which I will email you now for you to print out—take the animal to your home, and release it when I text you to do so.*

~ Where do I release pet?

~ *Anywhere the pet can be found.*

~ OK.

~ *If you are successful, I will give you other jobs. Small burglaries. Are you willing to do home invasions when nobody is home?*

~ For how much?

~ *I will pay you per job via a $1,000 gift card on Amazon.*

~ I prefer cash.

~ *You can use your Amazon gift card to buy jewelry to sell.*

~ That's all I have to do?

~ *You will have to drive to different cities in the Southeast.*

~ When will I meet you?

~ *You won't. Do you agree to these arrangements?*

~ Yes.

~ *In 5 minutes I will send you an email. Print out a copy of the attached ransom note to keep with you. When I text you an address, you must kidnap the pet within 24 hours. If you change your mind or search for me you will get hurt.*

~ When is my first job?

~ *December. Soon.*

~ This is risky. I want my pay up front.

~ *I will give you an Amazon gift card for $500 right now. You'll get it by email. Delete this conversation thread. Alpha.*

WWW.ONLINEWITHERSTON.COM

WITHERSTON ON THE WEB
Wednesday, December 14, 2015
8:00 a.m.

WEATHER

Temperatures will drop from a high today of 46 degrees Fahrenheit to a low of 20 degrees by midnight as a cold front moves into north Georgia. Witherston will be under a winter storm warning tomorrow, December 15, from 12:00 midnight to 10:00 a.m. The roads will be icy and dangerous with whiteout conditions possible in the early morning.

The sky is a hazy shade of winter.
Keep your eye on the weather guy.
~ Tony Lima, Weather Guy

ANNOUNCEMENTS

All Lumpkin County public schools will be closed tomorrow and Friday in the expectation of heavy snowfall.

Witherston City Hall will be closed tomorrow and Friday. Mayor Rich Rather recommends that you all stay home. The mayor's wife, Rhonda Rather, asks that you bring your pets into your house. She offers their home to any animals who need indoor shelter. I don't think she means chickens, but you'll have to ask her.

Founding Father's Creek Café will be closed tomorrow but open on Friday.

Witherston Inn, Witherston Inn Bar, and Witherston Inn Café will remain open during normal hours.

Gretchen Green's Green Grocery will remain open.

Scissors will be open tomorrow afternoon and Friday. Scissors owner Jon Finley asks his customers with appointments for tomorrow morning to come in at their convenience tomorrow afternoon.

Tony Lima says that his Mountain Band will practice tomorrow and Friday at 5:00 PM in Witherston Baptist Church's Reception Hall for their December nineteenth multi-faith holiday concert.

~ Catherine Perry, Reporter

LOCAL NEWS

Hempton Fairfield says that Fairfield Antiquities will hold its auction as scheduled at 8:00 this evening in Witherston Inn's Gold Nugget Hall. A cash bar will open at 7:00.

Harvey Goodridge will auction off antiques and Native American artifacts from Fairfield's collection. Mr. Fairfield will auction off a surprise item himself at the close of the auction.

Witherston Inn is filled with collectors from as far away as Seattle who have come for the event.
~ Catherine Perry, Reporter

LETTERS TO THE EDITOR

To the Editor:

If you haven't seen that yurt camp, Free Rooster, you should. It's on Tayanita Creek where Old Dirt Road intersects with Possum Road. What a disgrace to Witherston. The homeless people there—some ten or fifteen young folks—say they're living off the land, but they have refrigerators, cars, and computers.

Chickens run loose out there. They must drop their eggs all over the place.

I ask Mayor Rather: Please remove this eyesore. Send these folks away. Send them down to Athens where they will fit in.
~Red Wilker, Witherston

POLICE BLOTTER

Witherston Police Deputy Pete Senior Koslowsky arrested a high school sophomore, age fifteen, at 7:15 p.m. yesterday for hanging a squirrel's tail on the star atop Witherston Baptist Church's outdoor Christmas tree.

Pastor Paul Clement, who caught the boy in the act and reported him to the police, called the action a sacrilege. The boy said that the squirrel was already deceased when he took her tail.

The boy was fined $50 and released to his parents.

Witherston Police Deputy Pete Junior Koslowsky arrested two men in Rosa's Cantina at 11:30 p.m. yesterday for singing forty-two verses of the song "Ninety-nine bottles of beer on the wall, ninety-nine bottles of beer. Take one down and pass it around, ninety-eight bottles of beer on the wall." Elvis Smith, age forty-one, and his son Elvis Smith, Jr., age twenty-one, said that they were just entertaining the other patrons of the establishment when a local pastor got annoyed and called 9-1-1. The local pastor asked not to be identified. Smith and Smith were each fined $50 and released.

IN THIS MONTH IN HISTORY
By Charlotte Byrd

On December 14, 1830, Harold Francis (Harry) Withers, son of Hearty Withers and founder of Witherston, was born. Harry was to inherit the fortune his father had made in 1829 panning for gold as well as the forty acres of Cherokee land his father was to win in 1832 in the Georgia Land Lottery. He was also to inherit a lifelong hatred of the Cherokee people after witnessing his father's death at the hands of a Cherokee wielding a knife.

Harry's mother wrote in her diary on June 6, 1838, a week after the killing:

> *"We have to get rid of the Indians. We will never be safe as long as there is a single Indian left*

in Georgia. Fortunately, little Harry and I have our property. The Indian took my husband's life, but he didn't take our land or our gold."

Penance Withers and Georgia's other White settlers got their wish. In the winter of 1838-1839, in accordance with the Indian Removal Act of 1830, the federal government evicted 16,000 Cherokees from their homeland and marched them through snow and ice a thousand miles west to Indian Territory. On the way 4,000 Cherokees died of cold, starvation, and disease. Their journey to Indian Territory was called by survivors the "trail of tears," in Cherokee, nu na da ul tsun yi, "the place where they cried." The few who remained behind formed the Eastern Band of Cherokee Indians.

In 1890, on his eightieth birthday, a regretful John G. Burnett who had served in the mounted infantry that accompanied the Cherokees on the trek, wrote the following memoir for his children:

The long painful journey to the west ended March 26, 1839, with four-thousand silent graves reaching from the foothills of the Smoky Mountains to what is known as Indian Territory in the west. And covetousness on the part of the White race was the cause of all that the Cherokees had to suffer...

In the year 1828, a little Indian boy living on Ward Creek had sold a gold nugget to a white trader, and that nugget sealed the doom of the Cherokees. In a short time the country was overrun with armed brigands, claiming to be government agents, who paid no attention to the rights of the Indians who were the legal possessors of the country. Crimes were committed that were a disgrace to civilization. Men were shot in cold blood, lands were confiscated. Homes were burned and the inhabitants driven out by the gold-hungry brigands.

No wonder the Cherokee who slit Hearty Withers's throat was angry. But who can blame Hearty Withers's widow for being angry too?

And in 1937 Joanna McGhee Jones, a Cherokee resident of Miami, Oklahoma, told an interviewer collecting stories from the Trail of Tears this bit of family history.

> *"My mother was about twelve years old when they were forced to leave Georgia and I have heard her say that before they left their homes there the White people would come into their houses and look things over and when they found something that they liked, they would say, 'This is mine, I am going to have it,' etc. When they were gathering their things to start, they were driven from their homes and collected together like so many cattle. Some would try to take along something which they loved but were forced to leave it, if it was of any size. The trip was made in covered wagons and this made many of the women sick, but they were forced along just the same. When they reached streams and rivers, they did not want to cross and they were dragged on the boats."*

Why should this story matter to us Witherstonians? Because those of us living in the twenty-first century have inherited more than money and furniture from our ancestors. And we've inherited more than their genes. We have inherited perspectives and prejudices—through the stories we've heard at family dinners, the novels we've read, the songs we've sung.

We struggle through education to overcome these prejudices, but when we least expect it they reappear in our rhetoric, in our thoughts about each other, in our expectations of each other. Our heritage includes the mem-

ories that our parents and grandparents and great grandparents have bequeathed us. Some of us are descendants of the Whites who invaded the Cherokees' territory and took the Cherokees' land and gold. Others of us are descendants of the Cherokees who attacked the invaders. Our Cherokee friends and our White friends, as well as our friends of other cultural backgrounds, all have ancestral memories. The memories affect our behavior today, and the behavior of our children and our children's children.

Society is a relationship between those who are dead, those who are living, and those who are yet to be born, as the eighteenth-century philosopher Edmund Burke wrote. The past resides in the present. It's here, wherever we look.

MENU SPECIALS

Founding Father's Creek Café: Shrimp and grits, okra, coleslaw, chess pie.

Gretchen Green's Green Grocery (Lunch only): Baked acorn squash, sauteed purple cabbage, salad of mixed dark greens with balsamic vinegar from Modena, pumpernickel bread, apple sauce.

Witherston Inn Café: Barbecue ribs, fries, turnip greens, coleslaw, corn bread, pecan pie.

CHAPTER 1

Evening, Wednesday, December 14:

"And number twelve, Mr. Wilker, bids twenty-five hundred dollars for the Harpers Ferry Hall Rifle. Will somebody bid three thousand for it? Ladies and gentlemen, this rifle came from right here in north Georgia almost two hundred years ago. Mr. Wilker knows its value. He's a collector of fine weapons. So will someone give me three thousand for it? Three thousand. That would still be highway robbery. Nobody? How about twenty-eight hundred?"

Harvey Goodridge, wearing a tuxedo with a royal blue cummerbund, stood at the podium of Witherston Inn's Gold Nugget Hall. In a voice hoarse from high-speed auctioneering, the New York auctioneer described the weapon his beautiful assistant held up.

"This gun has a thirty-two-inch-long barrel. State of the art in 1831. And it was used by your ancestors, folks, when they protected the ladies and children from Indians and bears. Let's end this bidding, ladies and gentlemen. Twenty-seven hundred? Nobody? Twenty-six hundred? Nobody? Okay. Going…going…gone. Sold for twenty-five hundred to Mr. Red Wilker. Congratulations, sir."

Goodridge paused for breath and then, in a monotone, said, "Number twelve, please pick up your item and a certificate of provenance from Mr. Fairfield at the close of the auction."

Red Wilker stood up and waved to the crowd attending the town's first auction. He wore a red sweatshirt with a black hunting rifle on the front that advertised his store, Wilker's Gun Shop.

Goodridge got his breath back. His assistant brought out a Cherokee weapon this time.

"Here, ladies and gentlemen, is a four-foot-long river-cane Cherokee blowgun from the early nineteenth century. It's a prize. It's probably worth ten thousand dollars. You've had time to examine it and note the fine craftsmanship. And it comes with a thistledown dart." Goodridge held it up for the audience to see. "The Cherokee Indians, who lived in north Georgia and the Carolinas for a thousand years, employed the blowgun mainly for hunting small game. But for battle they poisoned the darts with viper venom."

"That's poison from a silly, slippery snake," whispered Jorge Arroyo to his twin brother Jaime.

"That would slither across the floor and slip under your door," Jaime whispered back.

"And slide up your leg."

"*Hijos*, be quiet." Paco said.

Mev—Detective Emma Evelyn Arroyo of the Witherston Police Department—could tell that her twin sons were getting restless. After the hour-long cocktail reception and silent auction, they'd sat still for another hour, watching Mr. Goodridge auction off expensive antiques before getting to the Cherokee artifacts.

Jorge and Jaime were genetically identical and indistinguishable from each other to most people. At almost fifteen years of age they were both five foot seven and a hundred and thirty-five pounds. They both had brown eyes and curly dark brown hair, which Jaime parted on the right side and Jorge on the left. They resembled their Spanish father more than their mother. Paco had brown eyes and curly black hair. The twins were both good students and, Mev thought to herself, good boys, though not particularly obedient. In the silent auction that preceded the live auction, Jaime had bid forty-one dollars on a faded pink silk rose for his girlfriend Annie Jerden. Jaime and Annie spent a lot of time with each other listening to sixties folk music, which Jaime was learning to play on his guitar. He was trying to persuade Annie to sing, since he couldn't. His voice was still changing.

Jorge didn't have a girlfriend, but he liked Mona Pattison, who was this year's Miss Teenage Witherston. She was also the new president of Keep Nature Natural, Witherston High School's environmental organization.

Harvey Goodridge glared at the boys. "Pay attention, ladies and gentlemen, and young men. This blowgun has probably killed more than a few of your forebears. And it could kill again. Your parents may want to bid on it."

Jorge and Jaime looked at their parents.

Paco shook his head firmly. "No," he mouthed.

"I will start the bidding at three thousand. Who'll give me three thousand dollars for this fine Cherokee blowgun? Three thousand, three thousand. Do I hear three thousand?"

A wealthy Atlanta collector held up her paddle. She was number twenty-nine. Her money came from stock in Lockheed Martin.

"The lady in blue bids three thousand dollars. She's number twenty-nine. Who will give me four?"

"Four dollars." shouted Thom Rivers, who stood along the wall with Waya Gunter, Atohi Pace, Atohi's wife Ayita, and their seven-year-old son Moki.

Hempton Fairfield, the antique dealer, rose out of chair at the side of the stage to point at Thom. "Who's he?" he demanded.

"I'll give you five dollars," Waya shouted. "That's more than you paid the Cherokees for it." He waved a hand-lettered cardboard sign with the words writ large *CHEROKEES WERE ROBBED.*

"May I ask you to arrest these delinquents for disturbing the peace?" Fairfield asked, addressing the one policeman in the room.

"I'll bid thirty-five hundred dollars if you'll arrest them," shouted Red Wilker, waving paddle number twelve.

Deputy Ricky Hefner did not respond.

"Arrest them," Fairfield said. "Now."

Mev knew both Thom and Waya, who were now young men. She had spoken to them at the reception and was amused by their antics. Obviously, Mr. Hempton Fairfield was not.

"Thirty-six hundred," shouted local attorney Grant Griggs, waving paddle number twenty-four.

"Thirty-six hundred, says the gentleman down front. Number twenty-four. Who will give me four thousand? Four thousand dollars for a rare blowgun. You'll never see another one like it. Four thousand?"

"Thirty-seven hundred," Red Wilker yelled.

"Who will give me four thousand?"

The art collector raised paddle twenty-nine again.

"Four thousand dollars says the lady in blue. Do I hear five thousand?"

Griggs held up paddle twenty-four. "Forty-five hundred."

A well-dressed older gentleman whom Mev had not seen before held up paddle number forty. "Forty-six hundred."

"Forty-six hundred dollars to the gentleman at the back table. Who will give me five thousand? It's a steal for five thousand. Five, do I hear five?"

"Right. It is a steal," Waya shouted. "First you wipe out our civilization because you think we're not civilized. Then you steal the things our civilization left behind, call them treasures, and sell them for thousands of dollars to rich people."

"That's enough," Fairfield responded. "Officer, I protest."

"You're selling our civilization. And we Indians have no money to buy it back. The only stuff we Indians own are memories passed down to us."

This time Deputy Hefner beckoned to Waya and Thom. Waya and Thom followed him out of the hall.

Grant Griggs waved paddle number twenty-four again. "Five thousand."

"Fifty-one hundred."

That was paddle number twenty-eight. Mev recognized her as Carolyn Foster, the newly appointed director of the Cherokee-Witherston Museum still under construction.

"Let me hear six thousand," Goodridge called out.

"Fifty-two hundred," Griggs said.

"Fifty-three hundred." Paddle number forty.

"Fifty-four hundred." Paddle number twenty-nine.

"Fifty-five hundred." Paddle number forty again.

Who was that gentleman? Mev wondered.

"Fifty-six hundred." Paddle number twenty-nine.

Goodridge got back into the game. "Ladies and gentlemen, let me hear six thousand dollars. Who will bid six thousand?"

"Six thousand," Gifford Plains said from the table next to Mev's. He held up paddle number twenty.

"Okay. The anthropologist—right?—bids six thousand dollars for this Cherokee blowgun. And the anthropologist must know blowguns! So will someone give me seven thousand? Seven thousand dollars. This Cherokee relic is a steal at seven thousand. Let's end this bidding, ladies and gentlemen. Seven thousand? Nobody? How about sixty-five hundred? Nobody?…Okay. Going…going…gone. Sold for six thousand dollars to the anthropologist. That's number twenty. Congratulations, sir."

"Woohoo," Jorge exclaimed. "Dr. Plains lives across the road from Aunt Lottie. We'll get to see the blowgun!"

"And the dart," Jaime said.

The auctioneer intoned automatically: "Number Twenty, please pick up your item and a certificate of provenance from Mr. Fairfield at the close of the auction."

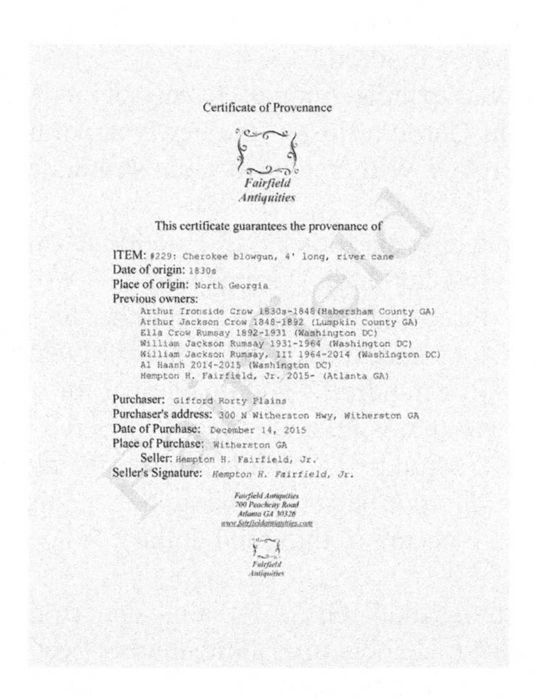

Certificate of Provenance

Fairfield Antiquities

This certificate guarantees the provenance of

ITEM: #229: Cherokee blowgun, 4' long, river cane
Date of origin: 1830s
Place of origin: North Georgia
Previous owners:
Arthur Ironside Crow 1830s-1848 (Habersham County GA)
Arthur Jackson Crow 1848-1892 (Lumpkin County GA)
Ella Crow Rumsay 1892-1931 (Washington DC)
William Jackson Rumsay 1931-1964 (Washington DC)
William Jackson Rumsay, III 1964-2014 (Washington DC)
Al Haash 2014-2015 (Washington DC)
Hempton H. Fairfield, Jr. 2015- (Atlanta GA)

Purchaser: Gifford Rorty Plains
Purchaser's address: 300 N Witherston Hwy, Witherston GA
Date of Purchase: December 14, 2015
Place of Purchase: Witherston GA
Seller: Hempton H. Fairfield, Jr.
Seller's Signature: *Hempton H. Fairfield, Jr.*

Fairfield Antiquities
700 Peachcity Road
Atlanta GA 30326
www.fairfieldantiquities.com

Fairfield Antiquities

Mev, Paco, Jaime, and Jorge had come to the auction just for fun. They had no interest in collecting art or antiques, but they took advantage of every form of public entertainment Witherston had to offer—high school sporting events during the school year, swim meets during the summer, outdoor markets, movies, fishing and hiking, and now the Fairfield Antiquities Auction, the first of its kind in town.

They were seated at a round table for eight with Mev's Aunt Lottie and their close friends the Lodges—Lauren, Jim, and son Beau. Although the Lodges were the only Black and White couple in very Whitish Witherston, they encountered little prejudice, for Dr. Lodge's patients cared less about his skin color than his medical skills and Judge Lodge's constituents cared more about their inheritance than her choice of a husband. Jim was a gynecologist, and Lauren was a probate judge. Mev believed that their acceptance in north Georgia signaled a decline in the racism that had long troubled the South.

Handsome, brown-skinned Beau, who had once been excluded from his classmates' birthday parties, had been elected president of the ninth grade on the basis of his leadership ability, his kindness, and probably his good looks. A collector of Cherokee artifacts, Beau had bid sixty five dollars on an ancient flint arrowhead in the silent auction.

Like the Arroyos, the Lodges had come to Witherston to stay, even though Lauren had to commute daily to Lumpkin County Probate Court in Dahlonega, twenty miles away.

Mev had counted interracial couples as well as same-sex couples among her friends at the University of Georgia. She herself had met the love of her life in Spain. She'd brought Paco back to Georgia before he could speak English, and she'd married him at her parents' home in Gainesville. A year later, she gave birth to her boys.

Aunt Lottie—known as Charlotte Byrd to readers of *Webby Witherston*, or rather *Witherston on the Web*—had moved next door to the Arroyos after her only son Brian had been killed in Iraq on Memorial Day of 2009. She seldom spoke of her sorrow. Retired as a distinguished history professor from Hickory Mountain College, Lottie devoted herself to the causes of animal rights, human rights, and a clean environment—whatever she believed would ease the suffering of this world. She drove a Smart Car, ate organic, and researched Cherokee history. In the evenings she worked on a book she planned to call *Invisible Persons*.

Lottie once said to Mev, "If you build something outside yourself, you build yourself." She was still building things outside herself.

Lottie leaned over to whisper into Gifford Plains's ear. "Congratulations, Giff. The blowgun is a great addition to your collection."

Gifford Plains and his wife Peg Marble were seated at the next table with twenty-one-year-old reporter Catherine Perry, Carolyn Foster, and two couples associated with the Cherokee-Witherston Museum.

"When Grant Griggs showed such desire for it, I decided I had to save it, for the sake of the Cherokees."

"I told Giff he was crazy. He didn't need more Cherokee weapons," Peg said.

Peg, Gifford's third wife who was half his age, had stayed in Atlanta when Gifford moved to Witherston upon his retirement from Emory University. She was a mystery writer and a collector of Cherokee antiquities, although she'd bid on nothing that evening. Meg thought she seemed more interested in reading and sending messages on her cell phone.

"Careful what you say, Peg," Gifford said. "Catherine is already writing an article about this auction for *Webby Witherston*."

Catherine smiled. "I am. I'll post it online before the evening is over. And then tomorrow I'll interview you, Dr. Plains."

A specialist in Cherokee culture, Gifford Plains was a fairly recent arrival to Witherston and the author of the widely acclaimed *A Nation Under Ground*. Although she didn't know him well, Mev found him interesting. She didn't know Peg at all, but she'd read Peg's books. She was amazed that Peg the fashionista knew so much about crime.

"Do any of you know paddle number forty?" Mev asked.

"David Guelph, from Seattle. A good man," Gifford said. "I know him slightly."

While Harvey Goodridge auctioned off other Cherokee relics—including an early twentieth-century rivercane fishbasket, which Carolyn Foster got, and an early-nineteenth-century black wood Cherokee mask from the Trail of Tears era, which David Guelph got—Mev thought about the Fairfields' recent arrival in Witherston. Hempton and Petal Fairfield had moved to Witherston within months of the small town's financial windfall. In the summer of 2015 every one of the town's four thousand residents had inherited approximately two hundred and fifty thousand dollars before taxes from the town's extraordinarily rich recluse Francis Hearty Withers. Upon his death, Withers had left one billion dollars to the municipality of Witherston and another billion dollars to the residents of Witherston to be divided equally among them regardless of age.

Mev, Paco, and their boys had each put their inheritance in the bank. She doubted that Jaime and Jorge would gamble away their fortune when they reached eighteen the way some of their older classmates had. The boys were already frugal.

Many Witherstonians said the Fairfields had smelled their money. But Mev figured the childless couple simply wanted to live in the beautiful north Georgia mountains. Hempton and Petal had bought Withers's hundred-and-fifty-year-old log home, gutted it, added decks and screen porches, reconfigured the interior, furnished it with Oriental rugs and Chinese antiques, and transformed it into a log mansion.

They moved in on Halloween and promptly held an open house for Witherstonians to admire their achievement. Mev guessed that Fairfield Antiquities in Atlanta was doing well.

"Grant and Ruth Griggs have zero interest in the Cherokee people," Peg said loudly to her table. "They're parking their money in whatever they think will rise in value."

At this moment Hempton Fairfield himself approached the mic. "I will auction off the last item myself," he said. Hempton wore a tux with a black cummerbund. With his carefully groomed flowing white hair, he was the epitome of the well-heeled antique dealer. "Petal, will you please bring out Doolittle?" he asked.

Fifty-year-old Petal emerged from behind the curtain wearing antique ruby-and-platinum earrings and necklace; a low-cut, long, black velvet dress that showed deep cleavage; and black patent leather high heels. She carried an eighteen-by-eighteen-by-twenty-four-inch silver bird cage to the podium.

The audience gasped. Inside the cage, with barely enough room to turn around, was a large gray parrot—well, mostly gray, Mev thought.

The bird had no feathers on his chest. He still had

gray feathers on his head and back, and red tail feathers, but he'd done serious damage to himself. "Oh my god," Lottie gasped. "An African Grey parrot!"

Hempton Fairfield spoke into the mic. "Ladies and Gentlemen, this is our beloved Doolittle. He is a young African Grey Parrot, a Congo African Grey parrot, who has lived with us for about a year. He's eighteen months old."

Jaime held up his hand. "Mr. Fairfield? Does he talk?"

"He sure does," Hempton replied, laughing. "Wait till you hear him swear at you."

"Can he fly?" Beau asked.

"No, his flight feathers are clipped."

Jorge held up his hand. "Why doesn't he have feathers on his chest?"

"He is molting," Hempton explained. "He's perfectly healthy and happy. He's like our child. Petal and I are selling him for one reason only. We travel up and down the East Coast all year, and we can't take him with us."

"And he doesn't like Tigress, our cat," Petal said, laughing.

"He looks sick," Mev murmured.

"*Pobrecito*," Paco said.

From across the room Lottie's friend Gretchen Green, owner of Gretchen Green's Green Grocery, yelled, "The bird is not healthy. Just look at him. And he doesn't belong in a tiny cage."

Hempton ignored Gretchen. "We got Doolittle last Christmas. He was six months old. We paid fifteen hundred dollars for him. But since we can't keep him, we have to sell him. Let's start the bidding at five hundred."

"You don't deserve to keep him," shouted Jon Finley, who was seated at a table with his life partner ecologist Gregory Bozeman, Gretchen, Gretchen's life partner Dr. Neel Kingfisher, Gretchen's Great Dane Gandhi, who lay quietly under the table, Gretchen's ex-husband Smitty Green, who was editor of *Witherston on the Web*, Smitty's wife Jane, and two young women Mev didn't recognize. Jon owned Scissors, Witherston's only beauty shop.

"Ladies and Gentlemen. Let's be civil here. Who will give me five hundred dollars for Doolittle?"

"You mean your child is for sale?" Jon asked. "Dear me. I thought the sale of children was illegal."

Lottie stood up. "I will give you two thousand to stop the bidding. And I will take Doolittle home with me now."

"Sold. And congratulations to Professor Byrd." Hempton Fairfield nodded to Petal.

"You will love Doolittle," Petal said to Lottie.

"I would have bid five thousand to take him out of your hands, Mrs. Fairfield," Lottie replied.

"Whoopee," Catherine Perry said. "I've got great stuff for my article."

"Does Doolittle come with a larger cage?" Gretchen asked.

"No," Hempton said. "But he does come with food."

"I'll get him for you," Gretchen called out to Lottie, who used a cane. She wove her way through the tables onto the platform, grabbed Doolittle's cage and the bag of Optimal Nutrition pellets, and spoke into the mic. "Before I die, I hope to see you too in a cage, Mr. Hempton Fairfield."

"May I speak with you, Dr. Byrd?" The young reporter for *Webby Witherston* wanted a quote from Lottie for her late-breaking online news article.

"Yes, Catherine, dear."

ꕥ

~ Alpha, iMessage, Wednesday, December 14, 9:49 p.m. Attention, Six. Stay in Witherston. You will receive your assignment tonight. Delete this message. Alpha

ꕤ

"It's a cold, dark night for you all to be walking," Jon Finley said to Gifford and Peg as they exited the building into a stiff wind. "Let Gregory and me give you a ride."

"Thanks, Jon." Peg accepted the invitation before her husband could decline it. Gifford liked to walk everywhere, despite his bad knee, no matter how inclement the weather.

Gifford protested briefly. "But my house is up near Lottie's. That's out of your way."

"No problem," Jon said.

The four of them climbed into Jon's white Ford Explorer, Gifford carrying the four-foot blowgun in his hand and Peg carrying the dart in a shoebox. As Jon turned on the engine he noticed the sleet beginning to hit his windshield.

"I'm glad I got this blowgun," Gifford said, "but I wonder where Hempton Fairfield got it. When Fairfield didn't tell us the provenance of the Ewi Katalsta pot, I started having doubts about the reported provenance of this blowgun."

"Well, you have a certificate listing previous owners," Gregory said. "You can do some historical research and check on them."

"And I will."

"I wonder about the provenance of little Doolittle," Jon said. "Lottie didn't get a certificate of provenance with him."

Jon slowly drove three blocks north on Immookali

Avenue, turned left on Ninovan Drive, turned right on Witherston Highway, and stopped in front of Gifford's A-frame house.

"Would you like to come in?" Gifford asked. "It's only ten o'clock, and nobody's going anywhere tomorrow."

"Do come in," Peg said. "I'm going upstairs to bed, but you all make a fire, open a bottle of wine, and enjoy the rest of the evening."

"Thanks, Peg. We'll watch the storm come in, but we'll leave before this house gets snowbound. We promise."

Peg went upstairs.

ೞೞ

Rhonda Rather took the ten o'clock call from Catherine Perry. "Mayor Rather is in the shower, Catherine," she said. "May I help you?"

"Hi, Mrs. Rather. I just wanted to give you all a heads-up. Chief Atohi Pace has petitioned a judge in Dahlonega to name his yurt camp off Old Dirt Road 'Tayanita Village.' He says he wants the community to be on Georgia's maps."

"Dear me. Chief Pace must not like the name 'Free Rooster Village.'"

"Will Mayor Rather give me a comment for *Webby Witherston*?"

"I'll have him call you in fifteen minutes."

"You all should have been at the auction tonight, Mrs. Rather. Dr. Plains bid six thousand dollars for a Cherokee blowgun and a dart. And Dr. Byrd bid two thousand dollars for a parrot named Doolittle who has no chest feathers."

"So the Fairfields are traders of birds, too? They will

buy and sell anything. If they'd lived in the nineteenth century, they'd have been traders of humans."

Rhonda loved animals—dogs, cats, donkeys, chickens. A year ago, well past the age of fifty, she'd unhappily gotten pregnant as a result of taking the drug Senextra. And then in June, she'd given birth prematurely to a baby boy and lost him. And although she was close to her daughter Sandra, she still wept for him. Since then, she'd devoted herself to the TLC Humane Society of Dahlonega. Giuliani, her female wire-haired terrier, was her constant companion. She spent more time with her than with her husband.

"I didn't mean to upset you, Mrs. Rather."

"Thanks, Catherine. That's okay. I'll tell Rich to call you. He'll probably be more interested in the blowgun than in the petition."

ᘓᘐᘓᘐ

Lottie was grateful for her friends' help with Doolittle. Gretchen and Neel put Doolittle on the back seat of their Jeep Wrangler because his cage, tiny though it was, wouldn't fit into Lottie's Smart Car. They squeezed Gandhi into Lottie's right front seat, to Gandhi's delight. Then they followed Lottie and Gandhi to Lottie's house, unloaded Doolittle, who had shrieked the whole way, and set the panicky parrot on the coffee table.

Gandhi promptly stretched out on the sofa.

As soon as Lottie opened the door to Doolittle's cage, Doolittle yelled, "Ugly bird!" His voice was unmistakably female.

"What? Did you hear that?" Lottie exclaimed.

"Bad, bad bird!" Doolittle screeched. "Doolittle is a bad, bad bird!"

Lottie tried to coax Doolittle out. "Come here, Doolittle," she said softly. "Do you want to go up?"

Doolittle lunged at Lottie from his one perch.

Lottie did not back off. After all, how much damage could an African Grey do if he bit? He could make her bleed a little but he couldn't take off her arm. Doolittle probably weighed a pound at most.

In September, Lottie had lost Darwin, her darling Pacific parrotlet. But she was ready to love another bird. She kept her left hand in front of the cage in a gentle invitation for Doolittle to hop up.

But Doolittle did not. Instead, he cowered against the back bars.

"Let me try," Gretchen said. "Doolittle, we love you," she cooed, putting her hand in front of the cage.

"Shut up," Doolittle responded, this time in a man's voice. Doolittle lunged at Gretchen. "Shut up! Shut the fuck up!"

Gretchen covered her ears with her hands. Gandhi jumped off the sofa.

Lottie removed the food and water dishes from Doolittle's small cage, gave Doolittle some clean water and a helping of the multi-colored pellets.

From the stone hearth, where he was about to light a fire, Dr. Neel Kingfisher said, "Doolittle has been abused." Neel had bought a Cherokee bone knife in the silent auction. He offered the wisdom he'd inherited from his Cherokee parents. "Listen to Doolittle with your heart, not your ears. What does your heart hear?"

"Fear," Gretchen said.

"Pain and suffering," Lottie added.

"Shut the fuck up! I'm gonna kill you!" Doolittle shrieked again—in Petal Fairfield's voice.

Then Lottie heard a commotion outside her front door. She opened it and welcomed her nearest and dearest kin: Mev, Paco, Jaime, and Jorge.

Jaime hugged her. "Hi, Aunt Lottie."

"We've come to see Doolittle," Jorge announced.

Doolittle growled.

Lottie left Doolittle alone with his cage door open while she uncorked and served her most elegant Spanish wine, a Mas la Mola Priorat, in honor of Doolittle's adoption.

"Here's to you, Doolittle." Lottie raised her glass. "May today be happier than yesterday."

"And don't let yesterday use up too much of today, Doolittle," Neel said. He had just gotten the fire going.

"*Salud*," Paco said.

Jaime offered his right hand to Doolittle. Doolittle promptly bit his finger.

"Ouch. That hurt." Jaime exclaimed. But then he offered Doolittle his left hand.

Doolittle climbed down to the bottom of the cage, and looked up at Jaime.

"Doolittle wanna apple?" asked Jaime, offering the parrot a bite-size chunk of apple.

"Fuck you," Doolittle said to Jaime, but this time softly.

Jaime put the chunk of apple into Doolittle's food dish.

"Look, everybody," Jorge said. He had his iPad open. "Mizz Perry's already got her story up on *Webby Witherston.* And it mentions you, Aunt Lottie."

"What does it say?"

"That you would have paid five thousand dollars to save the, quote, feathery little person's life."

"Let's see," Lottie said.

"Good story," Gretchen said.

"So now all *Webby Witherston*'s readers will know who paid what for those valuables," Mev said. "What if burglars read this?"

"They'll say, 'Thanks, Mizz Perry,'" Jorge said.

"*Hijos*, time to go home. It's eleven o'clock. Aunt Lottie has to get her beauty sleep."

"Aunt Lottie," Lottie said, "has to write her column for *Webby Witherston*."

As Jorge reluctantly closed his iPad, Doolittle stepped momentarily onto Jaime's wrist and then retreated into his cage.

WWW.ONLINEWITHERSTON.COM

WITHERSTON ON THE WEB
Wednesday, December 14, 2015
10:45 p.m.

LATE NEWS

Tonight, despite the dropping temperatures and approaching blizzard, Fairfield Antiquities held the first auction of antiques and Native American artifacts in Witherston's history. Gold Nugget Hall was filled to capacity. Sixty people came.

The event was memorable because of the much heralded surprise item. About 9:00 Hempton Fairfield began to auction off an African Grey parrot he called Doolittle. The parrot had no feathers on his chest. Dr. Charlotte Byrd bid $2,000 and got him. She said she would have bid $5,000 "to save the feathery little person's life."

The most valuable artifact sold during the live auction was a two-hundred-year-old Cherokee blowgun. Dr. Gifford Plains bid $6,000 and got it.

Waya (Eddie) Gunter, of Witherston, and Thom Rivers, of Dahlonega, were taken out of Gold Nugget Hall by police for disturbing the peace when they objected to the sale of the blowgun.

Other items sold during the live auction included the following:

Windsor rocking chair (1890s), $1,200, to Henry Avery Arbor of Charlotte

Antique silver hand mirror inscribed "Edith Rochester, Chattanooga, 1840," $1,900," to Carrie Rochester of Chattanooga

Cherokee Wood Mask (early 1800s), $2,300, to David Guelph of Seattle

Cherokee Quiver and Three Arrows (early 1800s), $925, to Carolyn Foster of Witherston

Harpers Ferry Hall Rifle (1831), $2,500, to Red Wilker of Witherston

Framed Cherokee Language Newspaper Sheet from Cherokee Phoenix (1830), $6,400, to David Guelph of Seattle

Cherokee Tomahawk (early 1800s), $2,100, to Grant Griggs of Witherston.

Thirty items were sold during the silent auction. Among those sold were:

Lot of 200 iron furniture keys (1800s-1900s), $95, to Christopher Zurich of Witherston

14-caret gold men's pocket watch (1890), $1,100, to Marcus Janson of Charlotte

Framed wood engraving from Harper's Weekly, "Broadway, February, 1868" by W.S.L. Jewett, $250," to Trevor Bennington, Jr. , of Witherston

Silver baby spoon and fork set (1900s), $160, to Sarah Sue Griggs, formerly of Witherston, presently of Atlanta

Chinese carved jade earrings on 18K gold (1890s), $965, to Karla Elsworth-Effington of Atlanta

Cherokee flint arrowhead (early 1800s), $65, to Beau Lodge of Witherston

Antique silk rose (1890s), $41, to Jaime Arroyo of Witherston

Framed marriage certificate (Withers Francis Withers and Obedience Olmstead, 1881), $60, to Dr. Charlotte Byrd of Witherston

Cherokee bone knife (early 1800s), $700, to Dr. Neel Kingfisher of Witherston.

One artifact not bought was a small Cherokee pot created by Ewi Katalsta in western North Carolina in the 1880s. Auctioneer Harvey Goodridge started the bidding at $1,500. After Dr. Plains raised questions about its origin, Mr. Fairfield declared it would not be sold.

According to Mr. Fairfield, the auction netted more than $50,000.

~ Catherine Perry, Reporter

ᘓᘓ

"Doolittle looks so sad," Jaime said to his brother, as they lay in their twin beds with the lights out. Mighty was already snoring beside him.

Mighty was the littermate of Ama, who lived with Neel, and Sequoyah, who lived with Beau. Beau had named Sequoyah after the early-nineteenth-century inventor of the Cherokee syllabary. Mighty, Sequoyah, and Ama were the unplanned offspring of Giuliani, Rhonda Rather's terrier mix female. Rhonda had given the puppies to Jaime and Jorge, Beau, and Neel at a party Jon and Gregory hosted the previous June. The three dogs looked like wire-haired Labradors, white, black, and reddish brown.

"Doolittle mutilated himself," Jorge said. "That's

what parrots do when they're unhappy. Monkeys, too. Even humans. I read about online. Parrots are social creatures. They live in flocks. If a parrot is stuck in a cage, he'll get lonely."

"I would, too."

"And if he's yelled at he'll get fearful."

"I would, too."

"And anxious. And depressed."

"Me, too."

Jorge sighed. "So to get his mind off his horrible situation, he'll pluck out his feathers."

"I don't have feathers. What would I do?"

"Bite your nails. Maybe scratch your arms till they bled. If you were an unhappy dog, you might lick a spot on your leg till it bled."

"Mighty's never done that."

"Mighty's happy. He gets a lot of cuddling."

Jaime was absent-mindedly stroking Mighty's back. Mighty opened his eyes briefly to register his contentment.

The boys listened to the sleet pounding the tin roof of the two-story cottage. For as long as they could remember they had ended their day with a bedtime conversation. Often they talked in the dark for twenty minutes before one of them turned on his side and said, "*Buenas noches, hermano*" and the other responded "*Buenas noches.*"

"Social animals need to be touched," Jorge continued.

"In a nice way."

"Yes, in a nice way. Social animals like to be preened by others."

"Want me to preen you, bro?"

"I'm being serious, Jaime. Monkeys like to be preened. Humans like to be hugged."

"And kissed," Jaime added. He knew about kissing. "I'm going to give Annie her flower tomorrow."

"So if a parrot lives with humans, he needs to be touched, in a nice way," Jorge continued. "And loved."

"All you need is love," Jaime intoned. He'd played the Beatles' song often on his guitar.

"Love is all you need," Jorge sang back. "If Doolittle gets love, maybe he'll grow back his feathers."

"He needs to get out of his cage. He needs to have some control over his life."

The boys were silent for a minute or two.

"Snow day tomorrow. What do you want to do, Jaime?"

"Play with Doolittle. Make him happier."

"And then let's go sledding on Old Dirt Road."

"With Beau."

"With Beau. And with Mighty and Sequoyah."

"And Annie, too. Okay?"

"Annie, too."

"*Buenas noches, hermano.*"

"*Buenas noches.*"

CHAPTER 2

Late evening, Wednesday, December 14:

"Cherokee brothers and sisters, it is eleven o'clock. I call this meeting to order."

Every Wednesday night in the Council House, Chief Atohi Pace led the fifteen members of Tayanita Village in an exploration of Cherokee history, a discussion of current affairs, and a prayer. As their elected leader, Atohi took responsibility for giving the young people pride in their culture.

Although none of the young people could claim to be a full-blooded Cherokee, they all identified themselves as Cherokee. They were dedicating two years of their life to living together with the ideals of their Cherokee ancestors. They ate locally, mostly from their vegetable garden, studied Cherokee traditions, took Cherokee first names, and obeyed the Cherokee Commandments, which they posted at the entrance to the Council House. Several were learning the Cherokee language. They called their community Tayanita Village—*Tayanita* being the Cherokee word for beaver—because it was on the banks of Tayanita Creek.

The community's imitation of the Cherokee way of

life was not perfect. These native Witherstonians all had smart phones, tablets, cars, and bank accounts. They lived in yurts instead of clay or mud houses. They enjoyed electricity and running water. And they all had day jobs, except for Amadahy Henderson, Galilahi Sellers, and Waya Gunter, who were students at the University of North Georgia in Dahlonega. Amadahy studied art, Galilahi studied early childhood education, and Waya studied biology. Atohi himself was a social studies teacher at Witherston Middle School.

CHEROKEE COMMANDMENTS

Honored by TAYANITA VILLAGE

Lumpkin County, Georgia

Remain close to the great spirit

Show great respect for your fellow beings

Give assistance and kindness wherever needed

Be truthful and honest at all times

Do what you know to be right

Look after the wellbeing of mind and body

Treat the earth and all that dwell thereon with respect

Take full responsibility for your own actions

Dedicate a share of your efforts to the greater good

Work together for the benefit of all mankind

Atohi, whose father owned the nine acres on which they'd established the village, had purchased the big yurt with his Withers inheritance. He outfitted it with a wood stove and chimney, two large clear vinyl windows, two large clear vinyl skylights, and a five-foot-seven-inch-high solid oak door opposite the chimney. And he furnished it with seven six-foot-long oak benches, which he placed in a circle, and traditional Cherokee wool rugs. In place of a third skylight, he sewed a canvas image of the Cherokee seal, so that, when his companions lifted their gaze in prayer, they could see the seven petals representing the seven clans of the Cherokee Nation. The yurt served Tayanita Village as the Council House.

Outside the yurt near the creek, Atohi installed free-standing solar panels to offset their electrical bills. A twenty-first-century Cherokee village needed electricity.

The other fourteen residents had each contributed ten thousand dollars to the village treasury to buy farm tools; seeds; a mule named Franny; a couple of nanny goats named Grass and Weed; a flock of twelve Buff Orpingtons, one of whom turned out to be a rooster; a chicken coop; and other equipment they shared, such as rugs, tables and chairs, pots and pans, dishes, glasses, and stainless steel flatware. Waya's father, Ned Gunter, gave the community a piglet named Betty whom they kept as a community pet. Betty spent cold days in the Council House by the wood stove.

During the summer, the residents had erected small yurts for sleeping quarters and constructed a log-sided kitchen and a log-sided community bathhouse with four shower stalls and four composting toilets. They cleaned up the old barn that had not been used for fifty years and filled it with straw for Franny, Grass, and Weed.

The Tayanita Villagers identified themselves as members of the Deer Clan, which in the Eastern Band of the Cherokee Nation once taught relaxation and unconditional love. They taxed themselves as needed. And they operated as a democracy.

"Brothers and sisters," Atohi said, standing in the center of the Council House. Snow had started to fall, but the yurt's interior was warm. "Today I filed a petition in court to give our community the official name of 'Tayanita Village.'"

"I thought that was already our name," Galilahi said.

"We can call ourselves whatever we want, right now. But to get our name on the map we need a judge's approval."

"I'm going to take down our 'Free Rooster' sign," Galilahi said. "Folks in town are calling us 'Free Rooster Village.' That's insulting. Anyway, Rooster Brewster takes good care of his hens, and I think he should stay."

"Me too," little Moki said, sitting cross-legged at his father's feet with one of the Village's innumerable cats in his lap and Betty Pig at his side.

"Okay, Rooster Brewster stays," Atohi said.

"Yea!"

The chief turned serious. "Tonight I want to talk to you all about something even more important than our name," he said. "Tonight Ayita, Moki, Waya, and I witnessed a sale of Cherokee culture."

"And a blowgun," Moki said.

Moki and Ayita lived in Cherokee, North Carolina, when school was in session. Both Ayita and Atohi wanted Moki to attend the tribally operated Cherokee Central School there, which immersed students in the Cherokee language and integrated Cherokee culture into the curriculum.

Moki, in second grade, was learning Cherokee history. He was also learning about Cherokee weapons.

"Tonight, Mr. Hempton Fairfield held an auction at Witherston Inn," Atohi continued. "Waya, Ayita, Moki, and I attended the auction to see what Cherokee treasures were being sold. Waya carried a sign that said 'Cherokees were robbed' to remind everybody that they were buying stolen goods."

"Let me tell what happened," Waya interrupted. "Mr. Fairfield did not appreciate my reference to historical events, and he asked Deputy Hefner to take me away. After a while, Deputy Hefner did. He took Thom and me to the police station for disturbing the peace. He fined us each fifty dollars, took my sign, and let us go. Deputy Hefner is part Cherokee, and he must have had some feelings about folks bidding for Cherokee stuff."

Amadahy Henderson raised her hand. "Chief Pace, what Cherokee stuff was sold?"

Atohi consulted his tablet. "A four-foot river-cane Cherokee blowgun, probably made nearby in the early 1800s. It went for six thousand dollars. A ceremonial wood mask, carved from poplar tree wood and painted black, also from the early 1800s, I guessed. It went for twenty-three hundred dollars. Bought by an older white man from Seattle, David Guelph. And then some less expensive things. A rabbit-skin quiver for nine hundred and twenty-five dollars. A woman named Carolyn Foster got it for the Cherokee-Witherston Museum. I was glad she got it. And a Cherokee bone knife that Dr. Kingfisher bought for seven hundred for his collection."

"Who bought the blowgun?" John Hicks, twenty years old, brown-skinned, six feet three inches tall, and muscular from his work as a carpenter and painter, stood up to ask his question.

"Professor Gifford Plains. You know him because you painted his house last summer. He lives over on Witherston Highway."

"I should have guessed. Yes, I do know him. And I know what he has inside his house. A collection of weapons that were made by our people and stolen from our people."

"That's why I carried my sign, John," Waya said.

John remained standing. "I should have taken those weapons from Professor Plains's display cabinets and given them to the Museum of the Cherokee Indian in North Carolina. Maybe someday I will."

"Was anything else sold, Chief?" asked Galilahi, whose Cherokee name fitted her well. It meant attractive.

"A tomahawk, bought by our local attorney Grant Griggs. And then something I would have liked to bring back to Tayanita Village. A page from the *Cherokee Phoenix* newspaper, which as you all know was published in New Echota between 1828 and 1834. The page was dated September 4, 1830. I have a photo of it that I took with my tablet. It carried a letter to the editor signed by three Cherokees about an injustice done to them by the state of Georgia."

Atohi looked at his tablet. "These three Cherokees were digging for gold on land that belonged to the Cherokee Nation along the Chestatee River. The Chestatee was the boundary line between Cherokee territory and Georgia. The Cherokees had already been forbidden to dig there by a Georgia judge, but they didn't consider a mandate from the state of Georgia binding on Cherokees digging on Cherokee land. The three were arrested by a sheriff, taken forcibly into the state of Georgia, marched for three days until they reached Watkinsville, fined ninety-three dollars by a judge there for contempt of court, and ordered to appear before the court in Gainesville two weeks later. One of the three men who authored the letter may have been your ancestor, John. His name was Elijah Hicks."

"Right. Elijah Hicks was my ancestor," John agreed. "My father told me about him. He edited the *Cherokee Phoenix*. After Elias Boudinot."

"By the way, that newspaper page was framed just like a painting to be hung on a wall."

"Who bought it?" asked Galilahi.

"David Guelph. Same man who bought the mask. He got it for sixty-four hundred dollars."

John stood up again. "So a rich White man whose ancestors perpetrated an injustice on our Indian ancestors decorates his wall with a page from the *Cherokee Phoenix* where our ancestors tell of the injustice. I view that newspaper page as a testament to the White man's crime. David Guelph views it as an historical curiosity. David Guelph, Gifford Plains, Hempton Fairfield—they're all alike. They're White traders buying Cherokee artifacts that are rare and valuable, too valuable for us Indians to buy." John sat down.

Atsadi Moon stood up. "I don't want to defend the White man's trade of our cultural treasures, John, but I have a point to make. Our culture's achievements must be preserved. The first newspaper written in the Cherokee language, and the blowgun, and the mask, they all must be preserved somewhere. Otherwise our culture will disappear. Like dust in the wind. As though the Cherokee Nation never existed. If rich people buy our treasures, at least they will take care of them. And scholars like Professor Plains will write about them."

"I disagree, Atsadi."

"I know, John."

"I don't want our history, or anybody else's history, to be converted into curios."

"Neither do I, John."

"You should see Gifford Plains's living room. He has our culture's weapons in glass cabinets, curio cabinets."

"In a perfect world, they'd be in museums, John. But we don't live in a perfect world. We live in a world where everything is for sale," Atohi said.

"Do you know what curio cabinets are? They're cabinets that display curiosities. Cherokee weapons are just curiosities to White folks who buy them," John said.

"Daddy, tell them about the parrot."

Atohi did. When he had concluded his account of Fairfield's sale of Doolittle to Charlotte Byrd, he said, "I am as distressed about humans' mistreatment of animals as I am about humans' mistreatment of other humans. Mistreatment of others—human or animal—comes from the inability to see the soul in the body of someone else. For Fairfield, Doolittle was just a commodity to be traded, like the mask, the blowgun, and the newspaper. For owners of slaves, Africans and Cherokees were just commodities to be traded, soul-less commodities."

"Commodities don't have souls, Daddy?"

"Not to their sellers, son," Atohi said.

"Were Cherokees slaves?" Galilahi asked.

"Yes, Galilahi, some Cherokees were kept in bondage before African slaves were brought to our continent. But Cherokees also kept slaves. They made slaves of war captives. Slavery is an old institution."

"How could anybody do that to other humans?"

"People who can't empathize with someone different can turn anyone into a commodity, or anything: people, parrots, land, water, and the remnants of once glorious civilizations."

"We bought chickens. We bought them for their eggs," Hiawassee Moon, Atsadi's sister, said. "We turned them into commodities."

"But we named them," Galilahi said.

"Allie, Lassie, Bonnie Laurie, Zany, Ginny, I forget the others," Moki said.

"And we let them range free in our village," Atsadi said. "They're in their coop only at night."

"To be safe from foxes," Moki said.

The fifteen Tayanita Villagers fell silent. They listened to the sleet strike the yurt's canvas top.

"It's eleven thirty, brothers and sisters. Snow is on the way. Let us pray," Atohi said.

The villagers stood, held hands in a circle, and looked up at the seal of the Cherokee Nation as their chief intoned, "Oh great spirit, who made the earth and the family of life, look kindly upon all the creatures who share your land. Take away the arrogance and hatred that divide and destroy us. Help us see ourselves as our neighbors—birds, deer, fish, and other humans—see us. And help us treat each other well, for we all need each other."

Then the villagers dispersed.

ᔓᔕ

Six got a message from Alpha at eleven forty-five.

~ Alpha, iMessage, Wednesday, December 14, 11:45 p.m. Go to 301 N Witherston Hwy. Charlotte Byrd lives there alone. Take the bird. Delete this message. Alpha.

ଓଃଓଃ

Mev sat in her living room with a cup of chamomile tea listening to the sleet. Paco was in the shower, and the boys were in bed. She was alone with her thoughts. She remembered the sign Eddie Gunter had carried into Gold Nugget Hall that evening: *Cherokees were robbed. Eddie*—she still thought of him as Eddie, though he'd asked to be called Waya—*was right. The Cherokees had indeed been robbed. At least their culture had been stripped of whatever valuables their conquerors, who were her ancestors, had coveted. To the victor go the spoils. Always and forever.*

Mev imagined how she would have felt if she'd seen her mother's jewelry auctioned off to a bidder from a society very different from her own, say China or Kuwait. How she would have felt if she'd seen her grandmother's wedding stemware auctioned off to wealthy buyers from China or Kuwait. If she'd seen her great grandfather's diary auctioned off to Chinese or Kuwaiti collectors of American artifacts. She understood Eddie's point.

Will the heritages of all the world's civilizations be auctioned off to the highest bidders, the victors, the ones with money? Mev wondered.

She had learned quite a bit about Eddie from Paco, who was fond of him. Little Eddie Gunter was not a full-blooded Cherokee, not even half-blooded. In fact, Eddie did not know he had any Cherokee ancestors at all until his senior year when his history teacher, Miss Whitbred, mentioned that the Trail of Tears went through Gunter's Landing in northern Alabama, a place now known as Guntersville. According to Paco, who was Eddie's homeroom teacher, Eddie got curious, did genealogical research for his term paper, and discovered he was descended from John Gunter, of Gunter's Landing, and

Ghe-Go-He-Li, a daughter of Cherokee Chief Bushyhead. Eddie graduated from high school, became Waya, and moved to Tayanita Village.

Now Waya was probably in jail with Thom just for annoying the wealthy Mr. Hempton Fairfield. She'd check on them in the morning.

Before going upstairs to bed, Mev glanced through her window at her aunt's house. She saw Lottie's kitchen light go out. Aunt Lottie must be going to bed too, she thought. And Doolittle must already be asleep. The two of them would be life partners, just as Aunt Lottie and her parrotlet Darwin had been. Doolittle was a lucky bird to have found Aunt Lottie. And Aunt Lottie was a lucky human to have found Doolittle.

The cuckoo clock the boys had given them last Christmas struck twelve. Twelve cuckoos. She'd become oblivious to the cuckoos over the past year, but now she noticed the time.

Gifford, Jon, and Gregory talked about the events of the evening while they finished the bottle of wine.

At midnight Jon looked out the window. "We should be going, Gregory," he said. "The sleet has turned to snow."

"Just a minute, Jon. I'm curious about something." Gregory pulled his mini tablet out of his jacket.

"Let's see your certificate, Giff," Gregory said. "I'm going to Google some of the previous owners of your blowgun."

"Here it is," Giff said. He handed it to Gregory and then answered a cell phone call. "Hi, Dave...Yes, indeed...We got what we wanted. I have some guests leaving now. I'll call you back."

"Well, I give up," Gregory said after two minutes. "You'd think there'd be some record of an Al Haash in DC. I can't find any reference to him on the web, not even an obituary in the Washington papers. It's as if he didn't exist."

"The first owner was from Habersham County," Jon said, looking at the certificate. "Lottie can find out who the Crows were."

"I think I'll give Lottie a call," Giff said. "And Hempton Fairfield too, to ask him where he got his Cherokee artifacts."

"Are you going to call Fairfield tonight?"

"Maybe."

Jon went to the window again. "We really have to go now, Gregory. The snow is sticking, and the wind is picking up."

Jon and Gregory left Gifford smoking his pipe by the hearth and cautiously drove home. They lived in an old farmhouse on Yona Road with a white standard poodle named Renoir, a long-haired black cat named Felix, and a short-haired calico named Felicia. After making sure that their outdoor animals Vincent Van Goat and Sassyass were warm enough in the barn, Jon and Gregory settled down by the living room picture window to watch the blizzard. Near one o'clock Jon's cell phone rang.

"I wanted to make sure you all got home safely," Gifford said. "I just heard a big tree limb crack in Lottie's yard across the road. The night is noisy."

"We're fine, Giff. Thanks. We're eating popcorn, drinking tea, and watching the storm."

"Just a moment, Jon. Well, I'll be! I'm looking out my window now, and I see that Lottie has company. She'll have them all night if they don't leave soon."

"Did you call Fairfield, Giff?...Hello. Are you there, Giff?...Hello?"

Jon lost the cell connection.

ଓଓ

"No more," Ignacio Iglesias said. "Time to go. I close.

It was twelve-thirty. Elvis Smith, Jr., and his party of three women had just left Rosa's Cantina, singing "She'll be coming 'round the mountain when she comes."

The two men still there were drinking beer margaritas at the bar. They had downed two in thirty minutes. The wind was picking up.

"Adiós," the short man said.

"One more, okay? One for the road," the tall man said.

"No. You drink too much. Pay and go."

The men conferred while Ignacio waited. He didn't understand English well.

The tall one dropped two bills on the table.

"Here's thirty."

"Gracias." Ignacio looked out the window of the tavern. "Look. Your trucks have snow. Get out of here. *¡Váyanse!*"

The men got up, put on their jackets, and walked unsteadily into the white night.

Ignacio watched their trucks head north on Immookali Avenue. He hoped they'd get home safely, wherever they lived. He was Mexican, undocumented, new to town, and in need of his job.

ଓଓ

Lottie sat up in bed when she heard someone open the front door, which she never locked.

"Who's there?"

"Be quiet, Dr. Byrd, and you won't get hurt."

She heard a man, two men, in the living room. "Get out of here! Get out of my house, now," she yelled.

"I'll tie her up, buddy. You stay here. Take the bird's picture. Here's my cell."

"Don't touch my bird!"

A tall man entered the dark bedroom. He was wearing a ski mask.

Lottie struggled to get out of bed. The man grabbed her.

Lottie kicked him as hard as she could, barefooted.

"Ow! Stop it, lady! Stop it!"

"Leave Doolittle alone!"

"Fuck you! Fuck you," Doolittle screamed.

"Fuck you, too, dumb bird!"

The tall man threw a blanket over Lottie and tied her up with duct tape. He then put duct tape across her mouth. She couldn't move and she couldn't speak.

"Hurry," she heard another man say from her living room.

"I'm almost done," the tall man said.

"Someone's coming."

The tall man left the bedroom. "She won't be going anywhere. Here give me the cage."

"Fuck you!"

"We're gonna be seen."

"No, we're not. Cool it."

ಌಌ

A cell phone rang. *OO EE AW AW*. The tall man took the phone call. It was one-fourteen. "Thanks, buddy. I'm okay. Are you okay?…I'll call you later."

Then he received a text message.

~ Alpha, iMessage, Thursday, December 15, 1:15 a.m. What's happening?

~ I have bird. Here is picture. But I had trouble.

~ What kind of trouble?

~ Bad.

~ Don't get caught. Do anything you need to do.

~ OK.

~ You understand?

~ Yes.

~ I will pay you well for whatever you have to do.

~ Right. I need money.

~ You'll get your money. Delete this message. Alpha

WWW.ONLINEWITHERSTON.COM

WITHERSTON ON THE WEB
Thursday, December 15, 2015
8:45 a.m.

LOCAL NEWS

Witherston is snowbound. According to Witherston Chief of Police Jake McCoy, the slow-moving traffic on both lanes of Witherston Highway came to a standstill at 1:30 a.m. in the blizzard. A southbound eighteen-wheeler chicken truck skidded on the ice on Witherston Highway a mile south of town, ended up sideways across northbound and southbound lanes, and stopped traffic in both directions. It is still stuck in the snow.

About the same time, a huge dead hickory tree fell across North Witherston Highway, two miles north of town, blocking both lanes of traffic just beyond Withers Retirement Village. It is still on the ground.

Officials from the Georgia Department of Public Safety, observing the situation by helicopter this morning, reported 14 vehicles trapped on this three-mile stretch of highway.

The driver of a Dodge minivan made the first 9-1-1 call at 1:32 a.m. He said he had rear-ended the Ford Focus immediately in front of him.

The elderly driver of the Ford Focus, Buck Heller, appeared to have suffered a heart attack and was still unconscious at 2:00 a.m., when deputies Pete Senior Koslowsky and Pete Junior Koslowsky arrived on the scene. Heller was taken by AirLife Georgia to Emory University Hospital in Atlanta.

The driver of the chicken truck was not hurt. Neither was his dog.

Mayor Rich Rather asks that drivers and passengers stay in their vehicles. Anybody who can donate or help deliver food or gasoline to the stranded travelers should email Rhonda Rather at rhondawoodrather@gmail.com.

Wreckers are on their way from Dahlonega and are expected to clear the highway by early this afternoon.

Raccoon Tree Service will remove the fallen hickory tree.

~ Catherine Perry, Reporter

POLICE BLOTTER
8:30 a.m.

Witherston Police are searching for one or possibly two individuals who released at least 40 white broiler chickens between 1:30 and 2:00 a.m. this morning from an eighteen-wheeler tractor-trailer truck that got stuck in the snow on South Witherston Highway about a mile below Witherston. The vandal or vandals moved some of the crates around inside the truck and tossed others onto the road. The truck was carrying the chickens to a poultry processing plant.

Deputies Pete Junior Koslowsky and Pete Senior Koslowsky discovered the vandalism when they were pecked by some runaway chickens.

Apparently, nobody in the stalled vehicles saw anybody in the blizzard.

Witherston Police escorted Thom Rivers, age nineteen, and Waya (formerly known as Eddie) Gunter, age twenty, out of Golden Nugget Hall last night after Gunter and Rivers disrupted the Fairfield Antiquities auction. Waya, who is of Cherokee descent, told Deputy Ricky Hefner that he was simply exercising his right of free speech when he held up a sign that said "Cherokees were robbed," and that he should not be arrested. Thom said that he had mistakenly put in an excessively low bid because he misunderstood the auctioneer.

The men were fined $50 each for disturbing the peace and released. Waya gave his address as Tayanita Village—lately referred to as Free Rooster Village. Thom, formerly of Witherston, gave his address as Hawk Nest Apartments in Dahlonega. Thom said he was returning to Dahlonega from Cherokee, North Carolina, and he had stopped in Witherston to see his high school friend.

Both men graduated from Witherston High School. Waya attends the University of North Georgia. Thom works at Corkscrew Wine and Spirits in Dahlonega.

WEATHER
8:00 a.m.

The record-setting blizzard of 2015 which started at midnight has so far deposited 10 inches of snow on Witherston. Winds have died down but have left big drifts across sidewalks and streets. Light snow is predicted to fall most of the morning. At noon skies will clear and by 3:00 PM temperatures will rise to 50 degrees or so.

If the snow starts to melt in the sunshine and freezes

again tonight, Witherston will be an ice village. So build fires in your fireplaces and get out your candles, folks. We may lose our electricity. I'm dreaming of a white Christmas.

~ Tony Lima, Weather Foreteller

LETTERS TO THE EDITOR

To the Editor:

Mr. Red Wilker is mistaken. We are not homeless. Tayanita Village is our home. We have shelter, food, and, most importantly, each other. We are a community. The fifteen of us live off the land in honor of our Cherokee forefathers. If the Cherokees could live off the land before White people gave them their "civilization," so can we.

Please, Mr. Wilker, use our proper name. It's Tayanita Village. "Free Rooster" is a sign we put up on Old Dirt Road to give away a Buff Orpington rooster to a good home.

And by the way, Mr. Wilker, our chickens do not lay eggs all over the place. In fact, they don't lay eggs at all in the winter months. Unlike commercial egg farmers, at Tayanita Village we don't force our chickens to lay eggs all year long by keeping lights on in their coop.

~ Waya Gunter, Tayanita Village

To the Editor:

Our chickens Hillary, Oprah, Frida, Harriet Beecher Stowe, and Lucille Ball take offense at Mr. Wilker's let-

ter. I would like to ask Mr. Wilker why he doesn't like chickens.

Mr. Wilker, owner of Wilker's Gun Shop, collects weapons. Other people collect chickens.

Dear reader, which makes you feel safer: bullets or eggs?

~ Scorch and Abby Ridge, Witherston

IN THIS MONTH IN HISTORY
By Charlotte Byrd

In December of 1826, Charles R. Hicks took authority over the Cherokee Nation when his predecessor Chief Pathkiller was on his deathbed. Pathkiller was the last hereditary principal chief of the Cherokees and the last full-blooded chief. Charles R. Hicks, who died shortly thereafter in January of 1827, was the first chief with European ancestry, that is, with some European ancestry. Chief Charles Hicks was succeeded by his younger brother, Chief William Hicks.

The shift in power from full-blooded Pathkiller to mixed-blooded Hicks was symbolically important to both Cherokees and whites, for it signaled the incipient integration of the Cherokee people into the white population. Charles Hicks was bilingual, well educated, and Christian, and his personal library was one of the largest in North America. As a Cherokee leader he advocated acculturation.

In 1832 Charles Hicks's son Elijah became the second editor of the Cherokee Phoenix. Elijah Hicks vigorously opposed the relocation of the Cherokees from Georgia to Indian Territory (in present-day Oklahoma).

MENU SPECIALS

Founding Father's Creek Café: Closed today.

Gretchen Green's Green Grocery (Lunch only): Pumpkin soup, sauteed spinach with cranberries and pistachios, celery-apple-walnut salad, hot cocoa.

Witherston Inn Café: Buffalo burger with mushrooms and onions, local greens, mud brownies.

CHAPTER 3

Thursday morning, December 15:

"Doolittle has been kidnapped," Jorge told his father over the phone. "Mom's called Chief McCoy." He explained how he, Jaime, and their mother had found Lottie tied up in the bathroom.

"I'll be there in five minutes," Paco said.

"We have a ransom note, Dad."

Paco arrived in four minutes, with Mighty. Lottie emerged from the bedroom, fully dressed in black wool slacks, a purple cashmere turtleneck sweater, and a faux white rabbit vest. She carried the scent of Paloma Picasso cologne. Mev read aloud the wrinkled computer-printed note they'd found under a refrigerator magnet.

> *Do this by 10:00 this morning: Go to ebay.com. Find pix of your pet labeled "Your Beloved #6" under Collectibles. "Buy It Now" for $2,000 with PayPal. You will then get your pet back. If you try to find me, someone you love will get hurt.*

"Doolittle's kidnappers didn't even have the courtesy

to call Doolittle by name," Lottie said. "They just call him my pet. We should notify the FBI."

"There was more than one intruder?" Mev asked.

"Yes, there were two. One tied me up. The other stayed in the living room."

"Did you recognize the one who tied you up?"

"No, he was wearing a ski mask. But I saw that he was a big man, over six feet tall I'd guess."

"Maybe this is a form letter," Jaime said.

"A form ransom note," Jorge said. "You know, a ransom note that kidnappers everywhere get off the web for free and customize for their purposes."

"*¡Hijos!*" Paco said. "This is not funny."

"They might be right, Paco. But maybe the burglars didn't know Doolittle's name," Mev said.

"They could have used the word 'parrot,'" Lottie said.

"Maybe the kidnappers kidnap pets for a living," Jorge said, taking his smart phone out of his pocket.

"They're not kidnappers, Jorge."

"Why not, Mom?"

"Legally, a kidnapping is a crime against a person. Doolittle is not a person."

"I beg your pardon," Lottie said. "Does the law allow only humans to be considered persons?"

"Well, yes."

"That's pre-Darwinian," Lottie said. "And 'speciesist.'"

"These burglars have given a lot of thought to obtaining the money electronically," Mev said.

"And I hadn't even gotten Doolittle till last night."

"So the kidnappers must have been at the auction."

"They're not kidnappers, Jorge," Jaime reminded him. "They're burglars."

"Who stole a little person," Lottie muttered. "A feathery little person with a soul."

"The burglars could have read Catherine Perry's article on *Webby Witherston*," Paco said.

"Look, folks." Jorge waved his smart phone. He'd found Your Beloved #6 on eBay. Sure enough, there was a picture of Doolittle in his tiny cage.

Your Beloved #6
Buy It Now for $2,000

Jaime examined the image. "This picture was taken in your living room, Lottie," he said. "On your coffee table."

"Just where I left my little friend when I went to bed."

They heard a knock.

"Come in, Jake," Mev called out. "Join us for breakfast." She had seen her boss circle the cottage, inspecting the doors and windows.

Chief Jake McCoy shook the snow off his coat as he entered through the back door. The drifts had piled high. "Good morning, folks. Good morning, Lottie. You look well." Jake removed his boots and hung his heavy coat on the rack.

"Let's eat while Lottie tells us what happened last night," Mev said, bringing a chair up to the table for Jake. "I'll make coffee."

"I'll scramble eggs," Paco said.

ൾൾ

"No, Peg, Giff is not here," Jon said. He'd been surprised by her early morning phone call. It was eight thirty. "He called us close to one o'clock this morning to make sure we'd gotten home okay. Didn't he go to bed last night?"

"No. I noticed this morning that his bed hasn't been slept in."

"I think you should call the police," Jon said.

He disconnected and turned to Gregory. "Gifford is gone. Peg has just now noticed."

"Loving couple," Gregory remarked.

"Why would he leave the house in the blizzard?"

ൾൾ

Jake took the call from his office while Paco poured his coffee. "Gifford Plains is missing? Where could he have gone in this storm?" He listened. "I'm here with Detective Arroyo at Dr. Byrd's house. The parrot Dr. Byrd bought at the auction is missing, too." He listened another thirty seconds. Then he said, "Mev and I will go over now. Gifford's house is just across the highway."

"What's going on?" Mev asked when Jake hung up the phone.

"Peg Marble called 9-1-1 to report her husband missing. She didn't notice until a few minutes ago because they sleep in separate bedrooms. Let's go."

Mev looked out Lottie's front window. "So much snow has fallen that we're not going to find any tracks."

"Look both ways before you cross the road, Mom," Jorge said.

The four cars stalled on the highway had obviously not moved for hours. They looked like four Indian burial mounds covered in snow with a little steam rising from each.

"Can Jorge and I come along, Mom?"

"And Mighty?"

"*Hijos*, stay here. We've got our own mystery to solve," Paco said.

"Doolittle's kidnapping," Lottie said.

ઌઌ

Six got the text message from Alpha at eight fifty.

~ Alpha, iMessage, Thursday, December 15, 8:50 a.m. Pix went up on eBay at 4 am. When ransom arrives in my PayPal account I will text you to release pet.

~ I am in trouble. I want $1000 now.

~ What kind of trouble?

~ Serious.

~ Do not get caught. Understand? This is a test of your abilities. I will send you a $1000 gift certificate.

~ Can you give me cash now?

~ No. Sorry. Delete this message thread. Alpha.

Six deleted it.

ꕥꕥ

"I'll look around outside if you'll look around inside," Jake said to Mev. "And take pictures."

With one of Lottie's canes, which he'd lifted before leaving her house, Jake jabbed at the snow banked against Gifford Plains's house. Then with his phone he snapped a picture of the white pickup in the garage, which he assumed was Gifford's, and the white Camry in the driveway behind it, covered with snow, which he assumed was Peg's.

Mev knocked on the front door. Peg Marble opened it while putting her cell phone in her pocket. She was wearing black jeans, a black Atlanta Braves sweatshirt, and moccasins. No make-up, but she looked good.

"Come in," she said. "You may look everywhere. Gifford's coat is missing. So are his boots and cap. I have no idea why he would have gone outside in this storm."

Mev had never been inside Gifford's contemporary cedar-sided A-frame. She was surprised at the cabin's spaciousness.

In the loft was a small bedroom and bath. On the main floor there were a larger bedroom and bath, a state-of-the-art kitchen, a great room with a fireplace on the north side and a dining room table with four chairs on the south side. Two facing navy leather sofas. Teak coffee table. Heart pine floors. Oak paneled walls. Floor-to-ceiling windows facing the woods to the east of the house.

A framed print of Robert Lindneux's painting *Trail of Tears* was on the mantle, and a fifty-by-twenty-two-by-eighty-inch glass curio cabinet displaying museum-quality Cherokee artifacts—arrowheads, masks, knives, arrows, bows, tomahawks, turtle-shell rattles, peace pipes, baskets, and pottery.

Add a few Cherokees, Mev thought, *and you'd have the makings of a nineteenth-century tribe*. She took pictures.

The certificate of provenance for the blowgun Gifford had bought lay on the kitchen counter. Mev pocketed it. But she found no blowgun, and no dart.

On the coffee table she saw the remains of the previous night's gathering. Three empty plates with bits of cheese and crackers, three empty wine glasses, an empty bottle of a 2011 Hedge Syrah from Terry Hoage Vineyards, a half-empty bowl of saltines, a half-empty bowl of dark chocolate-coated almonds. *Nice midnight snack.* Mev took a picture. "What time did you go to bed?" she asked Peg, as they sat down at the dining room table.

"I went upstairs at ten o'clock, showered, took a sleeping pill, and went to sleep. I didn't wake up till nearly eight."

"So you heard nothing all night long?"

"No. As I said, I took a pill. And Giff sleeps downstairs."

"When did you notice Giff was not here?

"At eight o'clock, when I came downstairs to make coffee. I called out to him because I was surprised he hadn't gotten up. When he didn't answer I opened his bedroom door and saw he'd never gone to bed."

"Could Giff have left with Jon and Gregory?"

"No, I phoned them."

Jake walked in. "Hello, Ms. Marble. I'm Chief McCoy. I hope that Detective Arroyo and I can be of help."

Removing his hat and jacket, Jake turned to Mev. "No signs of forced entry, no tracks, nothing but snow. Same story, second verse."

Mev turned back to Peg. "Had you and Giff had an argument?"

"No, of course not. We never argue."

"May I see your boots?" Jake asked.

"They're still damp from coming home last night, if that's what you want to know," Peg replied. "But here they are. See for yourself."

"Are you aware that Dr. Byrd's house was burglarized sometime after midnight?"

"Why, no. What was taken?"

"The parrot Dr. Byrd bought at the auction last night. Doolittle."

"Oh my goodness."

"I'm trying to see whether Gifford's disappearance and Doolittle's disappearance are connected."

"Are you implying that Giff stole Doolittle? That is ridiculous. Ridiculous."

"Doolittle is being held for ransom," Mev said.

"Well, Giff certainly has no need for more money. He has his retirement income and social security. And he inherited two hundred and fifty thousand dollars from Francis Hearty Withers just because he moved to Witherston before the geezer died."

"Why would Gifford leave the house in the middle of a snowstorm?"

"How should I know, Chief McCoy? I'm not my husband's keeper."

"We don't want to upset you," Mev said. "We're just trying to figure out this mystery."

"I'll stay here till Deputy Hefner comes," Jake said to Mev. "You go back to Lottie's house, and I'll pick you up when I'm through here." He turned to Peg. "Ms. Marble, I'll need a statement from you." Taking out a small recorder, he set it on the table. "Have a seat."

"Am I a suspect, or a person of interest, just because I reported my husband missing?"

"No, of course not. I just need a statement to rule you

out. Tell me your name and address. Date of birth. Marital status. Profession."

"My name is Margaret Ann Marble. I go by Peg Marble. I live at Chalk Light Condominiums in Atlanta. I was born in Atlanta on April 15, 1984. My first husband, Dr. Roy Garner, a cardiologist, died of a heart attack after our first year of marriage. Giff was my second husband. I am a lawyer. I passed the Georgia Bar, but I don't practice. I write novels. Murder mysteries, to be precise. Is that enough?"

"Where do you get your ideas for your stories?"

"I listen to the police scanner."

"Do you listen to the police scanner in Witherston?"

"Why would I? You all have no crime to speak of."

"When did you marry Dr. Plains?"

"On December, 15, 2010. Five years ago today, in Atlanta."

"Where were you between midnight and seven o'clock this morning?"

"In the loft, in bed. I told you I'd taken a sleeping pill."

"The Witherston Police will work hard to find your husband, Ms. Marble. If you can think of anywhere he might have gone, please let us know."

"Of course, Chief McCoy."

"His car is in the garage, so he can't have gone far."

Deputy Hefner knocked and opened the unlocked door. "Hello, Ms. Marble," he said. "My wife Angie is a fan of yours."

ↀↀ

"Will you pay the ransom, Aunt Lottie?" Jaime asked.

"Why should she, Jaime?" Jorge said. "Doolittle

wasn't really her pet yet. She hardly knew him."

Paco produced a platter with a dozen scrambled eggs, bacon, and toast. The boys gave themselves generous portions.

Lottie sipped her coffee. "Do you think that matters, Jorge? You're looking at Doolittle as a possession, a thing to be owned."

"But you bought him, so you own him."

"I bought him to take responsibility for his welfare, Jorge. I don't own him the way I own the chair you're sitting on."

"But will you pay two thousand dollars to get him back, Aunt Lottie?"

"Yes, Jaime, to liberate him from his kidnappers, just as I would pay any ransom necessary to liberate you from a kidnapper."

"How much would you pay for Dad?" Jorge giggled.

"Would you pay two million for Dad?"

"Of course, Jaime, though I'd have to borrow it."

"How much do you think Dad is worth?"

Jorge grinned. "Two million seven hundred sixty three dollars and forty-nine cents."

"*Gracias, hijo.*"

"And if he were not your dad, boys?"

"Seven hundred sixty three dollars and forty-nine cents."

Lottie got serious. "Boys, can you imagine being Doolittle? If you're able to see the world through his eyes, then you'll consider him a person. Not a human person, but a still a person. An avian person."

Jaime closed his eyes. "Okay, I'm being Doolittle. You know what I see?"

"Bars," Jorge answered.

"Yes.

"You get my point," Lottie said.

ɞɔɞɔ

"I'm back," Mev shouted, walking through the front door.

"*Hola, Mevita.*"

"Mom, Aunt Lottie is going to pay the ransom for Doolittle."

"I'm doing it right now," Lottie said as she typed her VISA number into the PayPal website. "Done. And it's only nine thirty."

"Oh my god, Aunt Lottie. Why did you do that?"

"Because I want the kidnappers to release Doolittle. He must be suffering."

"Burglars," Mev uttered automatically.

"Kidnappers," Lottie said.

"Whenever you pay a ransom, you reward the…well, the kidnappers…for their crime," Mev countered.

"And when I get Doolittle back, you can investigate. But not until I get him back. Please?"

"I can't promise that, Aunt Lottie. Chief McCoy is already on the case. And Catherine Perry monitors all police conversation for *Webby Witherston.*

"Catherine called me while you were gone. I told her the story."

"The story is online now," Jorge said. "I'm reading it on my smart phone."

ɞɔɞɔ

Six got the text message from Alpha at ten thirty.

~ Alpha, iMessage, Thursday, December 15, 10:30 a.m. I have the $2,000. Release the bird. Photo is off eBay. You will get Amazon card for $1,000. Delete this message.-Alpha

Six deleted it.

ഗ്ദ

Hempton Fairfield checked for his land line's caller ID, but found only the message, *Incoming Call*. "Hello?"

"Is this Mr. Fairfield?"

"Yes."

"The Hempton Fairfield who last night auctioned off my people's history?"

"With whom am I speaking?"

"You are speaking with John Hicks, Cherokee descendant of Elijah Hicks. I want to ask you a question."

"Who in the world is Elijah Hicks?"

"I figured you'd have no idea. Elijah Hicks was the second editor of the *Cherokee Phoenix*, after Elias Boudinot. Last night you auctioned off a page of the *Cherokee Phoenix* that you never even read. A page that carried a story that Elijah Hicks wrote about an injustice done to him and his two friends. A page ripped from a newspaper that advocated for the rights of the Cherokees when the US Government was evicting them from their homeland. A newspaper written by intelligent, educated individuals whose lives matter not at all to you, Mr. Fairfield, or to the person who sold the page to you, or to Mr. Guelph who bought the page from you."

"Look, Mr. Hicks. I don't appreciate—"

"You don't appreciate what? Being reminded that you're in the business of buying and selling things that have been stolen from the people who made them? Being reminded that you're turning what's left of the Cherokee civilization into decorations for people's walls? Being reminded that real persons with names created your merchandise?"

"Are you threatening me?"

"I'm asking you a question. Where do you get your merchandise?"

"None of your business."

"You don't care whether you're auctioning off a Cherokee tomahawk or a parrot. They're all the same to you. Just merchandise."

"I am calling the police."

"Do you think that's a smart move?"

ↀↀ

"Hello, Grant. This is Hempton."

"Well, hello there, Hemp," Griggs said. "Nice auction. And I'm happy with my tomahawk."

"I've just gotten a disturbing phone call from a John Hicks. Do you know who he is?"

"He's a painter and carpenter who lives in Free Rooster Village. And a computer geek. He's into Cherokee history big time. Sometimes he writes letters to the editor on *Webby Witherston.* He stained our deck last summer."

"I hope never to see him face-to-face. For his sake. Anyway, I'm calling to invite you and Ruth to dinner tonight. The roads are supposed to be passable by this afternoon. Are you all free?"

"What time?"

"Seven o'clock."

"We'll bring wine."

"We'll have lamb."

WWW.ONLINEWITHERSTON.COM

WITHERSTON ON THE WEB
Thursday, December 15, 2015
10:00 a.m.

BREAKING NEWS

Gifford Plains, of 300 North Witherston Highway, is missing. His wife, Peg Marble, called 911 at 8:30 this morning, December 15, 2015, to report him gone. Ms. Marble told Detective Mev Arroyo and Chief Jake McCoy that she had gone upstairs at 10:30 last night and had left Dr. Plains downstairs sharing a bottle of wine with their friends Jon Finley and Gregory Bozeman. She said he apparently never went to bed.

~ Catherine Perry, Reporter

At 8:05 this morning, Detective Mev Arroyo called Police Chief Jake McCoy to report an overnight break-in, assault, and burglary at the home of Charlotte Byrd, 301 North Witherston Highway. Detective Arroyo and her twin sons Jorge and Jaime had found Dr. Byrd in her bathroom, wrapped in a blanket, bound with duct tape, and gagged. Doolittle, the African Grey parrot Dr. Byrd bought at the Fairfield Antiquities Auction last night, was gone. So was his cage.

Detective Arroyo is Dr. Byrd's niece and next door neighbor. Jorge and Jaime had gone over to check on Dr. Byrd and see Doolittle. When Dr. Byrd didn't answer the doorbell, they returned home to get their mother.

Dr. Byrd said that there were two kidnappers who came after midnight. One of them, a man wearing dark clothes and a ski mask, grabbed her when she was asleep and tied her up. She described him as tall. She didn't see the other man.

The kidnappers left a note ordering Dr. Byrd to pay a ransom of $2,000 to retrieve Doolittle.

Dr. Byrd was unharmed.

Detective Arroyo and Chief McCoy are investigating the kidnapping.

~ Catherine Perry, Reporter

CHAPTER 4

Thursday afternoon, December 15:

Much to Daniel Soto's relief, the skies cleared about eleven thirty in the morning, and the sun brightened the snowy landscape. Dan was twenty-four years old, six-feet tall, black-haired, brown-skinned, brown-eyed, and clean-shaven, though after the long night in the cab of the eighteen-wheeler he needed a shave and a shower. He wore Levis, a red Georgia Bulldogs anorak, and a red wool beanie, not enough protection against the cold.

Finally the temperature had risen above freezing. People emerged from the line of southbound vehicles to clear their windshields, stretch, examine their cars, and talk with each other. A helicopter hovered overhead. Trevor Bennington III, who had come from town on his snowmobile, filled tanks with gasoline donated by Trig Morton and distributed probiotic drinks donated by Gretchen Green. Pete Senior and Pete Junior, who had come from town in the police department's Jeep Cherokee, checked on everybody's health.

Mayor Rich Rather, who had come from home in a silver Lincoln MKZ, shook hands with everybody he could meet. "Hello, there," he'd say. "I'm Mayor Rather, and I'd like to welcome you to Witherston, where everybody gets along with everybody else. We are friendly folks here, and we'd love for you to come back again and spend a more time with us. We sure would. Have a good day." And then he'd go on to the next car. He was not discouraged by the responses he received, or by the middle-finger waves. After all, he was a politician, as well as a used car dealer. He owned Rather Pre-Owned Vehicles in Dahlonega, which Witherstonians called "Rather Used Cars." And he was finishing a third year as mayor.

Dan leaned against the cab. His basset hound Muddy relieved himself against one of the eighteen tires.

"Hello, again, Mr. Soto," Pete Junior said. "I've come to talk with you about the release of your chickens."

"They're not my chickens, Deputy."

"Did you see anybody walking around your truck last night, Mr. Soto?"

"No, nobody."

"Did you hear anything?"

"No, nothing."

"What did you do all night?"

"Sat here with Muddy. Played my harmonica. Thought about my future."

"When did you find out you'd lost some of your chickens?"

"When the older deputy told me in the middle of the night. And they're not my chickens."

"How many chickens does your truck carry?"

"Two thousand, maybe more."

"How many crates?"

"Jeez. I don't know. Maybe four hundred. There are at least five poor chickens in every crate, some crippled, some blind, some with dislocated hips, some with broken legs. That's the way it is with hauling poultry. Some chickens are dead by the time I get to the processing plant. Dead from cold. Dead from heat. Dead from exposure. And the dead ones are the lucky ones. You know what? I'm a trucker, and I'm trucking tragedy. Wanna know more? You guessed it. I hate my job."

"Well, thank you, Mr. Soto. The wrecker is coming up from Dahlonega and should be here in an hour or so."

"Next time you eat a drumstick, Mr. Deputy, think about these chickens."

"Thanks, again, Mr. Soto. Thanks for talking with me." Pete Junior turned to walk away.

"And you can tell your boss that if I'd thought of liberating those chickens last night I would have, but I would have finished the job," Dan continued. "I would have liberated every single one of them. In fact, that's what I think I'll do right now. Maybe I can get arrested and go on CNN and talk about these chickens."

Pete Junior slogged back to the Ford Focus, some forty yards up the road. As he approached the snow-covered car, he noticed its distance from the eighteen-wheeler.

"Pop," he called out to his father. "Mr. Heller must have been behind a car that's no longer here."

"Or a truck, son."

"Or a truck."

Pete Junior looked carefully at the snow-covered roadway between the Ford and the eighteen-wheeler. It seemed undisturbed except for his tracks and the chickens' tracks.

Could a car have done a U-turn and gone north before the storm had deposited the ten inches? But a fairly deep ditch separated the southbound lane from the north-bound lane. Only an all-wheel-drive vehicle could have managed such an escape in the blizzard.

"Pop," Pete Junior shouted. "Must have been an all-wheel-drive vehicle."

"Maybe a truck."

ઌઌ

"Hey, Lottie. How are you holding up?"

"Oh, Gretchen. Thanks for calling. You saw the story on *Webby Witherston*?"

"Yes. Have you heard from the kidnappers yet?"

"No, and I paid PayPal with my VISA card three hours ago. Doolittle's picture is off eBay, so the kidnapper must have my two thousand dollars. Jaime and Jorge and Mighty are keeping me company. The boys are on my computer trying to figure out how PayPal works. Mighty is chewing on…well, something…something I don't recognize any more."

"Where are Mev and Paco?"

"Mev went with Jake to the police station. Paco is shoveling snow off my front walk."

"Neel is with me here at Green's Grocery," Gretchen told her. "We're bringing dinner over to you tonight—to you and the Arroyos and the Lodges and anybody else you'd like to invite."

"Would you like to bring your dogs? I suspect the boys will bring Mighty and Sequoyah. We may as well have everybody."

"Of course. Neel and I will see you all at six, with Gandhi, Swift, and Ama."

"I'll furnish the wine. And the dog food."

ઌઌ

"Thanks for keeping Scissors open this afternoon, Jon." Rhonda was already standing at the beauty shop's navy-and-mauve striped door by the six-foot-high stainless steel scissors when Jon and Renoir arrived in Gregory's red pickup. She was enveloped in an over-sized pink goose-down parka with a faux-fox-trimmed hood. Matching pink wool scarf. Black pants. Black boots. Black gloves. She embraced Renoir and Jon, in that order.

Jon unlocked the door and ushered her in. "Anything for you, Rhonda. You're one of my favorite customers. And you're already beautiful. You make my job easy."

Jon had lots of customers: women who just wanted to look pretty, others who just liked Jon, still others who just liked the dozens of pink and purple orchids flourishing under florescent lights. Everybody appreciated his up-to-the-minute knowledge of Witherston affairs.

"Today I'm cutting both your hair and Renoir's. Would you like to go first?"

"I'd like to go second. I'll keep Renoir company when he's in the chair." In truth, the sixty-pound poodle didn't routinely sit in the navy leather barber chair for his monthly lamb clip. Instead, he stood in front of a full-length mirror while his master trimmed his white curls.

So Rhonda sat down in the barber chair to watch. "Jon, what do you know about Gifford Plains?"

"Let's see. Giff is a scholar of Cherokee culture. He taught at Emory, then retired a year ago and moved here. He likes good wine and cheese. He smokes a Meerschaum pipe with McCranie's Red Ribbon Tobacco. He's about sixty-five years old. He has a grown daughter older than his wife. I hardly know Peg Marble, but just between you and me, he and Peg don't eat off the same plate."

"What's Peg Marble like? I read both *Interred Near You* and *Unburied*, which are set in north Georgia."

"Peg writes mysteries. That's what she does for a living, even though she has a degree from the University of Georgia Law School. Giff says she subscribes to true-crime magazines to get ideas for unusual murders. And she listens to the police scanner when she's driving."

Rhonda's cell phone interrupted their conversation. "Hi, Rich," she said. "What?…You're joking…Lord in Heaven…I'm coming out right now…To help…Go, Dan Soto…Yes, that's right, Rich. I'm coming out to help the trucker. Pete Senior can arrest me too if he wishes…I don't care if you *are* the mayor."

Rhonda disconnected and said to Jon. "You won't believe what just happened. The driver of the eighteen-wheeler—Daniel Soto is his name—is letting his chickens loose. I'll get my hair cut another time."

"Well, go there, lickety split."

ᘓᘓ

Rhonda cautiously drove her black Escalade east on Hickory Street, then southeast on Pine Cone Road, and then south on Hiccup Hill Road to the intersection of Hiccup Hill and South Witherston Highway, a quarter mile south of the stranded eighteen-wheeler. There she left it and proceeded on foot. Fortunately the snow was melting with the rising temperatures.

Trudging along the icy asphalt, she passed some fifty white chickens fleeing in all directions from a black and tan basset hound. When she reached the site of the accident, she spotted a tall good-looking man, apparently the trucker Dan Soto in front of the cab, engaged in an argument with Deputy Pete Senior Koslowsky and Mayor Rather. *Webby Witherston*'s ever present Catherine Perry held up a microphone.

Rhonda listened as she quietly climbed into the back of the trailer to complete the work Dan Soto had started.

"I am pleased to be arrested for committing an act of kindness," Dan said loudly, "an act of kindness that's against the law. The law supports the inhumane treatment of non-human animals."

"I am arresting you for destroying property that doesn't belong to you," Pete Senior said.

"If I liberate chickens, am I destroying property?" Dan asked, speaking into Catherine Perry's mic. "Whose property are they? Not God's?"

"The chickens are the property of Love Me Tender Poultry, Mr. Soto," Mayor Rather said. "Look at the sign on your truck."

"So the chickens don't belong to God? Well, I'll be damned."

"Don't get smart with us, Mr. Soto," Mayor Rather said. "Love Me Tender Poultry owns those chickens. They hired you to deliver their property to the poultry processing plant."

"So chickens are property under the law. Bless their little souls. Oops, my mistake, I guess property doesn't have a soul." Dan grinned.

Mayor Rather had gotten red in the face. "Do you want to be locked up, Mr. Soto?"

"Like the chickens? Yes, I'll show solidarity with them. By the way, some of the chickens have broken legs. Shouldn't we take those chickens to the vet? They must be suffering."

"May I interview you for *Witherston on the Web*, Mr. Soto?" Catherine Perry asked.

"I'd be happy for you to interview me, Miss…"

"Catherine Perry. I'm a reporter for *Webby Witherston*."

"Put your hands out in front of you, Mr. Soto," Pete Senior said. "I'm arresting you for destroying property and talking back to a police officer."

"Oh, I apologize. Profusely. I assumed we were just chatting about some creatures I thought belonged to God. I didn't mean any disrespect toward you, Officer. Or toward you, Mr. Mayor. Forgive me."

"Sure, sure," Mayor Rather muttered.

"If I'd known you all would pay me a visit, I would have brushed my teeth and combed my hair."

"I am arresting you for disorderly conduct."

"I'd prefer that you arrest me for civil disobedience, for refusing to carry out an injustice."

Rhonda heard everything as she opened a crate and released five chickens. They flew off the back of the trailer and scurried away. She opened another crate and released another five chickens, one of whom had a broken beak.

They too made their escape. She opened a third crate exposed to the wind outside and released one chicken. The other four had frozen to death.

The stench was awful. The air was thick with floating feathers and dust. But Rhonda was committed to her mission. She released thirty more chickens before she started coughing.

Suddenly, someone screamed. "What the fuck?"

Rhonda jumped. The voice seemed to come from inside the truck.

"I'm just looking around," she shouted.

"Fuck you!"

"Watch your mouth," Rhonda shouted back.

Rhonda heard a dog bark and then her husband yell, "What was that?"

Rhonda stood stock still. After a moment, the men resumed their conversation. So she resumed her work. She opened ten more crates before she discovered the cage with the African Grey parrot.

"Doolittle," Rhonda exclaimed softly.

"Doolittle is a bad bird," Doolittle responded softly.

Doolittle's cage was wedged into a space that four crates must have occupied, surrounded by chickens behind bars. Everyone was behind bars.

The truck was a maximum-security prison, Rhonda said to herself as she extracted Doolittle's cage from the shelf of cages. She climbed down from the platform, carrying Doolittle's cage in her left hand and took him to meet the men still arguing in front of the truck.

"Rhonda," the mayor exclaimed. "What are you doing here?"

"That must be Doolittle," Deputy Pete Senior said.

"Shut the fuck up!" Doolittle screamed.

"Where did that bird come from?" Dan asked.

"Where did my wife come from?" Mayor Rather asked.

"Chicken prison," Rhonda said.

"Mr. Soto, I'm now arresting you for burglary and extortion," Deputy Pete Senior said.

"What about Muddy? Are you going to arrest him?" Dan asked.

Muddy was off chasing the liberated chickens.

"Rich will take care of Muddy for you, Mr. Soto," Rhonda said. "Muddy will be safe at our house."

"Jesus, Rhonda. No, no, no. With all the animals you've rescued there won't be room for me in my own bed."

Rhonda ignored her husband. "Here, Muddy, come to Rhonda." Muddy came. Rhonda scratched his neck as Pete Senior handcuffed Dan. Then she opened the door of the Lincoln and lifted Muddy, appropriately named, into the back seat.

Catherine Perry walked a few yards away from the group and texted the news to Smitty.

~ *Catherine Perry, iMessage, Thursday, December*

15, 2:01 p.m. Doolittle discovered in eighteen-wheeler chicken truck. Trucker Daniel Soto arrested for burglary and extortion. CP.

When Catherine returned, Mayor Rather was pitching a fit. "For Heaven's sakes, Rhonda. Now, Pete Senior has to arrest you. You just did the same thing that Mr. Soto did."

"Like what, Rich? I didn't kidnap Doolittle."

"You released Love Me Tender's chickens. You destroyed property that didn't belong to you."

"I didn't destroy the chickens. I gave them life. Caging them is what destroys them."

"I'm afraid I have to arrest you, Mrs. Rather. I'm sorry," Pete Senior said.

"Go ahead," Rhonda said. "If you've been to jail for justice, you're in good company."

"I know that song," Pete Senior said.

"So do I," Dan Soto said from the back of Pete Senior's Cherokee. He pulled out his harmonica and started playing the tune.

"I'll drive myself to jail," Rhonda said. "You can hold my husband if I escape."

"What? Hey, no you can't. I'm the mayor."

A chicken squatted in the snow at his feet and pooped.

Catherine texted another message to her boss.

~ Catherine Perry, iMessage, Thursday, December 15, 2:17 p.m. Hold the presses! ;) I have big big big story!!!!!!!! Will email it to you. CP.

ꕥ

Rhonda and Dan sat side by side in the Witherston jail's holding cell. Mayor Rather had departed with Muddy.

Dan started playing "Jesu, Joy of Man's Desiring" on his harmonica.

"Tell me honestly," Rhonda interrupted Dan's solo performance. "Did you steal Doolittle?"

"No, of course not. Somebody must have put that bird in my truck after I crashed."

"Why are you in the chicken-hauling business, Dan?"

"I'll give you the short story. I grew up in Gainesville, where my parents worked in a chicken processing plant, went to the University of Georgia on a Hope scholarship, majored in Comparative Literature, joined a band called the Athens Armadillos—I played harmonica—and made some bad grades through no fault of my own. So I had to drop out of school my senior year. I could make more money driving an eighteen-wheeler than waiting tables, so I got my trucker's license, answered an ad from Love Me Tender Poultry in Tennessee, and started driving the rooster cruiser."

"I didn't see any roosters."

"The broilers I carry are only six weeks old. You can't tell a chicken's sex till they're three months old, and by that time the birds have been cooked and eaten."

"So your chickens…"

"They're not my chickens."

"So Love Me Tender's chickens have never laid an egg."

"No, Mrs. Rather. They're not old enough, so they've never had the pleasure. By the way, farms that raise egg-layers throw the males into a macerator that grinds them up."

At this moment, Chief McCoy entered their cell. "I'm fining each of you a hundred dollars and releasing you," he said. "I can't see how Mr. Soto could have stolen Doolittle. And I'm going to consider your chicken liberation activity to be vandalism rather than theft. So you all are free to go."

Rhonda shook Dan's hand. "I'm honored to know you. I'll ask Rich to meet you at your truck with Muddy. I can give you a ride there if you like.

"I like."

Rhonda turned to Chief McCoy. "I will pay both fines." Then she quietly said to Dan, "We're a team."

ଓଓ

Lottie opened her front door. Mev stood there with Doolittle.

"Doolittle," Lottie cried out. "Doolittle, where have you been?"

"In his cage, Aunt Lottie," Jorge called out from the living room.

"Come in, dear, come in, come in. Where did you find Doolittle?"

Mev set Doolittle's cage on the coffee table. Lottie opened the cage door. Doolittle cowered in the back.

Jaime seated himself on the floor by the parrot.

"Doolittle was sequestered in the middle of four hundred chicken crates in the eighteen-wheeler that blocked Witherston Highway traffic," Mev told her.

"Who put him there?"

"Pete Senior thought the trucker, Dan Soto, did it. But Jake and I don't think Soto could have done it. At least not without an accomplice."

"Did you hear an eighteen-wheeler pull up outside your house last night, Aunt Lottie?" Jorge asked with a giggle.

Mev ignored him. "Pete Senior was arresting Soto for letting the chickens out of their crates when Rhonda Rather came out of the truck with Doolittle. So Pete Senior arrested Rhonda, too, for letting chickens out of their crates."

"Rhonda's in jail? Who will color her hair? I'll call Jon," Paco said.

"Go, Mrs. Rather," Jorge said.

Mev sighed. "Rhonda's no longer in jail. She and Soto were each fined a hundred dollars and released."

"Look at Doolittle," Jaime exclaimed. Doolittle was perched on his wrist.

Jorge snapped a picture with his smart phone. "I'm emailing this to Smitty Green," he said.

WWW.ONLINEWITHERSTON.COM

WITHERSTON ON THE WEB
Thursday, December 15, 2015
3:00 p.m.

BREAKING NEWS

At mid-day today Deputy Pete Senior Koslowsky arrested Daniel Soto for destroying property, disorderly conduct, burglary, and extortion. Mr. Soto, driver of the eighteen-wheeler tractor-trailer truck that blocked both lanes of traffic on South Witherston Highway at 1:30 a.m. this morning, was carrying the missing African Grey parrot named Doolittle among the 2,000 chickens he was hauling for Love Me Tender Poultry.

Doolittle was stolen last night from Dr. Charlotte Byrd, who paid a ransom of $2,000 this morning.

The mayor's wife, Rhonda Rather, discovered Doolittle in the trailer of the truck while releasing chickens from their cages.

Deputy Pete Senior arrested Mrs. Rather for destroying property.

This is what happened. Deputy Pete Senior caught Mr. Soto releasing chickens he was supposed to deliver to a poultry processing plant. When he was arrested for destroying property, Mr. Soto said he was committing an act of civil disobedience of a law that supports the inhumane treatment of non-human animals. He said that the chickens with broken legs should be treated by a veterinarian.

Mrs. Rather came to the scene when nobody was looking and climbed into the back of the truck. She freed almost a hundred more chickens and then found Doolittle's cage among the chicken crates. When Deputy Pete Senior arrested her for releasing the chickens she sang, "If you've been to jail for justice, you're in good company."

~ Catherine Perry, Reporter

Chief Jake McCoy has announced that Witherston Highway has been cleared. The eighteen-wheeler chicken truck has been pulled to the side of the road where it will not block traffic. And the hickory tree that fell across the highway near Withers Retirement Village has been removed. Traffic is now flowing.

~ Catherine Perry, Reporter

CHAPTER 5

Thursday afternoon and evening, December 15:

Just as Rhonda and Dan reached the chicken truck, Rhonda spotted Atsadi Moon and his younger sister Hiawassee Moon loading crates of chickens into the back of a newish red pick-up. On its bumper was a sticker that said *IF YOU DON'T BELIEVE IN GOSH, YOU'RE GOING TO HECK.*

"They're stealing your chickens," Rhonda said to Dan. "Good for them."

"They're not my chickens," Dan said. "They're God's chickens."

"Gosh's chickens. I think I'll help those kids."

"Who are they?"

"They are young Witherstonians with Cherokee blood who have created a yurt settlement to honor their Cherokee ancestors. Some of us call it Free Rooster Village because they put up a sign advertising a free rooster at its entrance on Old Dirt Road. They're petitioning to be officially named Tayanita Village."

"What does *Tayanita* mean?"

"Beaver, in the Cherokee language. Anyway they say that White American culture is obliterating Cherokee culture, so they're trying to make the Cherokee people more visible. They're growing their own vegetables like their ancestors, but they live in green canvas yurts, not like their ancestors. Their ancestors lived in clay huts."

Dan stepped out of Rhonda's Escalade. "Do you all need any help?"

"We're rescuing these chickens," Atsadi said.

"We know all about chickens because we keep Buff Orpingtons for eggs. They roam free. And so will these chickens," Hiawassee said.

Rhonda climbed into the back of the chicken truck where she'd found Doolittle. She was handing a crate of five chickens to Dan when Catherine Perry drove up.

"Hey," Catherine said.

"Hey," Rhonda said.

"Hey," Dan said. "Did you follow us?"

"Yes, of course. I'm a reporter," Catherine replied.

"Would you like to interview me?" Dan asked her. "Because I'd love to interview you."

"Sure."

Then Rhonda saw her husband pull up in his Lincoln. Muddy was leaning out of the back window.

"Jesus, Rhonda," Rich exclaimed. He heaved himself out of the car, opened the back door for Muddy, and yelled at his wife, "What on God's green earth are you doing here again?"

"I'm helping these nice young people save the chickens from certain death," Rhonda said.

"Well, let's everybody scram before the Petes come. Scram," Rich shouted. "Scram."

"I'll bring food for the chickens," Rhonda shouted. "For the lucky ones running free and for the unlucky ones still stuck in the truck."

Atsadi and Hiawassee left.

Dan climbed into the eighteen-wheeler's cab with

Muddy and Catherine. Rhonda carefully picked up an injured chicken, wrapped her pink scarf around the clucking bird, carried the bird to her Escalade, and deposited her in the right front seat.

"I'm taking this chicken to the vet," Rhonda said to her husband.

Rich put his car in gear, turned around, and yelled, "I don't give a hoot where you take that broiler, Rhonda, just so long as you don't bring it home."

"We'll see you soon, hon," Rhonda said to her husband as he departed. "Both of us."

A moment later Jon pulled up in Gregory's truck. He grinned. "Hi, sweet baby. I hear you've been to jail for justice."

"Hi, Jon. Do you want to save some more chickens from injustice?"

"Sure. Gregory and I will give those chickens a nice home. Sassyass and Vincent van Goat will be delighted to have the company."

Rhonda and Jon went to work.

ꕥ

Jorge, Jaime, Annie, and Beau were hiking through the packed snow up Old Dirt Road with their sleds when a red pickup and a cloud of white feathers slowly passed them. Mighty and Sequoyah raced after the truck.

"Hey, boys," Atsadi stopped the truck to speak to them. "Would you all like to help us unload some chickens?"

"Sure," Jaime said.

"Yes."

"We're coming."

The four teenagers followed the pickup past the free rooster sign into the settlement. Atsadi parked the truck near the barn, and he and Hiawassee jumped out. When Atsadi lowered the tailgate they saw chicken crates stacked high and deep and heard a chorus of clucking.

"Woohoo," Jorge shouted, dropping his sled by the fence.

"Woohoo!"

"*Woof.*"

"Let's put the dogs in the truck cab," Atsadi said. They did. The dogs steamed up the windshields with their barking.

Under Hiawassee's direction, the boys unloaded thirteen crates and set them on the snowy ground. Annie opened the latches and freed the prisoners. In five minutes fifty chickens were fleeing north, south, east, and west.

"You all are real chickens now," Jaime said. You all are free."

"Free to run where you please, free to roost where you like, free to stretch your wings," Hiawassee said.

"But don't let the foxes get you," Beau said.

"Or the bear," Jaime said.

"Or the kidnapper," Jorge said.

"Or the cook," Annie said.

"How much would you pay if a kidnapper put one of these chickens on eBay, Jorge?" Jaime asked.

"I'd ask Aunt Lottie to pay two thousand dollars."

"And she would."

Waya came out of the barn. "What's happening?" he asked.

"We borrowed your truck," Atsadi said. "We couldn't find you, but we found the key in the ignition, so we borrowed it."

"We're going to clean it up, Waya," Hiawassee said.

"That's not my truck. Looks like it, but it's not mine. It's Thom's."

"We'd better get rid of the feathers before Thom sees the truck."

"Or smells it."

"Whenever. No big deal," Waya said.

ᘓᘓ

"Have you all thought about going vegetarian?" Jaime asked Annie, Jorge, and Beau as they walked out of Tayanita Village. They had leashed up Mighty and Sequoyah in consideration of the chickens.

"I have," Annie said. "But when I told my parents I wanted to go vegetarian, they told me I'd go hungry. They said I'd have to watch them eat meat at the dinner table."

"You can eat with me if you like," Jaime said. "I don't think I can eat chickens anymore. I'm going to talk to my parents tonight. Maybe I'll go vegetarian with you, Annie."

"So you'd give up bacon, sausage, hamburgers, hot dogs, and steak, Jaime?" Jorge asked his brother.

"Maybe I would just give up chicken, bro."

"And parrot."

"And dog," Beau said.

"How old do you think a person should be to decide for herself what to eat? I'm fifteen years old, and I've been president of Keep Nature Natural," Annie said. "I taught my parents about pollution. They didn't care about the environment until I started talking about the five-legged frog you all found in Founding Father's Creek last summer."

"Maybe they'll care about chickens in chicken trucks if you tell them what you think," Jorge said.

"This is what I believe," Beau said. "Old people like our parents formed their views about the world when they were our age. Over the years, they focused on work and not ideas, and they became afraid to change their minds. Then we kids come along and say their views are out of date, and they get all upset and defensive. That's what's happening at your house, Annie, when you tell them you won't eat what they eat."

"Maybe they don't want to give up meat themselves," Jaime said.

"Maybe they don't want their daughter to have opinions different from theirs," Annie said.

"You know all those sixties protest songs we listen to, Annie?" Jaime said. "Aunt Lottie, who was our age in the sixties, told us her parents wouldn't let her listen to that music in their house. She said that they hated Peter, Paul, and Mary, who sang peace songs. How could anyone hate peace songs?"

"Because peace songs make people feel guilty about supporting war. That's why some people hate pacifists when a war is going on," Beau said.

"I think I'm a pacifist," Jorge said.

"So is Aunt Lottie."

"Aunt Lottie has a huge collection of sixties records."

"People who don't like pacifists and vegetarians think that pacifists and vegetarians are siding with the enemy," Beau said.

"Enemies like the Holsteins and the Guernseys."

"And the Herefords."

"And the Orpingtons."

"And the Bantams."

"So many enemies."

"We just don't want to kill," Annie said. "We don't want to kill other people or other animals, either. I'm a pacifist and an environmentalist and a feminist and a soon-to-be vegetarian."

"You are everything your parents are not. No wonder they feel threatened by you. They think you want to overturn their world," Beau said.

"I do."

"Your parents must think everybody is either with them or against them, and you're against them because you're not with them," Jorge said.

"Aunt Lottie is always talking about having empathy for others. Do your parents have empathy for people who are different from them, Annie?" Jaime asked.

"I don't think so. At least they don't have empathy for chickens."

"Do you have empathy for your parents, Annie?"

"You got me, Beau. I don't."

"It's hard to have empathy for people who think differently from us," Beau said. "But if you don't have empathy for people who think differently, you're not really a pacifist."

"I think I'll stop eating meat at home and just get skinny. I'll worry my parents, and then maybe they'll ask me why I don't want to eat chickens and cows," Annie said.

"What will you tell them?"

"That I don't want to eat anybody with thoughts and feelings. If I can look into an animal's eyes and see a person there, then I'm not going to eat him. That's what I'll tell my parents."

"Aunt Lottie says that Doolittle is a person. I say that chickens are persons, too," Jaime said.

"So are cows," Annie said.

"We have to eat something," Beau said.

"We can be nice to the animals," Jorge said. "We can be nice to them before we kill them, cut them up, roast them in the oven, put salt and pepper on them, stab them with a fork, and put them into our mouths."

"And digest them," Jaime said. "We sacrifice them for us. Cows are peaceful. We humans eat them to get big and strong so that we can kill our enemies."

"Enemies like cows."

"I'll bet eaters of cows can beat up eaters of carrots," Beau said.

"I guess the army won't go vegetarian," Jorge said.

"I think I'll join the Peace Corps," Annie said.

They reached the top of Old Dirt Road.

"Sledding time," Jorge shouted. He unleashed Mighty and Sequoyah.

"I'll race you down."

❧❧

Thirty-year-old Tony Lima sat on a high stool facing his six Mountain Band singers in Reception Hall of the Witherston Baptist Church. He softly strummed the spruce and rosewood acoustic guitar he'd bought with his Withers inheritance. Pastor Paul Clement stood with his double bass. Rhonda Rather sat at the piano.

"So that's the story of my incarceration, friends," Rhonda said, after telling the choir about her rescue of Doolittle. "The chickens were incarcerated because my fellow humans want to eat them. So humans have to restrict their freedom. I was incarcerated because I sided with the chickens and gave them their freedom. They had to restrict my freedom so I wouldn't do it again."

"Would you do it again?" Mona Pattison asked.

"Of course," Rhonda said.

"Could I go with you?"

"Of course. If another chicken truck ever stops in Witherston."

"Which is not likely," Pastor Clement said.

"If it does, I'll mobilize Keep Nature Natural."

"Why did the kidnapper choose the snowiest night in the past five years to take Doolittle, do you suppose?" asked Tony. "I forecast the blizzard."

"Maybe the kidnapper lives out of town and didn't read your forecast on *Webby Witherston*, Mr. Lima," Mona Pattison said.

"But then he wouldn't have known that Dr. Byrd had bought Doolittle."

"Or she," Mona said. "The kidnapper could have been a she."

"Mona is right," Rhonda said. "Sometimes women do just as bad things as men. Though not often."

"I'm serious," Tony said. "Somebody in Witherston knew that Doolittle had gone to Dr. Byrd's house."

"Must have been somebody at the auction."

"My money's on Peg Marble," Angie Hefner said. "She may not have been the kidnapper, but she attended the auction."

"*Interred Near You* is about a kidnapping," Bonnie Koslowsky, Pete Senior's wife, said. "And a killing."

"Of a human," Rhonda said.

After a moment of thoughtfulness, Tony said, "Time for practice, folks. Let's start with 'Light One Candle.'"

Soon the singers were belting out the chorus to Peter Yarrow's Hanukkah song.

ᨀᨀ

Because the Lodges arrived everywhere fifteen minutes early, Lottie had told them to come for dinner at six thirty. Gretchen and Neel arrived everywhere fifteen minutes late, so she had told them to come at six. And she'd told Mev's family to come at six-fifteen.

Between five-thirty and six-fifteen Lottie donned a purple velvet tunic over black silk slacks, moved Doolittle to the kitchen counter and opened his cage door, unfolded a red linen tablecloth, set the table for ten, lit the all-blue lights on the Christmas tree, put on a Nana Mouskouri Christmas album, and got out six cans of Alpo. She uncorked two bottles of her favorite Rioja, the 2011 Muga Reserve, and a bottle of her favorite local wine, a Chardonnay from Frogtown Cellars near Dahlonega. This was going to be a night of holiday celebration. She switched on the outdoor lights, for darkness had already fallen.

Lottie's calculations were perfect. Everybody arrived at six fifteen. That is to say, Beau, Jim, and Lauren, Gretchen and Neel, and Mev, Paco, Jaime, and Jorge reached her front door then. Swift, Ama, Gandhi, Sequoyah, and Mighty chased each other in the snow, skidding every which way possible on the icy sidewalk and plunging nose-deep into the snow banks. Lottie brought her human guests inside and left her canine guests outside. She would invite her canine guests inside at Alpo-time, after her human guests had had dessert.

While Gretchen and Neel arranged the dinner on the table—mushrooms sautéed in balsamic vinegar; a spinach, apple, and pecan salad; roasted sweet potatoes; carrots and parsnips; baked rainbow trout; fresh whole wheat bread; and chocolate-covered almonds—Lottie poured the wine.

Lottie was surprised that Gretchen and Neel had brought so much trout, enough to feed twenty, but she knew that the teenagers would consume most of it. Gretchen, her best friend, had become a pescatarian after taking a yoga class and was committed to doing no harm to animals, or to anyone else under the sun.

Gretchen once saved a huge ant that Lottie had started to crush, saying only, "Let's practice non-violence, sugar." She kept her friends close, brought fun to every occasion, and lived in the present with few regrets and few fears. She frequently quoted Omar Khayyám, the eleventh-century Persian poet who sang wine's praises. Above the entrance to her grocery store, Gretchen had posted a brass plaque inscribed with the verse:

Ah, fill the Cup: what boots it to repeat.
How Time is slipping underneath our Feet.
Unborn To-Morrow, and dead Yesterday,
Why fret about them if To-day be sweet.

Lottie was happy that Gretchen and Neel had gotten together. They were kindred spirits. Neel had come to Witherston two years ago from Tahlequah, Oklahoma, where his north Georgia grandparents, Mohe Kingfisher and Penance Louise Withers, had sought refuge in 1930 after Penance was disinherited for marrying a Cherokee. Neel moved to Lumpkin County in search of his ancestral roots and found them. A physician by vocation, having trained at the University of Oklahoma College of Medicine, and a philosopher by avocation, Neel had resigned from Withers Retirement Village in July because he no longer wanted to administer drugs for a living. After he and Gretchen fell in love, he bought a plot of land several miles north of Witherston, named it Green Acres, and started growing vegetables, organically of course. Under Gretchen's influence, he too abandoned meat, except for venison. Neel and Gretchen were both fifty-six years old and now no longer lonely.

Neither was Lottie lonely, not any more. In the depression she suffered after Brian's death, she could not have imagined the joy she felt this evening surrounded by her favorite people and confident of their affection for her. She looked around. This was her family, the one she'd created for herself. "Here's to you all," she said as she raised her glass of Rioja. "You all have come into my heart, and you are here to stay."

"Here's to you, Aunt Lottie, the kindest, smartest, most loving aunt in the whole wide world," Mev said.

"Here's to Aunt Lottie."

"Here's to Lottie."

"Here's to our hostess."

"Merry Christmas, dear friends," Neel said. "Thank you all for opening your hearts to me."

"*Salud, queridos amigos.*"

"Time for a group hug," Jorge said.

The ten of them group-hugged.

Jaime pulled up a kitchen stool to sit by Doolittle. Jorge and Beau sat down cross-legged on the floor at the coffee table. Jorge began drawing a cartoon on paper and Beau opened up his tablet.

"I found a large parrot cage for you to buy for Doolittle, Dr. Byrd," Beau said. "It's thirty-two inches wide, twenty-two inches deep, and sixty-four inches high. The picture on the web shows an African Grey in it."

"I'll order it for you, Aunt Lottie."

Lottie handed Jorge her credit card.

"It will arrive on Wednesday."

Of the twins, Jorge was the artist, writer, political activist, and journalist-in-training. Even though he was in ninth grade, he'd written an online column titled "What's Natural" for *Webby Witherston* for the last six months, and he occasionally contributed a cartoon or a photograph. He liked the attention he got from *Webby Witherston*'s readers. He'd told only a few people that the photograph accompanying his column was of his identical twin brother. He figured it didn't matter. He and Jaime were inseparable. He'd never perceived much of a dividing line between them.

Jaime was the naturalist of the family, the animal

lover, and the musician. He played the guitar. He planned to major in biology at the University of Georgia, get a PhD in ecology, and become a professor. Since the previous June, when Founding Father's Creek proved to be contaminated with dangerous pharmaceuticals, he'd wanted to study the ways humans polluted nature. And he understood animals. If anybody could make Doolittle happy, Jaime could.

Beau wanted to be a scholar like Lottie. Having an African American father whose slave ancestors worked in the Dahlonega gold mines during the 1828 Gold Rush, Beau planned to write a history of the Black people in north Georgia whose lives were entangled with the Cherokees, the gold seekers, and the White settlers of the state. Beau believed that some of his relatives had been force-marched to Indian Territory with the Cherokees on the Trail of Tears. Last June when he helped Jorge and Jaime figure out old Francis Hearty Withers's family tree, Beau realized that he relished being a detective of the past, uncovering what really happened, and learning how the events of years ago led to the events of the present. Like Jorge and Jaime, Beau was a straight-A student at Witherston High.

And Paco was a popular teacher at Witherston High. He taught biology—in the classroom, in the lab, and in the field. He was famous, at least in Witherston, for taking his students to Founding Father's Creek to see for themselves not just the individual organisms but also the ways the organisms interacted in the ecosystem. Paco embraced the ecological principle of the organisms' interdependence, which he saw as the basis for ethics. "If all of us creatures are interdependent," he'd tell his classes, "then we are all better off if we help each other." His students had great fun repeating Paco's mantra with Paco's Spanish accent, but they took it to heart.

As a detective, Mev benefitted from her extended family's various intellectual talents. The Arroyo team, which included all of Lottie's guests, had helped her solve the biggest mystery in Witherston's history—the murder of Francis Hearty Withers over Memorial Day weekend. Tonight everybody wanted to know about Doolittle's rescue.

Mev conveyed what she'd found out. "Here's to Doolittle," she said after telling the story and raised her glass of Rioja. "and to Aunt Lottie. May Doolittle and Aunt Lottie have a long life together."

"*Salud,*" Paco said.

"*Salud,*" everyone else echoed.

Doolittle kept quiet. He watched Jaime.

"Doolittle is a good bird," Jaime said softly. "Doolittle, wanna go up?" Jaime held out his hand.

Doolittle stayed in his cage.

"I'd like to offer a toast to Rhonda Rather for liberating the chickens," Gretchen said.

"And to Dan Soto, who did his share of the work before Rhonda got there," Lottie said.

"And to the person who started the liberation in the middle of the night, whoever he or she may be."

"*Chin, chin.*"

They all clicked glasses.

"And to Jorge, Jaime, and me, who uncrated fifty chickens at Free Rooster Village this afternoon," Beau said.

"And to Annie, who set them free."

"Free Rooster Village?" Paco asked. "Is that where you were?"

"Here's to chicken liberation," Jorge said, raising his glass of ginger ale to Beau's. "Let's make road signs that say, 'Welcome to Witherston, Free Chicken City.'"

"Jorge can draw the chickens," Beau said.

"That's what I'm doing," Jorge said.

Gretchen raised her glass. "Here's to Witherston, where chickens have a life."

"*Chin, chin.*" Clicking all around.

As Lottie and her company sat down for dinner, they heard Swift bark. Fiercely. And then the other dogs.

"Last night's burglar must have forgotten something," Jorge said.

"Could be the UPS man," Jaime said.

"Delivering ground beef," Beau said.

"''Tis some visitor, only this and nothing more.'" Lottie opened the front door. In the glow of the porch light, she could see the five dogs digging into the snow bank beside the driveway. Then Swift dragged something obviously heavy into the driveway. "Oh, no," she cried. "There's a body out there."

Mev grabbed her jacket and went outside. Jim followed. Mev brushed snow off the body. It was Gifford Plains. Jim felt his neck for a pulse, found none, and pronounced him dead at seven o'clock.

ઌ

After Deputy Hefner had taken pictures, Chief McCoy squatted on his haunches and brushed more snow off the body.

"The cause of Plains's death is probably hypothermia," Jake said to Mev. "Dirk will tell us."

Dirk Wales was the Lumpkin County Coroner in Dahlonega.

"Why would a healthy man freeze to death within thirty feet of Lottie's front door?" Mev asked. "Wouldn't Lottie have heard him make a noise if he slipped on the ice?"

"She may have been tied up when Plains came over."

"Well, he couldn't have come much later than one o'clock, because there's not much snow underneath his body and there's almost a foot of snow on top.

"Any broken bones?" asked Mev. "Cuts? Head injuries?"

"There's a bruise on his left temple," Jake said, removing Gifford's navy wool beanie. "Maybe he fell on the ice, lost consciousness, and froze."

"But he was lying on his right side."

"Maybe he got smacked by a falling branch."

"So where's the fallen branch?" she demanded.

"Maybe he was knocked down by Doolittle's kidnapper."

"Or hit in the head."

"If that's what happened, we're looking at a case of manslaughter."

"I'll give the sad news to his wife," Mev said to Jake. "Will you come with me?"

ઌઌ

Dan Soto and Catherine Perry sat at a candle-lit corner table in Witherston Inn Café. Muddy lay at their feet hidden by the red tablecloth. Dan and Catherine ordered grilled catfish and coleslaw with a bottle of Montaluce Chardonnay from a local winery. To the puzzlement of the waiter, they also ordered a buffalo burger.

"Please hold the onions, mushrooms, and local greens," Dan said to the waiter. "Just buffalo and bun."

After the waiter had brought their food and wine, Dan slipped Muddy's plate under the table. Muddy ate his dinner quietly, while Dan and Catherine told each other about their past, their present, and their ambitions for the future.

Catherine had grown up in Dahlonega, studied journalism at Brenau College in Georgia, worked summers for *Webby Witherston*, and now had a real fulltime job with the online news source. She hoped to become an investigative journalist, get married, and have two children.

Dan wanted to quit driving a chicken truck, immediately, then and there, buy an apple orchard in north Georgia as soon as possible, get married, and have two children.

"If you're going to quit driving that chicken truck immediately, Dan, what will happen to the freezing, starving chickens still stuck in their crates?"

"How about you coming with Muddy and me to free the rest of the chickens, feed them, and give them water?"

"And if you get caught again?"

"I've thought about that. I'm sending a check to Love Me Tender Poultry for four thousand dollars—that's two dollars per broiler—to pay for those chickens. I've already texted my boss. Then they'll be my chickens. And my gift to Witherston."

"Who's your boss?"

"I call him 'Mr. Tender,' and he thinks that's funny. His name is Rand Comstock. He's a nice man. He's just in a business I don't like, a family business his father started forty years ago."

"Does he like the business?"

"I haven't asked him. He'd like to make Love Me Tender Poultry a chicken-friendlier place. But he's stuck in a system he can't change. He has to compete with poultry producers throughout the Southeast to bring chickens cheaply to a chicken-hungry population. And for way too many people in the South, chicken is the only protein-rich food they can afford."

"I eat chicken, Dan, two or three times a week. Or I did, till now."

"Anyway, the times are changing, and we're discovering what goes on in animals' minds. So in the future we may be kinder and gentler to chickens, as well as to pigs and cows."

Catherine's cell phone rang. She listened. "I'm headed to Dr. Byrd's house right now," she said into the phone. Disconnecting, she turned to Dan. "That was my boss. He says that Gifford Plains has been found. Dead. In Dr. Charlotte Byrd's front yard."

"Jeepers. Where have I landed?"

"In the friendliest town in north Georgia, where everybody gets along with everybody else, as the mayor says. That reminds me. I'd better call Mayor Rather for a comment."

"Muddy and I will spend the night here at Witherston Inn. But I'd be grateful for a ride to my truck tomorrow morning."

"You'll get it. Here's my cell phone number." Catherine handed Dan her business card. "Call me. And be sure to check *Webby Witherston* when you wake up." She kissed him lightly on the cheek.

ꕥ

Mev and Jake sat together on one of the sofas facing Peg.

Peg was crying. "Giff wanted to live in the mountains, and I wanted to live in the city," she said between sobs. "So Giff bought this house in Witherston, and I kept our condo in Atlanta. At first I came up every weekend, but when I was promoting *Interred Near You* I didn't have time. I came up on Tuesday to go to the auction with Giff because we both collect Cherokee paraphernalia. I hadn't seen him since October."

"Do you know why he might have gone to Dr. Byrd's house so late in the evening?"

"I have no idea. Maybe he just wanted to look in on her. They were about the same age."

"Were you and Giff happy together?" Mev asked.

"Yes. Today we were going to celebrate our fifth anniversary."

"I am so sorry, Peg."

"Oh, I almost forgot to tell you. I found the blowgun and dart."

"Where?"

"In his closet. They're still there."

Jake interrupted their conversation. "Ms. Marble, did your husband keep a copy of his will here?"

Peg got up, went into Gifford's bedroom, and emerged with a large brown envelope. It was sealed.

"May I take it?" Jake asked politely.

"Of course. And you may read it. You'll see that I am the executrix."

❧❧

Jake and Mev sat together in Jake's squad car staring at Gifford Rorty Plains's will.

"Very, very interesting," Jake said. "Peg Marble is not the executrix, and she's barely an heir. Look at the date this will was executed."

"October thirtieth of this year, probably just after they last saw each other—before she came up this week, that is."

"And the main beneficiary, besides his daughter, is the Native American Artifacts Recovery Foundation in Seattle. Gifford Plains didn't leave his wife any of his money. Or any of his Cherokee relics, and she's a collector."

"Hmm. There was a bidder at the auction from Seattle, Jake. David Guelph. Strange coincidence."

He read the will out loud.

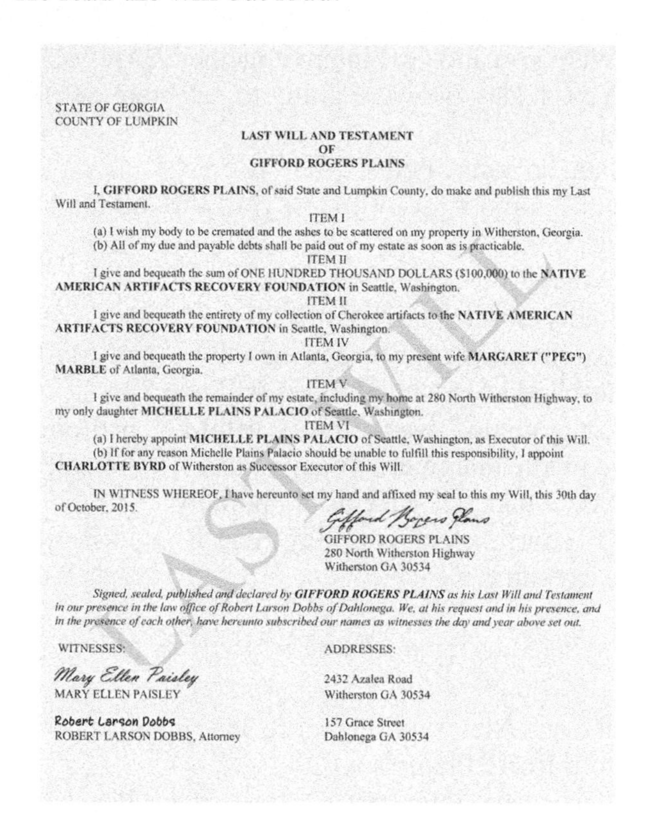

STATE OF GEORGIA
COUNTY OF LUMPKIN

LAST WILL AND TESTAMENT
OF
GIFFORD ROGERS PLAINS

I, **GIFFORD ROGERS PLAINS**, of said State and Lumpkin County, do make and publish this my Last Will and Testament.

ITEM I

(a) I wish my body to be cremated and the ashes to be scattered on my property in Witherston, Georgia.

(b) All of my due and payable debts shall be paid out of my estate as soon as is practicable.

ITEM II

I give and bequeath the sum of ONE HUNDRED THOUSAND DOLLARS ($100,000) to the **NATIVE AMERICAN ARTIFACTS RECOVERY FOUNDATION** in Seattle, Washington.

ITEM II

I give and bequeath the entirety of my collection of Cherokee artifacts to the **NATIVE AMERICAN ARTIFACTS RECOVERY FOUNDATION** in Seattle, Washington.

ITEM IV

I give and bequeath the property I own in Atlanta, Georgia, to my present wife **MARGARET ("PEG") MARBLE** of Atlanta, Georgia.

ITEM V

I give and bequeath the remainder of my estate, including my home at 280 North Witherston Highway, to my only daughter **MICHELLE PLAINS PALACIO** of Seattle, Washington.

ITEM VI

(a) I hereby appoint **MICHELLE PLAINS PALACIO** of Seattle, Washington, as Executor of this Will.

(b) If for any reason Michelle Plains Palacio should be unable to fulfill this responsibility, I appoint **CHARLOTTE BYRD** of Witherston as Successor Executor of this Will.

IN WITNESS WHEREOF, I have hereunto set my hand and affixed my seal to this my Will, this 30th day of October, 2015.

Gifford Rogers Plains
GIFFORD ROGERS PLAINS
280 North Witherston Highway
Witherston GA 30534

*Signed, sealed, published and declared by **GIFFORD ROGERS PLAINS** as his Last Will and Testament in our presence in the law office of Robert Larson Dobbs of Dahlonega. We, at his request and in his presence, and in the presence of each other, have hereunto subscribed our names as witnesses the day and year above set out.*

WITNESSES:	ADDRESSES:
Mary Ellen Paisley MARY ELLEN PAISLEY	2432 Azalea Road Witherston GA 30534
Robert Larson Dobbs ROBERT LARSON DOBBS, Attorney	157 Grace Street Dahlonega GA 30534

"I'll contact the daughter. And I'll tell her about the will," he said when he'd finished.

"She'll probably ask for it to be probated soon, Jake. Remember to give her Lauren's contact information."

Mev got out of Jake's car to return to Lottie's party.

"Good night, Mev. Enjoy the rest of your evening."

As Jake turned on the ignition, his cell phone rang. "Hello, Catherine," he said. "No grass grows under your feet."

ও৩ও৩

While Hempton stoked the fire and Petal brought in the tray of after-dinner liqueurs—Frangelico, Drambuie, Limoncello, and Cointreau—Grant studied the Fairfields' living room. He saw wealth.

Antique oriental chairs, some of them reminiscent of small thrones, and highly polished rosewood end tables lined the forest green walls. A set of antique carved rosewood screens adorned with carved ivory birds filled one corner. A six-foot-long cabinet of carved Chinese elm filled the other. A carved ivory chess set occupied an ivory inlaid rosewood coffee table. A set of two-foot-high, intricately carved elephant tusks, now illegal to buy or sell, framed the gray marble fireplace. Two tall brass floor lamps provided the lighting for the room. A wall-hung black lacquered wood curio cabinet, probably thirty inches by thirty inches by two inches, displayed sixteen exquisite Japanese netsuke, tiny carved ivory figurines. Wrought iron bars on the newly installed picture windows ensured the safety of these treasures.

Hemp and Petal really liked ivory, Grant thought. Good thing Gretchen would never be invited here.

"Tell us about the tusks," Ruth said to Petal. "Who carved them?"

"I don't know. Someone in China a long time ago. Hemp got them from another dealer."

"Have you been to China, Hemp?" Grant asked. "You obviously like things Chinese."

"Actually, I have not. I'm a collector, not a traveler. And if you make me a good offer on anything you see here, I'll sell it to you."

"The tusks too?"

"Yes, the pair for ten thousand dollars."

"No, Grant. Don't even think of it," Ruth said.

The Fairfields' phone rang, their landline.

"I'll get it," Hempton said to Petal. "Hello?...Hi,

Rich." Hempton listened a moment. "That's shocking. But I can tell you who did it. John Hicks. He's already threatened me for selling Cherokee artifacts." Hempton hung up and turned to his guests. "Gifford Plains is dead. John Hicks must have killed him for buying the blow-gun."

"So he might go after us too."

"Keep your tomahawk handy, Grant. He may go after you."

☙❧

By nine o'clock Gifford Plains's body had departed by ambulance to Chestatee Regional Hospital in Dahlonega for an autopsy. Deputy Hefner had departed as well.

Catherine Perry arrived to find Lottie, Mev, Paco, Lauren, Jim, Gretchen, and Neel drinking peppermint tea at the dining room table, Jorge drawing on the coffee table, Jaime holding Doolittle, and Beau lying on the living room carpet with five tired dogs. *What a nice extended family*, she thought. "Detective Arroyo," she said, after Mev had invited her to take a seat on the sofa. "Can we talk about Dr. Plains?"

Mev told her what she knew.

As Catherine donned her scarf, coat, and gloves and prepared to leave, Jorge got up from the coffee table. "Mizz Perry, could you please take this cartoon to Mr. Green to put on *Webby Witherston*?"

"Wow, Jorge. That is good. Really, really good."

"I've been thinking, Mizz Perry. Do you know Scorch and Abby Ridge?"

"Yes. Scorch sculpted the statue of Francis Hearty Withers."

"Well, Scorch and Abby keep chickens, and they've

named them. They call one of them Harriet Beecher Stowe. Scorch says that chickens have feelings and thoughts and memories. So why do we treat chickens worse than parrots?"

"Because chickens aren't as smart as parrots," Jaime said. He had Doolittle on his hand.

"Scorch told me that each of his chickens has a different personality, and when he calls a chicken by her name the chicken comes to him," Jorge said. "Scorch says that chickens recognize different people as well as different chickens. They know who's above them and who's below them in the pecking order."

"So do lots of animals. Dogs, wolves, deer," Jaime interjected.

Lottie frowned. "Jaime, even if chickens aren't as smart as parrots, should they be treated worse than parrots? Would you say that a human who is not smart should be treated worse than a human who is smart?"

"No."

Doolittle suddenly lunged at Jaime's arm. Jaime jerked his wrist to distract Doolittle. Doolittle then concentrated on maintaining his balance. Apparently the bird enjoyed riding on Jaime's wrist. He couldn't fly, though he still had his flight feathers. He simply didn't know how to use his wings.

"Would Doolittle like to step up on my arm?" Catherine asked, pushing up her sweater and offering the bird her left arm.

Doolittle hopped onto it while Catherine held her arm very still. Then Doolittle bit her hand.

"Ouch," Catherine cried. "That hurt."

"That hurt?" Doolittle asked.

"Yes, Doolittle. That hurt, but not very much."

Jaime held out his hand and took back the bird.

"It's not because chickens aren't smart that we treat

them badly," Beau volunteered from his place with the dogs on the floor. He was lying on his back and resting his head against Gandhi, who was asleep. "It's because we eat chickens. We don't think about the intelligence of anybody we eat. If we consider chickens stupid, we don't mind treating them badly."

"We don't empathize with anyone we want to eat, or use for leather, or employ as a pack animal," Lottie said. "Or keep as a slave."

"Or conquer," Gretchen said.

"Right, Gretchen," Neel said. "When your White ancestors sent my Cherokee ancestors to Indian Territory, they didn't consider my ancestors to be real people. But now you and I love each other. Proof that integration helps society overcome historical prejudices."

"My mother's ancestors enslaved my father's ancestors because Whites had power," Beau said. "And Whites needed Blacks to work in their fields. Also, Whites thought they were smarter than Blacks. But that was because the Blacks couldn't read. Did you know it was illegal for slave-owners to teach slaves to read?"

"People have always thought that those who looked like them were better than those who didn't," Jim said. "Smarter, more moral, more deserving, more sensitive, more blessed by God, holier—you name it."

"It's like the way we act with animals," Beau said. "Humans think that everyone who's not human is not smart or sensitive. So humans think it's okay to treat nonhumans any way they like."

"OO EE AW AW," Doolittle whistled.

"Doolittle, you're weird," Jaime said and then imitated the bird. "OO EE AW AW."

"I just thought of something. Pigs are smart and we eat them," Jorge said.

"OO EE AW AW."

"I don't," Gretchen said.

"I don't," Lottie said.

"I don't," Neel said. "At least not anymore."

"I do," Paco said. "Just not here in Lottie's house."

"*Salud*," Doolittle said.

"Doolittle," Jaime exclaimed. "*Salud* to you."

Beau sat up. "Since people don't keep pigs or chickens as pets, people don't know about their feelings."

"Free Rooster Village keeps a pig named Betty as a pet," Gretchen said.

"When we name anybody, we're saying that he or she is a person," Lottie said. "But then I think that all the feathery and furry animals who share our space on Earth are persons, whether or not we humans have named them." Lottie winked at her niece.

"I do too," Gretchen said.

"By the way," Lottie continued, "parrot parents use different calls for their different offspring. Scientists say that's equivalent to naming the chicks. And scientists who record parrots' calls say that different parrot families have different accents."

Neel grinned. "I know someone who has named a roach in her house 'Bobby,' and since all roaches look alike, she calls them all 'Bobby,' and she doesn't kill them."

"My lovable Neel is talking about me," Gretchen said.

Mev cocked her ear. "Aunt Lottie, you said your parrot was kidnapped. Would you say that those chickens on Dan's truck were kidnapped?"

"I would," Lottie said. "And I'd like to prosecute Love Me Tender Poultry for kidnapping two thousand chickens and then inhumanely stuffing them into Dan's truck to be transported over a state line and murdered.

That adds up to kidnapping, which is a federal offense, and murder, which is a state offense."

"Murder is the crime of killing a person with malice aforethought," Mev said. "An animal is not a person, Aunt Lottie, so an animal can't be murdered—just killed."

"If a bird can be kidnapped, a bird can be murdered. No matter what kind of bird the victim is—a parrot, a sparrow, an ostrich, or a chicken." Lottie smiled. "What do you say, Judge Lodge?"

Lauren smiled back. "I'm a probate judge, Lottie. If a bird had a will, I'd probate it just as I would any other person's will."

"Aha. You said 'any other person.'"

"Right, Lottie. I'm on your side."

"If I were not a human, I'd want to be a parrot, so I could tell people about my feelings," Jaime said.

"Do you think that mattered to Doolittle's previous owners? I don't," Lottie said.

"Doolittle is a fucking bad bird." Doolittle said.

"Time for me to go," Catherine said. "Let's see if your drawing evokes a response, Jorge."

"Time for us all to go," Mev said. "You've had a long day, Aunt Lottie."

"But a happy one, dear."

Jaime returned Doolittle to the rope handle on top of his cage and said to the parrot, "Doolittle is a good bird. I love you."

Doolittle repeated, in Jaime's voice, "Doolittle is a good bird." Then, "Doolittle wanna apple."

❧❧

Mev disconnected and turned to Paco. "I can't believe what's happening. David Guelph died last night outside Witherston Inn. He may have frozen to death."

"Like Gifford?"

"Or he may have been struck."

"Like Gifford."

"Very much like Gifford."

"Who is David Guelph?" asked Paco.

"He's the older gentleman from Seattle who bought the page from the *Cherokee Phoenix* and some other stuff at the auction. A collector. The night manager found him under a rhododendron near the front entrance. Not all the snow had melted off the bush, but enough was gone for him to notice the partially covered body."

"*Caramba.* How many more bodies will we find when the snow is all gone?"

"Anyway, since the two housekeepers were not at work today, it was the night manager who noticed that Guelph hadn't checked out. He went into Guelph's room and found the bed still made and Guelph's suitcase still there. So he went outside to look around. With a flashlight."

"Chief McCoy's there?"

"Yes, he's there, and so is Catherine. But Guelph is not. His body has already been taken to Dahlonega for autopsy. I'll meet Jake at nine tomorrow morning."

ঞঞ

"How could anybody kidnap pets for a living?" Jorge asked Jaime as he turned the lights out, moved Mighty from his pillow to the foot of his bed, and crawled under the covers.

"Don't know. Can you imagine being a little kid thinking 'When I grow up I want to kidnap a parrot'?"

"Like thinking 'When I grow up I want to be a criminal.'"

"Like 'When I grow up I want to kill someone.'"

"No little kid wants to grow up and be bad."

"But some turn bad, Jorge. Our high school has seven hundred students. And we like almost everyone there. But two or three of them may turn bad. And we can't guess who they are."

"I'd say that bad things happen to people, and if they can't handle their trouble, they accidentally turn bad. One thing leads to another."

"How do we keep from turning bad?"

"We consult each other."

"Right, we're a team," Jaime agreed.

"What if you didn't have me, or anybody?"

"I don't know. Hard to imagine."

The boys were quiet for a few minutes.

"What do you want to do tomorrow?" Jaime asked.

"Find Doolittle's kidnapper."

"Me too."

"*Buenas noches, hermano.*"

"*Buenas noches.*"

WWW.ONLINEWITHERSTON.COM

WITHERSTON ON THE WEB
Friday, December 16, 2015
8:00 a.m.

LOCAL NEWS
Two Deaths in Witherston

Gifford Plains, of 300 North Witherston Highway, is dead. The retired anthropologist was found at 7:10 p.m. yesterday by Charlotte Byrd in a snow bank in her front yard at 301 North Witherston Highway. Chief Jake McCoy, judging from the snow piled on top of the body, estimated the time of death between 1:00 and 2:00 a.m., early Thursday morning.

Mayor Rather expressed his sorrow over the death of Dr. Plains. "In November, Professor Plains joined me on the very important board of our new Cherokee-Witherston Museum, which I chair. He will be missed."

David Guelph, of Seattle, is also dead. His body was found under a bush at Witherston Inn at 9:45 p.m. on Thursday evening. Mr. Guelph had attended Hempton Fairfield's auction Wednesday night and had purchased several Cherokee relics.

Chief McCoy said, "The kidnapping of the parrot Dr. Byrd bought at the auction and the deaths of Dr. Plains and Mr. Guelph, who also bought items at the auction, may be related. Witherston Police would like to in-

terview anybody who may have seen the two men out in the storm either late Wednesday night or early Thursday morning."

Chief Jake McCoy fined Daniel Soto and Rhonda Rather each $100 for vandalism and released them from jail yesterday afternoon. Deputy Pete Senior Koslowsky had arrested them for letting loose more than a hundred chickens from Mr. Soto's eighteen-wheeler tractor-trailer truck.

Mr. Soto was hauling 2,000 live chickens from Love Me Tender Poultry farms in Tennessee to a processing plant near Dahlonega when the truck went out of control in the blizzard and blocked South Witherston Highway.

Later, in the afternoon, more chickens were released from the truck. It is rumored that many chickens have been taken to the grounds of Tayanita Village and to the home of Jon Finley and Gregory Bozeman.

The eighteen-wheeler has been towed to the side of the road. The snow that fell on Witherston Highway has melted, and traffic is flowing normally. Doolittle, the African Grey parrot found in the truck, has been returned to Dr. Byrd.

By the way, lots of chickens are running loose near the intersection of South Witherston Highway and Hiccup Hill Road. You can't see them in the snow, but you can hear them. They sound happy now, but they will need to be fed. See the drawing of the chicken truck and the photo of Doolittle, both by Jorge Arroyo, on today's WITHERSTON ON THE WEB.

~ Catherine Perry, Reporter

ANNOUNCEMENTS

Tony Lima's Mountain Band will practice tonight at 5:00 in Reception Hall of Witherston Baptist Church. They will be joined by Mayor Rather who will sing Alvin's part in the Chipmunks' Christmas song, Pete Senior Koslowsky who will sing Theodore's part, and Pete Junior Koslowsky, who will sing Simon's part.

WEATHER

The skies are clear, the sun is out, and the temperature will rise into the 50s today, after a low of 28 degrees last night. Tonight's low will be 41.

Old Dirt Road is still good for sleds, and for a one-horse open sleigh.

Weave, weave, weave me the sunshine out of the falling snow.

~ Tony Lima, Singer Sledder

LETTERS TO THE EDITOR

To the Editor:

On Wednesday night, Mr. Hempton Fairfield auctioned off to the highest bidders a Cherokee blowgun, a Cherokee tomahawk, a Cherokee quiver, a Cherokee ceremonial mask, and a page from the Cherokee Phoenix, which was the first Native American newspaper in the history of our continent. None of the highest bidders was a Cherokee.

The Cherokee people cannot afford to buy back what our own people—our own great, great, great, great grandfathers and grandmothers—created with their hands and their hearts.

Our civilization has been destroyed twice. The first time was the removal of our people from north Georgia because we occupied land that Whites wanted for its gold.

The second time was the theft of our artifacts, which are now bought and sold by dealers like Mr. Fairfield to wealthy individuals, usually White, who want tokens of a culture they find exotic.

Who should own the vestiges of a destroyed people? Their descendants, few as they may be? Or the descendants of their destroyers?

~ Chief Atohi Pace, Tayanita Village

To the Editor:

Do you not find it strange that Mr. Hempton Fairfield puts up for bid both an American weapon that was used by Whites to kill Cherokees and a Cherokee weapon that was used by Cherokees to kill Whites?

And that Witherston's own Mr. Wilker bid on both—the long rifle and the blowgun—without any apparent concern for the murderous circumstances of their deployment?

Are these weapons, both from the 1830s, both from Georgia, no longer emblems of the bloody history of our state?

Are they simply items for trade in the antique business, where age, rarity, and demand determine price?

~ Neel Kingfisher, Witherston

Doolittle in the chicken truck by Jorge Arroyo

Doolittle, in home of Dr. Charlotte Byrd
Photo of Jaime Arroyo
by Jorge Arroyo

WITH CHICKEN TRUCK DRIVER
by Catherine Perry

Last night this reporter interviewed Daniel Soto, driver of the 18-wheeler tractor-trailer truck that skidded across South Witherston Highway about 1:30 a.m. on Thursday. It was carrying 2,000 chickens at the time of the accident. The kidnapped parrot Doolittle was found in the truck yesterday afternoon.

CP: Thank you for allowing me to interview you, Mr. Soto.

DS: Please call me Dan.

CP: First, may I ask you to describe your cargo?

DS: My cargo? Broiler chickens. Chickens bred to be broiled. So they're called broilers. What an insulting name to give an animal who thinks and feels! Anyway, broilers have white feathers, yellowish skin, and red comb and wattles.

CP: How old are they?

DS: Forty-five days old, most of them, when I pick them up from Love Me Tender Poultry.

CP: How much do they weigh?

DS: Five pounds each—at only six or seven weeks of age. They've been fattened so fast they can hardly stand when they're loaded into their crates. They're like a two-year-old human toddler who weighs more than three hundred pounds.

CP: So they're not healthy?

DS: Hell, no, they're not. They have skeletal deformities, bacterial infections, and chronic pain—let me say it again, chronic pain—all because the poultry industry needs to turn chicks into food as efficiently as possible to satisfy humans' demand for fried chicken, roasted chicken, stewed chicken, broiled chicken, and chicken nuggets.

CP: Do you eat chicken?

DS: Never. I identify too much with these beautiful birds to eat them for dinner. Can you imagine being a chicken on my truck, confined to a crate, unable to stand, freezing cold, terrified?

CP: You're speaking as if chickens were people.

DS: I live in a world where humans think we're the only ones on the planet who have thoughts and feelings, who have a mental life. See that hawk circling above us? Don't you think he has thoughts and feelings, and maybe a plan to kill one of these chickens?

CP: Let me ask you another question. Did you kidnap Doolittle, the parrot? Or do you know who did?

DS: No, and no.

CP: How do you explain Doolittle's getting into your truck?

DS: I don't. Only thing I can think of is that someone put him there to hide him. Maybe when I had my wreck. You know that someone got into the trailer and let some chickens loose last night? In one minute, some of those lucky birds went from being broilers in the truck to chickens in the wild, in one single minute, all because I skidded on ice. Luck. Luck shapes everybody's life. I could have been born a chicken. You could have. Rand Comstock could have.

CP: Who is Rand Comstock?

DS: He is the owner of Love Me Tender Poultry. He's a decent man. He's just stuck in an indecent industry.

CP: Are you also saying that chicken truck drivers are stuck in an indecent industry?

DS: Yes, everybody who raises chickens, transports chickens, processes chicken, packages chicken, sells chicken, or eats chicken is stuck in an indecent industry. And almost everybody in the indecent industry is decent. So we have to change the whole industry. Same with the pork industry and the beef industry.

CP: How can that be done?

DS: I don't know. But good people who are smarter than I am are trying. As for me, I'm opting out. I want to live on an apple farm in these beautiful mountains right near your beautiful town, Miss Perry.

IN THIS MONTH IN HISTORY

By Charlotte Byrd

On December 16, 1981, Smithfield Green became the fourth editor of the Witherston Weekly, founded in 1931, which he turned into the online WITHERSTON ON THE WEB *in 2009. Smitty came to Witherston from Athens, Georgia, at the age of twenty-two with his wife Gretchen Hall Green. They had just graduated from the Grady College of Journalism at the University of Georgia.*

Smitty recalls Witherston in 1981. "With a population of 2,173, Witherston had one gas station, one church, one restaurant, one grocery store, one elementary school, one high school, one fire truck, one patrol car, one tavern which was Rosa's Cantina, one bowling alley, and a seldom-used jail attached to the police station and mayor's office. Witherstonians went to Dahlonega if they needed a doctor. I had little to fill the pages of the Witherston Weekly other than the consequences of intoxication reported in Police Blotter. I would have enjoyed a shooting. The most exciting section was the Letters-to-the-Editor page, which was dominated by complaints against Mayor Bullet Wilker for doing whatever the wealthy Francis Hearty Withers told him to do. Jimbo McCoy was police chief. He had no deputy. Now we have three deputies and four police vehicles. Rosa's Cantina is still the only tavern."

Smitty and Gretchen divorced in December of 1982. According to Gretchen, they couldn't eat at the same table. She could eat no meat and he could eat no fish, so they parted company. After unsuccessfully opposing Mayor Wilker for election in 1984, Gretchen established Gretchen Green's Green Grocery.

MENU SPECIALS

Founding Father's Creek Café: Oven roasted herb chicken served with new potatoes and asparagus, wilted lettuce salad with bacon, banana pudding.

Gretchen Green's Green Grocery (Lunch only): Hot gingered carrot soup, freshly baked whole wheat bread with homemade butter, collard greens with cranberries and pine nuts, spinach-celery-apple-walnut salad, lemon sorbet.

Witherston Inn Café: Tarragon chicken over white rice with fennel, turnip greens, carrot cake.

CHAPTER 6

Friday morning, December 16:

Good morning, Doolittle," Lottie said, exiting her bedroom.

Before she plugged in her coffeemaker, Lottie opened Doolittle's cage door. To her surprise Doolittle climbed out and made his way to the rope handle.

"Doolittle is a good bird," Lottie cooed.

"Doolittle is a bird," Doolittle said softly.

"Doolittle is a good bird," Lottie repeated.

"Cluck, cluck." Doolittle clucked like a chicken. "Cluck, cluck, cluck, cluck."

Lottie offered her left hand to Doolittle, but Doolittle lunged at it. "No, no," she said quietly, turned her back on the parrot, found some dry roasted unsalted peanuts, and put them in Doolittle's food dish with fresh pellets.

"No, no," Doolittle said quietly.

Lottie called Mev. It was seven thirty in the morning, but she knew her niece would be up and about. "Doolittle is clucking like a chicken," she told Mev when Mev picked up. "I wonder what else Doolittle can tell us about his kidnapping."

"Zongzingzing." Doolittle mimicked the arrival of a text message.

"Aunt Lottie, something terrible has happened. David Guelph, the older gentleman who bought the Cherokee newspaper page at the auction, was found dead outside Witherston Inn last night."

"Good lord."

"I'm going over there now. Jake thinks he had been dead for some time."

"Good lord."

"Good lord," Doolittle repeated.

"Both Giff and David Guelph bought items at the auction."

"And I got Doolittle there."

"Right." Mev paused. "Maybe Hempton Fairfield can help us out."

"The bird abuser."

"Aunt Lottie, I have the certificate of provenance Giff got with his blowgun. If I brought it over in a few minutes, would you take a look at it?"

"I'll be happy to help with your investigation, dear. Your boys can help, too."

"I'll ask Paco to send them over as soon as they get up. I have to go to Witherston Inn now."

Then Lottie heard a small voice. "Doolittle wanna apple."

"I'll see you later, dear," she said. "Doolittle needs my attention."

ꕥ

By the time Mev reached Witherston Inn's Room 201, at nine o'clock in the morning, Chief McCoy and Deputy Hefner were already there. So was Catherine.

"Hello, Catherine. You don't miss anything."

"I listen to the police scanner, Detective Arroyo, and so does Smitty. We know where the action is."

"I've found the Cherokee stuff, boss," Ricky said. "It's all here in the closet, with his clothes."

"Tell me what you've found," Jake said.

Mev took out her notebook. Catherine took out her Android tablet.

Ricky dictated. "One framed old newspaper page, one wooden mask, three arrows, one small Cherokee pot—which I wish I'd bought for my wife, it's really nice—and one small basket. Also a certificate of provenance for the newspaper page."

Mev examined the certificate first. "The previous owner was Al Haash of Washington, DC," she observed. "He had it for a year before Mr. Fairfield got it." Then she looked at the framed page two from the *Cherokee Phoenix*. She took a picture of it and then turned it over. "This is interesting," she said. "Here is a label from the framer. And the date of the framing in pencil."

FOREVER FRAMES, Washington DC
2013

"So it was framed by Al Haash," Mev said. "I wonder whether he framed each page of the newspaper individually."

"Mr. Haash could have sold the other pages on eBay and made a bunch of money," Catherine said.

"Or he could have sold them in auctions," Mev said.

Mev turned to Jake. "May I take the certificate of provenance, Jake? I'd like Aunt Lottie to examine it."

"Photograph it, Ricky. Photograph what all you've found. Mev can take the certificate to Lottie and the rest of the auction items back to the station. And Ricky, photograph the clothes in the closet, the bed, the bathroom, everything. Also, the framed newspaper page. Robbery doesn't seem to have been the motive. At least not robbery of these valuable artifacts."

"Guelph's wallet and cell phone are here in the bedside table," Mev said. She tossed the wallet to Jake and opened the cell phone. No password was needed. "Well, this is interesting," she said. "I'm looking at his recent calls. He called Carolyn Foster at eleven thirty last night and Gifford Plains at twelve. Then somebody named Carlos Palacio in Snohomish, Washington, at twelve forty-five a.m. And Delta Airlines at one twenty-five. So he must have been alive at least until one twenty-five this morning. And his bed has not been slept in."

"Carlos Palacio. Maybe Michelle Plains Palacio's husband?"

"Mr. Guelph's body clock may still have been on Pacific time. That's three hours earlier," Catherine said.

Jake pulled out Guelph's driver's license. "Guelph was born on November 8, 1945."

"No text messages," Mev said. "I'll check his email. Hmm. His phone is not connected to email."

"He's old," Catherine said. "Maybe he just uses his phone as a phone."

"Seventy is not old," Jake said. "But maybe you're right."

"He was a smoker," Mev said. "Here's a package of Marlboros, opened."

"But this is a non-smoking room. Anyway, I don't smell smoke. He must have gone outside to smoke," Jake said.

"His clothes smell smoky. I don't know how he got so old being a smoker."

"Catherine, seventy is not old."

ও৩ও৩

"Boys, please see if you can find an Al Haash on the web."

Lottie sat at the dining room table studying the blowgun's certificate of provenance. Jorge stared at his iPad. Jaime, right beside him on Lottie's living room rug with Doolittle perched on his left wrist, looked over his brother's shoulder. Mighty lay asleep on the sofa.

"Aunt Lottie, I can't find any reference at all to an Al Haash," Jorge said. "Or to any Haash in Washington, DC. I've checked obituaries, death notices, marriage announcements. No Haash."

"Not cornbeef Haash?" Jaime asked.

"Not even Haash browns."

"Sounds like a made-up name," Jaime said.

"Good lord," Doolittle said.

"Good lord!" Lottie repeated.

"Doolittle is a fucking good bird."

"Lucky good bird. Doolittle is a lucky good bird," Lottie said.

"Lucky good bird."

Lottie changed the subject. "Boys, according to this certificate, a Mr. Arthur Ironside Crow from Habersham County was the first owner."

"But the blowgun was made by a Cherokee, not a White man. Why isn't the Cherokee listed as the first owner, Aunt Lottie?"

"Because Mr. Arthur Ironside Crow stole it from a Cherokee," Jorge said.

"And he didn't know the Cherokee's name."

"He didn't ask."

"That was not polite."

"He didn't care. The Cherokee was just an Indian."

"He should have said, 'Mr. Cherokee Indian, while I'm sticking my pistol into your esteemed ribs and taking your blowgun, would you please tell me your name?'"

"Boys, let's focus," Lottie said.

"We are focusing, Aunt Lottie," Jorge said.

"Good lord," Doolittle said.

Jorge continued. "Aunt Lottie, we're saying that Whites didn't treat Cherokees with respect back then."

"Whites didn't treat the Cherokees as persons," Jaime added. "They stole their stuff."

"They stole their land, dug up their gold, and sent them packing to Oklahoma."

"It wasn't Oklahoma then, bro. It was Indian Territory."

"Well, the Whites didn't send other Whites to White Territory."

"White Territory was here."

"Where the gold was in the ground," Lottie said. "But in Indian Territory oil was in the ground. If President Andrew Jackson had known that oil would be discovered there in 1859, he would have sent the Indians somewhere else."

"Like Death Valley," Jaime said.

"Anyway, boys, let's think about this certificate of provenance. Arthur Jackson Crow is probably the son of Arthur Ironside Crow. Ella Crow Rumsay is probably the daughter of Arthur Jackson Crow. William Jackson Rumsay is probably the son of Ella Crow Rumsay. And William Jackson Rumsay, III, is probably the grandson of William Jackson Rumsay. So if the blowgun was in the family of the Crows and the Rumsays for almost two hundred years, how did it get into the hands of Al Haash?

"Whoa. Check this out, Aunt Lottie. I just looked for Haash on eBay and found an A-L-H-A-A-S-H." Jorge spelled out the word. "Alhaash Antiques Online. I'll click on American Antiques. Look. Etchings, rare books. A watch."

"Click on Native American Artifacts," Jaime said.

"Huh. Just a few Native American things. Arrows, arrowheads, a hatchet."

"Do you suppose Mr. Fairfield is getting his antiques here? On eBay?" Lottie asked.

"You paid Doolittle's ransom on eBay, Aunt Lottie," Jaime said.

Mighty suddenly barked and raced to the back door.

"Hello, everybody." Mev entered the house. "I have more work for you all."

"Hey, Mom."

"Hey, Mom."

"Hello, dear." Mev took off her coat and pulled out the certificate of provenance for the framed page from the *Cherokee Phoenix*. "Your mission, should you all choose to accept it, is to figure out what the two certificates have in common."

"We accept, Mom."

"We accept, Mom. Can Beau come over?"

"And Annie?"

"We accept, Mev dear. We've already made an important discovery."

"By the way, folks," Mev said, "on the brown paper backing of the frame there was a label from a business called 'Forever Frames' in Washington, DC. The framing was done in 2014."

"So Forever Frames turned a valuable historical document into a souvenir," Lottie said.

"The newspaper may have been intact when Forever Frames framed that single page," Mev said. "What a loss. This Mr. Al Haash may have had the whole issue of the *Cherokee Phoenix* and taken it apart to sell each page separately."

"To make more money," Jorge said.

"Is the whole newspaper a souvenir, Aunt Lottie?" Jaime asked.

"Well, I myself would use it as an historical document to get a better picture of the past. But that's because I'm an historian. But I'd have to say yes to your question, Jaime. Even historical documents are little more than souvenirs. All we have from the past are souvenirs," Lottie said. She looked at the framed photograph of her son Brian taken at his high school graduation. "At least now we have photographs."

"So Mr. Fairfield was auctioning off souvenirs," Jorge said. "Expensive ones."

ᏣᏣ

After leaving the site of David Guelph's murder, Catherine met Dan and Muddy in the Witherston Inn lobby. "Do you want to go to Free Rooster Village, Dan?"

"Sure. But we have to go to my truck first. Remember? I want to check on my chickens."

"Your chickens?" Catherine smiled.

"I should have said God's chickens." Dan smiled. "Or Witherston's chickens. They're no longer Mr. Love Me Tender's chickens."

Catherine drove the two miles down Witherston Highway from Witherston Inn. Muddy leaned out the open window of the 1990 Ford's right rear seat, his mouth open, his tongue hanging out, his long ears flapping in the wind.

As they approached the eighteen-wheeler, Muddy started barking. Muddy had spotted the hundreds of chickens eating the chicken feed Rhonda was scattering on the snow.

Dan sang a song from *Mary Poppins*, "Feed the

birds, tuppence a bag, tuppence, tuppence, tuppence a bag."

Catherine laughed. "Pretty-in-pink Rhonda hardly looks like an old bird lady."

"I needn't have worried about hungry chickens."

"Or hungry animals of any kind when Rhonda is around."

Catherine made a U-turn by the eighteen-wheeler and pulled up behind Rhonda's black Escalade. Inside the vehicle, she could see a half-dozen fifty-pound bags of Eggstra chicken pellets. Plus Giuliani, who waited patiently in the front seat. Catherine and Dan got out, leaving Muddy in the back seat with the window down.

"Hey, Mrs. Rather," Catherine shouted.

"Hey, Mrs. Rather. You are a saint."

"Hello, cellmate," Rhonda said to Dan. "And hello, Catherine. Scorch and Abby donated all this chicken feed. Wasn't that nice of them."

Suddenly the white chickens, each clucking at the top of her lungs, fled in all directions across the snowy ground. Muddy was racing into their midst.

"Muddy!" Dan yelled. "Muddy! Come here!"

The basset hound ran as fast as his short legs could take him and quickly overtook the slowest of the chickens. Feathers flew.

Rhonda covered her eyes with her hands.

Muddy brought the dead chicken back to Dan. He wagged his tail.

"Mrs. Rather," Catherine said, pulling out her tablet and leaning against the Escalade. "You've just witnessed a predator kill his prey. Muddy is happy and the dead chicken is…well, dead. You like both dogs and chickens. So who gets to eat?"

"Both, I guess. At least that poor chicken had twelve hours of freedom in her short life."

After leaving a hand-written *FOR SALE* sign on the now chickenless eighteen-wheeler, Catherine and Dan, with Muddy in the back seat, drove slowly up Hiccup Hill Road. The asphalt was still slick from the melting snow.

"Two deaths in tiny Witherston in the middle of the night, the same night," Dan commented. "While I was stuck in the blizzard."

"Maybe the blizzard had something to do with the deaths."

"What did Gifford Plains and David Guelph have in common?"

"They both bought Cherokee relics at the auction."

"Yes, and they knew each other."

Catherine told Dan about what she'd learned in Guelph's hotel room.

"You're going to solve this mystery?"

"I am. And then I'll get a better job, maybe with the *Atlanta Journal-Constitution*."

"Would you live in Atlanta?"

"I wouldn't live there. I'd live here and work for the *AJC* online. Maybe I could write obituaries from here. That reminds me. I need to write obituaries this afternoon."

After going a couple of miles Catherine turned left onto Old Dirt Road and then right onto North Possum Road, where they saw a freshly painted *TAYANITA VILLAGE* sign. She drove into the compound of snow-covered green yurts. They were greeted by a bronze-feathered rooster, a dozen white chickens, a few brown chickens, and a beautiful young woman with a long black braid.

"Hello," Catherine said, stepping out of the car. "I'm Catherine Perry. I'm a reporter for *Witherston on the Web*."

Dan stepped out too. "And I'm Daniel Soto, the former driver of the chicken truck. Or the driver of the former chicken truck. I'm happy these chickens have found a home."

Muddy barked.

"Oh, yes, and that's my dog Muddy. He'll stay in the car."

Dan went back to the car and rolled each window down half way. For the time being Muddy would have plenty of fresh air but no freedom.

"I'm Galilahi Sellers. I used to be Helen Sellers, but I wanted a Cherokee name, so last year I changed my name legally to Galilahi. Chief Atohi Pace chose that name for me."

The rooster crowed.

"And that's Rooster Brewster," Galilahi added. "We've decided to keep him. I just replaced the *FREE ROOSTER* sign."

"You'd have had better luck giving Rooster Brewster a new home if you had put up a sign saying 'Buff Orpington Rooster for Sale: $50.' Folks don't value what's not worth money."

"You're probably right," Galilahi said.

"Could we sit down somewhere out of the cold?" Catherine asked. "I would like to ask you about the petition to call your settlement 'Tayanita Village.'"

"Let's go to the big yurt. It's got a wood stove. But we may have company. It's the only warm yurt in the village."

Galilahi led Dan and Catherine past the *CHEROKEE COMMANDMENTS* sign into the big yurt. The three of them, with Galilahi in the middle, sat down on one of the seven benches. Catherine noticed they did have company. Someone wrapped in a blanket was snoring on the bench nearest the wood stove across from the entrance. A pig was sleeping on the rug in front of the wood stove. So were several cats.

"Ignore him," Galilahi said, referring to the human. "He's a White friend of ours who stays here when he comes to Witherston. We do have White friends you know."

"Why does your village need an official name?" asked Catherine.

"We need a Cherokee name. We want Cherokees to be visible, and Cherokee culture to be remembered," Galilahi said. "We're part of a movement to revive Cherokee history. Cherokees occupied these mountains for a thousand years before White settlers arrived and replaced our names with theirs."

"What about Dahlonega?"

"The name *talonega* means yellow, for the gold that was in the ground. The White settlers who occupied the Cherokee towns sometimes kept the Cherokee names, but when they divided the land into counties they named the counties after themselves." Galilahi shook her head, as if in dismay. "Dahlonega is in Lumpkin County, named after Wilson Lumpkin. Lumpkin, when he was governor, gave away Cherokee land to White settlers in the Georgia Land Lotteries in the early 1830s. Ellijay, which came from the Cherokee word *elatseyi*, meaning 'new ground,' is in Gilmer County. George Gilmer, when he was governor, evicted the Cherokees from Georgia and sent them on the Trail of Tears."

"So the map shows both who was here first and who made the first people disappear," Dan said.

"Made them invisible," Galilahi corrected.

"Do you know Dr. Charlotte Byrd?" Catherine asked her. "She knows a lot about Cherokee history. She's an historian."

"No, but I know her across-the-street neighbor, Dr.

Plains. He gave a lecture last year at University of North Georgia, where I go to school, and brought some of his Cherokee weapons for us to look at."

"He's dead, Galilahi," Catherine said.

"What? Oh, no. How did he die?"

The sleeping body stirred. Catherine lowered her voice.

"He died in the snow outside of Dr. Byrd's house. He may have gone over to see her in the blizzard. And he may have been killed."

"Who would have killed him?"

"I don't know. Neither does the police. Do you?"

"No, no, Miss Perry. No. I tell you, no Cherokee would have killed him, or anybody. At least no Cherokee from Tayanita Village. Did you see our commandments? We try to follow them."

"You're kidding," Mev exclaimed.

"I'm not," Jake said.

Jake sat behind his desk at the police station, looking at his computer monitor. "I'm reading an email from Dirk. Says he will send us autopsy reports shortly. Then he asks this question: 'Where could the little white feathers on David Guelph's wool coat have come from?'"

"Could Guelph have been in the chicken truck?" she asked.

"Could he have kidnapped Doolittle?"

"But he was old," Mev said.

"Seventy is not old."

"Let's assume that this dignified gentleman who flew here from Seattle to buy expensive Cherokee artifacts did not leave his comfortable hotel room in his rental car in the blizzard to kidnap Doolittle, hide Doolittle in the chicken truck, and then return to Witherston Inn to make phone calls."

"Okay. But he must have had contact with chickens. Or with chicken feathers."

"Hmm. Maybe he ran into someone who had been in the chicken truck," Mev said.

"Someone who gave him a hug?"

"No, Jake. Think."

"Could that someone have been Dan Soto?"

"No. Dan was stuck in the cab of his eighteen-wheeler all night. Must have been someone else."

"Someone strong enough to knock him out and drag his body under the rhododendron."

"A man."

"That's the way it seems." Jake shrugged. "Men do most of the violence in this world."

Pete Junior entered Jake's office. "The mayor is here to see you," he said. "Should I send him in?"

"Oh, Lordy," Jake said. "Yes, you might as well."

"I'll be around," Mev said, heading toward the door.

"Hello, Detective Arroyo. How nice to see you."

"Good morning, Mr. Mayor. I'm just on my way out."

Mayor Rather walked in and settled his large body in the chair Mev had vacated. "I'm here to give you a tip on your murder investigation, Chief McCoy" he said. "You should interview John Hicks. And soon, very soon."

Jake listened to the mayor and promised to question John Hicks.

ꕤ

"You won't believe this," Catherine said to Dan and Gretchen.

She was reading an email on her Android while they

waited for Gretchen to fix their lunch. Catherine and Dan had seated themselves at one of the two rickety tables in the back of Gretchen Green's Green Grocery by the kitchen, near where Gandhi was sleeping. Muddy had taken his usual position under the table.

Gretchen never provided a menu, but her fare was always good. Today she was serving hot gingered carrot soup, freshly baked whole wheat bread with homemade butter, collard greens with cranberries and pine nuts, spinach-celery-apple-walnut salad, and lemon sorbet.

She brought the bowls of soup to Dan and Catherine and pulled up her own chair.

"I emailed the *Seattle Post-Intelligencer* and learned they've already prepared an obituary for Mr. Guelph," Catherine said. "I'm reading it now. Guess what? He's Dr. Guelph. The old man had a PhD."

"How did they know he was going to die, Catherine?" Dan asked.

"Newspapers write obits ahead of time for very important people. And Dr. Guelph was a very important man in Seattle," Catherine said. "He was really rich, really smart, and really interested in Native American culture." She showed Dan and Gretchen the obituary attached to the message. "I'll get his obit into *Webby Witherston* tomorrow."

CHAPTER 7

Friday afternoon, December 16:

The fire in the big yurt must have started soon after Catherine and Dan left Tayanita Village for Gretchen's Grocery.

Catherine got Smitty's call at twelve-twenty, when they were finishing their soup, and she knocked over her chair in her hurry to reach her car. Dan and Muddy followed her and managed to pile into the old Ford before she took off.

They arrived at the village entrance only minutes after the Witherston Fire Truck had entered and minutes before Deputy Pete Junior pulled up.

"Stay," Dan commanded Muddy, locking the dog in the car while Catherine ran up the muddy road to the Council House. Smoke poured out the open door. She joined Galilahi, Amadahy, and Atohi, who were watching the fire in horror.

Fire Chief Mike Moss and his two volunteers unrolled the fire hose, pushed in a window, and sprayed the interior with foam.

"Help," Thom Rivers cried out from the yurt's entrance. He was carrying Waya in his arms. "Help us, for

God's sake. Help us." He coughed. His face was black with soot.

"Help," Galilahi shouted to Chief Moss. She ran to Thom.

Thom set Waya on the snowy ground and started mouth-to-mouth resuscitation.

"Let me try," Chief Moss said. He tried. Finally, he sat back on his heels. "He's dead. I'm sorry."

"No, no, no, no, no! Please, God, no, no, no!" Thom sobbed.

Galilahi put her arm around Thom and cried with him.

"Waya came in to save me," Thom said. "He's my best friend. Now he's dead."

Atohi sat down next to Waya, closed the young man's eyes, and kissed him on the forehead. Then he looked up. "What happened, Thom?" he asked quietly.

"I was asleep on the bench near the wood stove. Betty squealed and woke me up. The rugs were on fire. At first I couldn't see anything for the smoke. Then I saw Waya running toward me. I guess he came to rescue me. Maybe he tripped on the rug and hit his head on a bench. I don't know. Anyway he fell. I picked him up. I thought he was still breathing."

"Is Betty in there?" Deputy Pete Junior shouted. "I'll go get her."

"Don't go. You can't see anything. The rugs are on fire and the smoke is blinding."

"But we have to save Betty."

"Betty is a pig," Amadahy exclaimed. "Her name's Betty Pig."

"A pig?"

"A pig. A nine-month old, two-hundred-pound pig," Amadahy replied.

"I don't deserve to live," Thom moaned.

"But you tried to save Waya, Thom," Galilahi said with her arms still around him.

"I should have died in there with him," Thom said. "I've got no reason to live."

"You need to get medical treatment for smoke inhalation," Atohi said. "Do you have family we can call?

"No, nobody. Nobody. Waya was my family."

"We can be your family," Galilahi said.

Thom coughed again.

Atohi turned to Pete Junior. "You've got to get Thom to a hospital."

"I'm calling the ambulance now," Pete Junior said, pulling out his cell phone. "It will get him to Dahlonega in a half hour. To Chestatee Regional Hospital."

"I don't need to go to the hospital. I don't want to go."

Atohi turned to Amadahy. "Amadahy, can you get us some blankets?"

Amadahy ran off in the direction of the nearest small yurt.

By now the firemen had put out the fire. They rolled up the hose, said their goodbyes, hopped onto the fire truck, and drove away slowly down Old Dirt Road.

Amadahy returned with two blankets. She put one of them over Waya's body. Then she looked around for Thom. He was gone. She watched his red pick-up disappear down Possum Road.

"We will gather here this evening at seven," Atohi said. "Galilahi, can you contact the other villagers?"

"I will," Galilahi said. "But where are Ayita and Moki?"

"In Dahlonega. I'll call them. And I'll call Waya's father."

"Waya was only twenty," Galilahi said. "He turned twenty just two weeks ago."

"Let us pray." Atohi bowed his head. "Let us have a moment of silence for Waya. Let us remember him as he was, a good young man, funny, loyal to his friends.

Atohi, Amadahy, and Galilahi brought Catherine and Dan into their circle.

Atohi knelt beside Waya's body. He bowed his head, as did everyone there.

After a minute of silence Galilahi looked up. "Here comes the detective."

Mev had left her CRV on the road and walked up the hill. She shook hands with each of the villagers, as well as Catherine and Dan.

"I am so very sorry," Mev said. "My husband taught Eddie, I mean Waya, and loved his sense of humor. I know his father. By the way, who called nine-one-one?"

"I did," Amadahy replied. "I saw the smoke, so I called nine-one-one."

"I was in the kitchen. I ran over when I saw the smoke," Galilahi said. "I didn't know that Waya had gone into the yurt."

"Where are the other villagers?" Mev asked Atohi.

"At work. We'll meet at seven o'clock for a memorial service. You are welcome to come, Detective Arroyo, and bring your family. Anybody who knew Waya is welcome to come."

"Thank you for the invitation, Chief Pace. My family will be here. But I must tell you that the medical examiner will want to have Waya's body autopsied."

"Why?"

"It's routine. In Georgia autopsies are usually performed in cases of accidental death. The ambulance will take Waya to Chestatee Regional."

"I'll tell Mr. Gunter."

"And Police Chief McCoy will want to examine the scene of the accident. He's on his way."

Deputy Pete Junior finished roping off entrance to the big yurt. He glanced inside. "The rugs are ruined," he said. "But the benches are fine. And so are the canvas walls. They must be fireproof. The skylights need cleaning."

"We need to get Betty Pig out," Galilahi said. "Poor Betty."

"Chief McCoy and I will be through here by four o'clock," Mev said. "Then you can prepare the yurt for the memorial service. Again, please accept our deepest condolences."

Catherine was taking notes on her Android. "May I put an announcement of the memorial service on *Webby Witherston*?"

"Certainly," Atohi said.

Catherine texted her boss.

The ambulance arrived.

ꕥ

After they had eaten their sandwiches of organic cashew butter and raspberry jam, Lottie cleared the dining room table so that she, Jorge, Jaime, Beau, and Annie could study the two certificates of provenance. Annie and Beau had joined them for lunch, and Beau had brought Sequoyah. Sequoyah and Mighty dozed on the sofa. Doolittle perched on the rope handle of his cage near Jaime.

"Good lord." Lottie was staring at the certificate of provenance Mev had given them. "The page from the *Cherokee Phoenix* that Mr. Guelph bought was also previously owned by Al Haash."

"Good lord," Doolittle said.

Jaime told Annie what they'd learned about Al Haash and Alhaash Antiques Online that morning.

"Mr. Fairfield must be a really good customer of Mr.

Alhaash," Annie said. "A really, really good customer."

"Or maybe Mr. Alhaash and Mr. Fairfield have some sort of deal," Beau said.

"Maybe Mr. Alhaash is Mr. Fairfield's main supplier," Lottie said.

Jorge went again to Alhaash's eBay store and looked at the buttons. He read aloud, "HOME, AMERICAN ANTIQUES, NATIVE AMERICAN ARTIFACTS, CONTACT US, ABOUT US"

"What's the difference between "antiques" and "artifacts"? Beau asked.

"Antiques were bought," Jorge answered. "Artifacts were stolen. From their makers."

"Antiques were made by so-called civilized people. Artifacts were made by so-called uncivilized people," Jaime said.

"Antiques are collected for parlors. Artifacts are collected for museums," Jorge said.

"Wait, folks," Lottie said. "It's way more complicated than that."

"Well," Beau said. "I'm African American, or at least half African American, so did my ancestors make antiques or artifacts?"

"Let's see." Jorge Googled AFRICAN AMERICAN ANTIQUES.

Beau looked over his shoulder. The first item that came up was BLACK AMERICAN COLLECTIBLES on eBay.

"They made collectibles."

"Good lord," Doolittle said.

"Right, I should have guessed. African Americans didn't make antiques," Beau said. "Or else they made antiques for White people. Like desks and cabinets."

"Slaves had no money to make fine things for themselves, Beau," Jaime said.

"True," Beau said.

"Folks," Lottie interjected. "Let's concentrate on Mr. Guelph's certificate of provenance."

"Who was Elias Boudinot?" asked Jaime, peering over Lottie's shoulder at the document. "He was the first owner."

"Can you look him up, Jorge?"

"Look him up on Wikipedia."

"Oh, this is interesting," Jorge said. "There were two Elias Boudinots, a White man and a Cherokee. The White Boudinot was president of the Continental Congress from 1782 to 1783. The Cherokee liked the White Boudinot and took his name. The Cherokee Boudinot was the first editor of the *Cherokee Phoenix* from 1828 to 1832."

"So Cherokee Boudinot edited the edition of the *Cherokee Phoenix* that David Guelph bought at the auction," Lottie said. "Boudinot probably kept the whole edition, not just page two."

"Here's more," Jorge said, still skimming the Wikipedia article. "Boudinot was fired in 1832 and replaced by a man named Elijah Hicks."

Jaime leaned closer to the monitor. "And then Boudinot gave the September 4, 1830 newspaper to Samuel Worcester. Who was Worcester?"

After a moment, Jorge reported, "Worcester set up the printing press and created the type for the *Cherokee Phoenix*."

"And Erminia Nash Worcester?"

"Worcester's second wife," Jorge said. "Apparently Worcester and his first wife moved to Oklahoma. After she died he married Erminia."

"And Dustu Rogers?"

"Can't find anything on Dustu Rogers. But there were some Cherokee chiefs in Oklahoma named Rogers."

Lottie looked up from the certificate. "Looks like the

newspaper stayed in Cherokee hands until Alhaash got hold of it."

"Think of all the people who read this newspaper from 1830 till now," Annie said.

"And who didn't," Lottie said. "Whoever took it to Forever Frames was more interested in the page as a souvenir than as an account of events. You know, that's what a souvenir is, a relic that no longer communicates its original meaning."

"A lightweight relic," Jorge said.

"I want to read what's on the page," Annie said.

"I'll ask Mom to email it to us," Jaime said. "She took a picture."

ശ്ശ

Jake shook hands with the chief. "Hello, Chief Pace. I am so very sorry about Waya's death."

"Thank you, Chief McCoy. Waya got into mischief from time to time, as you know, but he was a very good man. A good Cherokee."

Jake nodded. After a moment's silence he asked, "Is John Hicks here? I'd like to talk to him about a different matter."

"John Hicks left this morning. Said he was going to Atlanta to do some research."

"Does he have family there?"

"I don't think so. His parents, Bobbi and Lester Hicks, are veterinarians in Dahlonega."

"Do you have a cell phone number for him?'

Atohi wrote it down on his own business card. "Here it is. John Hicks is smart with computers. You should get him on your team."

"Thanks," Chief Pace said. "Again, my condolences."

"Take all the time here you need."

Jake shook hands with Atohi again and walked over to the Council House.

Mev had skirted the burned rugs to reach the far side of the yurt. "Hey, Jake. Here's Thom's cell phone," she called out. "This must have been the bench where Thom was sleeping."

"What's the number?"

Mev turned on the phone, went to settings, and read Jake the number.

"I'll call to see if it still works," he said.

OO EE AW AW.

"That's a weird ring tone," Jake said. "Like a signal from outer space."

"I've heard that sound before, Jake. Now where? Oh, I remember. From Doolittle."

"The parrot?"

"Yes. Think, Jake. Doolittle must have heard this ring tone. Doolittle must have been in Thom's presence when a call came in. Thom must be Doolittle's kidnapper. We have a witness."

"Maybe we can find Thom through Hicks. I'll text Hicks."

"I'll take Thom's phone to the office."

"Thanks."

"Will the testimony of a bird stand up in court?"

"Probably not, but yours will."

ଓଓ

~ Chief Jake McCoy, iMessage, Friday, December 16, 2:55 p.m. Hello, John Hicks. This is Police Chief McCoy. I would like to speak with you.

~ OK. R U investigating Fairfield.

~ Why would I investigate Fairfield?

~ He sells stolen stuff. Stolen from Indians.

~ *May I call you?*

~ Sure.

~ *Where are you?*

~ At Waffle House on 400. Near Cumming.

~ *I will call you.*

ᏫᏫ

"Hello, Mr. Hicks. Thanks for taking my call."

"No problem, Chief McCoy."

"I have a few questions for you related to your phone call to Hempton Fairfield Thursday night."

"Go ahead."

"Why did you call him?"

"To ask him where he was getting his curios."

"Did you threaten him?"

"No, of course not. But I did accuse him of treating Cherokee treasures as merchandise. He took offense."

"Where are you headed now?"

"To Atlanta. To check out Fairfield's antique shop. I want to see what Cherokee treasures he's offering for sale to his wealthy Atlanta clientele. And at what price."

"Do you have an address for the shop?"

"Yes, 700 Peachcity Road, wherever that is. North Atlanta somewhere."

"I apologize, but I must ask you where you were between midnight and two o'clock on Wednesday night."

"In Tayanita Village. In bed. Why?"

"Do you have any witnesses?"

"No witnesses. No mistresses. I sleep alone. Is that okay? What's this all about?"

"Did you know that Gifford Plains is dead?"

"What?"

"His body was found outside Charlotte Byrd's house last night."

"Really? I'll be damned. He collects Cherokee stuff."

"John Hicks, I have to give you some bad news."

"You're arresting me? I didn't kill him."

"No. I'm not arresting you. There's been a fire at Tayanita Village. Your friend Waya Gunter is dead."

"Oh, God, no. No, no, no, no."

"A memorial service will be held in the Council House at seven tonight."

"What happened?"

Jake told him. "Thom Rivers is missing," he added when he finished. "Do you know anything about that?"

"No. He was at Tayanita Village yesterday. I saw him. He was hung over, or maybe strung out. Not in great shape. He spent most of the day sleeping in the Council House."

"He disappeared after the fire. Took his truck. Do you know where he'd go?"

"Probably Dahlonega. He lives there. Hawk Nest Apartments. I don't know him well. He was Waya's friend."

"Thanks."

"I'm turning around. I'll be at the memorial service."

WWW.ONLINEWITHERSTON.COM

WITHERSTON ON THE WEB
Friday, December 16, 2015
3:00 p.m.

BREAKING NEWS

Waya (Eddie) Gunter died today in a fire in the Council House of Tayanita Village. According to Thom Rivers, who carried Gunter's body out of the big yurt, a pig named Betty had bumped into the wood stove that heated the large yurt and caused sparks to ignite the Cherokee rugs. Rivers said he was asleep on one of the benches and woke up when Gunter ran in to save him from the flames. He said his friend tripped over a rug and fell. Rivers left the Village shortly thereafter and so was unavailable for a comment. Family and friends of Mr. Gunter are invited to his memorial service at 7:00 this evening in the Council House of Tayanita Village.

~ Smitty Green, Editor

Waya (Eddie) Gunter
Photo by WithSchoolPhotos.com

CHAPTER 8

Friday evening, December 16:

After seeing Waya Gunter's picture, Ignacio Iglesias made a decision. He called the office of *WITHERSTON ON THE WEB* and, in broken English, told his story to the editor. He hoped the editor would honor his request for anonymity. He'd heard that, in the United States, journalists were not required to reveal their sources to law enforcement agencies.

Smitty honored his request. He called Jake. "I have a confidential source who tells me that Wednesday night a man resembling Waya got drunk with another man, somebody very tall, at Rosa's Cantina. Said they left at twelve-thirty in red pickup trucks. If this individual is telling the truth, then Gunter and Rivers could be the two kidnappers of Doolittle."

"It's beginning to look that way, Smitty."

Jake called Mev and relayed Smitty's news.

"Now Waya is dead and Thom is gone," Mev said.

"If Thom killed Gifford Plains, then Waya was a witness."

"That's what I'm thinking, Jake."

"And Waya is dead."

ᘓᘓ

"May this prayer be yours, Waya," Atohi said.

"I give you this one thought to keep.
I'm with you still. I do not sleep.
I am a thousand winds that blow.
I am the diamond glints on snow.
I am the sunlight on ripened grain.
I am the gentle autumn rain.
When you awaken in the morning hush,
I am the swift uplifting rush,
Of quiet birds in circled flight.
I am the soft stars that shine at night.
Do not think of me as gone
I am with you still, in each new dawn.
Do not stand at my grave and weep.
I am not there, I do not sleep.
Do not stand at my grave and cry.
I am not there, I did not die."

Mev watched Jaime and Jorge during Atohi's recitation. The boys sat in rapt attention, and she knew why. Since Francis Hearty Withers's burial in a very pricey coffin in May, the boys had questioned their culture's encasing of the dead in airtight, waterproof, wormproof caskets. They had embraced Aunt Lottie's philosophy that humans were as much a part of the ecosystem as all the other animals who replenished the soil with their remains.

"Aunt Lottie would love this," Jaime whispered to Jorge after Atohi had concluded the poem.

"Waya will be cremated," Jorge said. "No coffin."

"*Hijos*," Paco whispered. "*Silencio*."

"Sisters and brothers," Atohi said in his deep baritone. "We have come to the end of our memorial service. The residents of Tayanita Village thank you all for joining us this evening to bid farewell to Waya. Now we invite you to have a cup of hot apple cider before going into the cold night."

"Chief Pace didn't mention Betty Pig," Jaime whispered to his brother.

"Betty Pig is cooked."

Mev looked at the small crowd gathered in the Tayanita Village Council House. In addition to John Hicks and the other villagers, she saw Catherine Perry and Dan Soto, Trevor Bennington, III, and Pastor Paul Clement of the Witherston Baptist Church. Then she spotted Ned Gunter, who sat on the bench by the wood stove.

"Paco," she said. "Let's go speak to Waya's father."

Mev and Paco made their way to the far side of the yurt.

"I am so sorry," Paco said to Ned. "Eddie, I mean Waya, was a beautiful boy. He was full of mischief, like most smart teenagers, but he was full of kindness too. He was one of my favorite students."

"I have no other children," Ned said. "No other child of my own."

"I am so sorry."

"We are so sorry," Mev added.

"Eddie and I lived alone on the farm with each other for a decade after his mother died. But a year ago, right before his senior year, Thom came to live with us. We became a family. Then last summer Thom got into gambling in North Carolina, and maybe into drugs too. He changed. I asked him to move out. He went to Dahlonega to live. Eddie left too. He changed his name to Waya and moved to Tayanita Village. So I lost both of them."

"Is there anything we can do to help?" Paco asked.

"No. Thanks, anyway. I don't know what I'll do."

Mev's cell phone rang. She moved out of earshot and took the call from Jake.

"I'm in Dahlonega outside Hawk Nest Apartments, where Thom supposedly lives. He's not there. Could he have a girlfriend in Dahlonega?"

"I don't know. And Waya, who could have told us, is dead. Thom could be dangerous. Mr. Gunter thinks he's into gambling and drugs."

"And possibly murder. I'll put out an all-points bulletin."

At that moment, Mev heard *ZONGZINGZING.* It came from her pocket. She pulled out Thom's cell phone.

"Hold on, Jake. Thom's phone just got a text message. I'm looking at it now."

~ Alpha, iMessage, Friday, December 16, 8:03 p.m. Did you kill Plains? Don't get caught. Do you want another job for $10,000?

"I need Thom's password to get the rest of this message."

"Try his cellphone number."

"It works." Mev read the rest of the text message to Jake. "'Delete this message. Alpha.' So Thom worked for somebody named Alpha. I'm going to reply."

~ What is the job?

"How do we track down Alpha?" he asked.

"I don't have the skills myself, Jake. But let's check Thom's emails tomorrow morning. I'll meet you at the office at nine o'clock. Right now I'm going to find Galilahi. She may hear from Thom."

"She won't hear from him, because you have Thom's phone."

"I'll keep it on me."

"Check Thom's incoming calls."

"They're all from Edward Gunter—that's Waya. The latest came at one-fourteen Thursday morning. That must have been when Doolittle heard Thom's outer-space ring tone."

"If Waya called Thom at one-fourteen, Waya and Thom must have separated after kidnapping the bird. Thom must have still had the bird."

"So Thom parked Doolittle in the eighteen-wheeler chicken truck."

"And then left the highway."

"Which means that Waya could not have killed Guelph."

Mev returned Thom's phone to her pocket.

ZONGZINGZING.

"Wait, Jake. Here's another text message for Thom."

~ Alpha, iMessage, Friday, December 16, 8:06 p.m. I have just given you $1000 in advance of the job. You do it right, I keep you out of jail, and I give you an additional $9000. Tell me where you are. Delete this message. Alpha

Mev read it to him.

"Alpha really wants to know Thom's whereabouts," he said.

"I think we need to find Thom right away, before Alpha finds him."

Mev put Thom's phone back in her pocket, where it immediately beeped.

"Wait, Jake. Thom has an email message...from Amazon. Let's see. Oh my goodness. Thom has just gotten an Amazon gift card. Should I claim it?"

"Hell, yes. Then we can find out who sent it."

"I'm putting in the code: EFZS-N8UY3C-E64T. And now I'm clicking on the REDEEM NOW button. Uh oh. I have to put in Thom's email address."

"His email address is thomasrivers2014@gmail .com."

Mev typed it in.

"Oh my god, Jake. It worked. Thom has received a thousand dollars—from Anonymous."

"So that's how Alpha pays Thom."

"If Alpha sent it, he'll get an email from Amazon saying that Thom has received the gift."

"So what's our next step, Mev?"

"You find Thom."

"Right. And you find a computer geek."

"I live with two. May I consult Jorge and Jaime?"

"You may. I always say, if you need help with computers, ask somebody young."

ೞೞ

Moments after she'd disconnected from Jake, Mev got another call.

"Detective Arroyo? This is Sandra Rather Anders. Did you know I'm now a nurse at Chestatee Regional?"

"Yes, Sandra. Your mother told me. You inherited her ability to care for others. Only she cares for animals and you care for humans."

"Well, I'm taking care of Mr. Heller, the man who had the heart attack in the blizzard."

"Buck Heller."

"Yes. Mr. Heller is recovering, thank goodness. Anyway, he says that he was rear-ended by the minivan behind him because he'd hit the brakes to avoid rear-ending a red pick-up. I thought you might like to know that there was a red pick-up between Mr. Heller's car and the eighteen-wheeler chicken carrier."

"That's very helpful information, Sandra. Thank you very much."

"I'll call you if he says anything else, Detective Arroyo."

"Thanks so much, Sandra."

"Did you know that Mom's giving Phil and me a chicken coop for Christmas?"

"I didn't, but I should have guessed."

Mev called Jake. "Now we have a witness to Thom's being on Witherston Highway, Jake. A human witness."

"Better than a bird witness."

ᘓᘓ

"Hi, Galilahi. This is Thom."

"Thom, where are you?"

"At Miss Effie's Tavern in Dahlonega. I lost my cell phone. I need to talk to you. Where are you?'

"In the Council House. The ceremony to say goodbye to Waya has just ended. Why aren't you here?"

"Long story. Can you come to me?"

"Miss Effie's Tavern on the Chestatee River?"

"Yes. Can you come?"

"Okay. Are you all right?"

"No. No, I'm really not all right. I'll tell you when you come. How soon can you get here?"

"I'll see you in thirty minutes."

"Don't tell anyone where you're going, please."

"I won't. I promise."

ᘓᘓ

Catherine reported to Mev what she'd overheard Galilahi say to Thom.

Mev thanked her and called Jake.

Jake drove to Miss Effie's Tavern to make the arrest. As he got out of his car, he saw the locally famous purple neon sign in the window, *WE WON'T TELL IF YOU DON'T TELL.* He entered and found Effie Crockett behind the bar, where she'd spent six nights a week for forty years. "Good evening, Miss Effie," he said. "I'm Chief McCoy of the Witherston Police Department. Have you seen Thom Rivers here tonight?"

"No, Chief."

"Do you know Thom Rivers?"

"No, Chief."

"Have you seen a tall man in a navy blue jacket?"

"No, Chief."

"Would you tell me if you knew him?"

"Can't say I would, can't say I wouldn't."

"Well," Jake said, "thanks all the same."

"Care for a drink, Chief? I won't tell."

"I'm sure you won't, Miss Effie. But no, thanks. I'm on duty tonight. But I'll hang around a bit. That is, if you don't mind."

"Well, Chief, can't say I do, can't say I don't."

ഗ്ഗ

Thom was waiting in his red pickup across the street from Miss Effie's when he saw Chief McCoy enter the tavern. He turned the engine off and dropped down in his seat. He wouldn't need to see Galilahi's 1995 yellow Corvette when she arrived. He would hear it.

And he did. Galilahi roared into Miss Effie's parking lot and, a moment later, knocked on his window. She must have spotted him. He signaled for her to go around, leaned over, and let her into the cab.

He took her hand. "Thanks for coming, Galilahi. I wanted to say goodbye."

"Are you going away, Thom?"

"Yes. For a long time."

"Where are you going?"

"To prison."

"To prison, Thom? Why?"

"I'm a murderer."

"Who did you kill?"

"You'll find out soon. But now I need you to talk to Mr. Gunter. Please tell him that he's been the only father I've known, that I love him, and that I'm sorry for all the things I've done to disappoint him."

"Okay, Thom. But tell me what you've done."

"Terrible things. That's all I'll say. I should die. I hope I die. I don't deserve to live. So I've decided to get arrested. Tonight. To confess what I've done. Could you please tell Mr. Gunter I'm in jail?"

"Okay. I love you, Thom."

"And that I need a lawyer."

"Okay."

"I love you, Galilahi. Now kiss me goodbye and go home."

Galilahi kissed him on the lips, hugged him, and left.

When the Corvette was out of sight, Thom walked to the door of Miss Effie's, ran into Chief McCoy, and put his hands into the air.

"I need to talk with you," Thom said. "Please arrest me. I'm a murderer. I want to confess."

"You are under arrest, Thom Rivers," Jake said as he cuffed Thom. "You have the right to remain silent. Anything you say or do can be used against you in a court of law. You have the right to consult an attorney before speaking to the police and to have an attorney present during questioning now or in the future. If you cannot afford an attorney, one will be appointed for you before any questioning, if you wish. If you decide to answer any questions now, without an attorney present, you will still have the right to stop answering at any time until you talk to an attorney. Do you understand?"

"I understand," Thom said. "I want to talk."

"Do you have any relatives you'd like me to call?"

"No. Nobody."

"Any friends?"

"No."

Jake settled Thom into the back seat of his police vehicle, moved a few feet away, and called Mev. He told her that he had Thom.

"Jake, if I'm going to be answering Thom's text messages we've got to keep his arrest out of the news."

"Just a sec, I have an incoming call from Catherine."

"Ask her please, please not to write anything about Thom's arrest."

"Will do. You handle the text messaging with Alpha. I'll see you tomorrow."

Jake answered Catherine's call. "Hi, Catherine. You're up to speed, as always."

Jake watched Thom as he talked. Thom had closed his eyes. Finally, Jake said, "Catherine, I always tell you what's going on. You know you can trust me. But tonight I ask you, please, do not report anything in *Webby Witherston* about Thom's arrest. Thom worked for somebody, and we need to catch that somebody."

"I won't, until you tell me it's okay."

"Thanks, Catherine. If you'll come by the office tomorrow morning at nine thirty, Mev and I will brief you confidentially. And please ask Smitty not to put anything about this in *Police Blotter*."

"Sure. Can I bring him tomorrow?"

"Yes, you can bring Smitty."

ꕥ

ZONGZINGZING.

Mev was sitting on the sofa with a glass of chardonnay when the text message came in. Paco looked up from the hearth.

"*Oye, Mevita.* Who can that be?"

"I wonder," she said.

She pulled Thom's cell phone out of her pocket. Another message from Alpha. She would respond.

~ *Alpha, iMessage, Friday, December 16, 9:17 p.m. Where are you?*

~ If you tell me who you are, I will tell you where I am.

~ *No. Can you do the job this weekend?*

~ Yes.

~ *I will get back to you. Delete this message. Alpha.*

Mev did not delete the message. "Boys," she called. "Could you please come downstairs? I need your computer skills for this murder case."

"Sure, Mom."

"Sure, Mom."

They came down immediately, Jaime with his guitar and Jorge with his iPad. Mighty followed. The three of them settled down on the floor.

"If you get money by way of an Amazon gift card," Mev asked, "how can you find out who gave it to you?"

"Let's try this experiment," Jorge said. "You or Dad send Jaime and me each a gift card with fifty dollars anonymously. We'll try to figure out who sent it to us. Okay?"

"Twenty-five," Paco said.

"Forty," Jaime said.

"Thirty," Paco said.

"It's a deal," Jaime said. "Bro, you and I will each get thirty dollars as compensation for our expertise."

Mev and Paco pulled out their phones. Thirty seconds later, Jaime and Jorge each got an email from Amazon announcing their thirty-dollar gifts from Anonymous.

They each went to the Amazon redeem center, applied the code, and added thirty dollars to their accounts.

"Thanks, Dad," Jaime said.

"Dad, the email doesn't tell who sent us the gift. It just says Anonymous."

"No return address?"

"Just dc-orders@gc.email.amazon.com," Jaime said.

"Is there any other research you'd like us to do, Dad?"

ꕥ

Jorge transferred Mighty to Jaime's pillow, piled up his own pillows to make a back rest, and opened up his iPad. It was almost midnight.

Jaime sat on the floor playing "Dueling Banjos" on his guitar, softly.

"What are you Googling now?"

"I'm writing down what we know about Witherston's crime wave."

Jaime continued playing.

Jorge moved over beside Jaime, so that Jaime could see, and wrote:

> *Facts:*
>
> *Doolittle is kidnapped by two men—Wed night.*
>
> *Doolittle is found in Mr. Soto's eighteen-wheeler chicken truck—Thurs afternoon.*
>
> *Dr. Plains is found dead in snow at aunt lottie's house—Thurs night*
>
> *Mr. Guelph is found dead in snow at Witherston Inn—Thurs night.*
>
> *Both bought Cherokee stuff.*
>
> *Both certificates of provenance show Al Haash as owner before Mr. Fairfield.*

Al Haash is really Alhaash, who does business online, which is fishy.

Common denominator is auction.

"Put down Doolittle's weird ransom note."

"Onkey donkey."

Doolittle's ransom note was weird.

It didn't mention what kind of pet was kidnapped.

It used PayPal on eBay to get ransom money.

"How about adding that Waya and Thom were arrested at the auction?"

"Good idea. Also, the fire. Do you think the fire had anything to do with this crime wave?"

Jaime stopped strumming. "Well, Waya died in it."

Jorge wrote:

Waya Gunter and Thom Rivers were arrested for acting up at auction.

Waya died in yurt fire.

Thom disappeared

"Whoa, bro. Do you think Thom killed Waya?"

"If he didn't, why didn't he go to the ceremony? Now I'm writing down some questions."

Questions:
Who kidnapped Doolittle?
How did Doolittle get in chicken truck?
Who is Al Haash or rather Alhaash?
How does Mr. Alhaash get his stuff?

How does Mr. Fairfield get his stuff from Mr. Alhaash?

Are deaths of Dr. Plains and Mr. Guelph related?

Were they murdered?

Then he added to the questions:

How did Doolittle's picture get on eBay?

Who got ransom money from PayPal?

Jorge stopped writing and looked at his brother. "What else?"

"How about Dr. Plains dying about the same time Doolittle was kidnapped?"

Jorge added:

Did one of kidnappers bump off Dr. Plains?

Did same kidnapper bump off Mr. Guelph?

What do their deaths have to do with auction?

"Here's what could have happened," Jaime said. "The kidnappers kidnapped Doolittle Wednesday nig—"

"You mean Thursday morning, since it was after midnight. Lottie said she went to bed at midnight."

"Right. The kidnappers kidnapped Doolittle early Thursday morning during the blizzard, like about one o'clock. They got surprised by Dr. Plains. So they killed him. Then they got on Witherston highway to go south and got stuck behind Daniel Soto's chicken truck. They didn't want to get caught with Doolittle in their car."

"Or truck."

Jaime nodded. "They didn't want to get caught with Doolittle in their car or truck so they stashed Doolittle with the chickens and got off Witherston Highway."

"They must have had an all-wheel-drive vehicle, or

they wouldn't have been able to cross over to get off the highway."

"And north-bound traffic was stopped, too. At the same time. Remember?" Jaime said.

"Yes, so they couldn't leave Witherston."

"Then they went to Witherston Inn and killed Mr. Guelph."

"Why would they do that?" Jorge asked.

"Maybe they needed a place to stay. Jorge, shouldn't you write this down?

Jorge nodded:

Theory:

Kidnappers kidnapped Doolittle between twelve and one.

They bumped into Dr. Plains and bumped him off.

They tried to make getaway on Witherston Highway.

They got stuck behind stuck chicken truck.

They hid Doolittle among chicken crates.

Then they went to Witherston Inn to try to spend the night.

They bumped into Mr. Guelph and bumped him off.

"So where did they sleep?"

"Good question, since Witherston has only one hotel."

"They must have known someone in Witherston."

"Someone friendly enough to let them in at one-forty-five in the morning? During the blizzard?

Jorge added to his questions:

Where did kidnappers sleep?
Did they have accomplice in Witherston?
Are they from Witherston?

"Do you think we know them?"

"I'll bet we do. Or at least Mom and Dad do. They know everybody."

"I'll email Mom these notes."

"I'm going to sleep."

"Me too." Jorge emailed the notes and put his iPad into the drawer.

Jaime put his guitar into its case and turned off the lamp.

"*Buenas noches, hermano*."

"*Buenas noches*."

After five minutes, Jorge said, "Jaime, are you still awake?"

"Yes," Jaime mumbled.

"What do you think is the connection between the auction and Doolittle's kidnapping?"

"Can we do this tomorrow?"

"*Buenas noches, hermano*."

"*Buenas noches*."

WWW.ONLINEWITHERSTON.COM

WITHERSTON ON THE WEB
Saturday, December 17, 2015
8:00 a.m.

LOCAL NEWS

Former Witherston High School basketball captain Thom Rivers is being sought for questioning in the kidnapping of the parrot Doolittle. Chief Jake McCoy asks that anybody seeing Rivers report his whereabouts immediately to Witherston police.

Rivers was credited with trying to save the life of his best friend Waya Gunter, who died yesterday in the fire at Tayanita Village. He disappeared shortly thereafter.

The 2014 Witherston High School yearbook features Rivers as "Most Popular." The quotation under his class photo is "Solitary Man."

~ Catherine Perry, Reporter

WEATHER

The sunny skies of yesterday have been followed by the rainy skies of today. Rain will fall steadily until this evening, when high winds from the west will bring temperatures down into the twenties. Rhonda Rather, wife of

Mayor Rather, reminds us to bring our animals inside.

Listen to the rhythm of the falling rain.

~ Tony Lima, Prognosticator

POLICE BLOTTER

Yesterday afternoon, Mayor Rich Rather complained to Witherston Police that somebody had put up a wooden sign in front of City Hall that said "Free Chicken City." Mayor Rather said he suspected that the culprit was a member of Keep Nature Natural.

LETTERS TO THE EDITOR

To the Editor:

Why in the world is Webby Witherston *so obsessed with chickens? For God's sake, Mr. Green, please fire Catherine Perry. Her interview with that trucker Daniel Soto proves what I have long said:* Webby Witherston *is biased against business.*

Let me tell the other side of the story. The population of the United States is about 317 million. Each year the 317 million of us consume 8 billion chickens. We are a nation of chicken eaters. How can our country satisfy this demand for chicken without mass production?

Furthermore, folks: We can divide the world between people and food for people. CHICKENS ARE NOT PEOPLE! So guess what they are. That's right, they're food. Just food.

~ Grant Griggs, Witherston

To the Editor:

Go, Dan Soto! Chickens do have inner lives. So do pigs. Tayanita Village's pig Betty knows her name, and she also knows my name.

Betty Pig sits when you tell her to sit and comes when you tell her to come. She tells you, with a special oink when it's time for dinner.

She pushes the latch to open the door to the big yurt, so she can go inside where it's warm. And she's careful not to knock anything over.

Everybody on Earth has feelings. Most humans don't know that because they think only about themselves.

I like you, Dan Soto. Please come visit Tayanita Village.

~ Galilahi Sellers, Tayanita Village

[Editor: This letter from Galilahi Sellers was submitted before the Tayanita Village fire took Betty Pig's life.]

To the Editor:

Jorge Arroyo's drawing of the chickens escaping from the chicken truck is cool.

Everybody in Georgia should break into chicken trucks when they are at truck stops and LET THE CHICKENS GO!

~ Christopher Zurich, Witherston

OBITUARIES

Gifford Plains

Gifford Rorty Plains, age 65, died on Thursday, December 15, in Witherston. The cause of his death has not yet been determined.

Dr. Plains was born in Chattanooga, Tennessee, in 1950. After earning his B.A. and Ph.D. in Anthropology from Vanderbilt University, he joined the faculty of Emory University, where he specialized in the Cherokee civilization of the Southeast. He was the author of the books A Nation Under Ground; Cherokee Remains; and Cherokee People: So Proud to Live, So Proud to Die.

Upon his retirement from Emory last spring, Dr. Plains moved to Witherston. He became known here as a collector of Cherokee artifacts. He was a supporter of the new Cherokee-Witherston Museum here and the Lumpkin County Library in Dahlonega.

Dr. Plains leaves behind a daughter, Dr. Michelle Plains Palacio, who teaches Native American history at the University of Washington in Seattle, and a wife Margaret "Peg" Marble, a novelist in Atlanta.

David Ewing Guelph

David Ewing Guelph, PhD., former CEO of Xlent Software, died in Witherston, Georgia, on December 15. He was 70 years old.

Dr. Guelph was born and raised in Seattle, Washington, where his parents, Jim and Nelle Guelph, were public school teachers. Dr. Guelph got his BS in physics at the University of Washington in 1966 and his PhD in electrical engineering at the California Institute of Technology in 1971. He returned to Seattle to work for Boeing, left Boeing in 1980, and a year later founded Xlent Software, Inc., now a multinational corporation.

In 2008, Dr. Guelph sold his shares in the company, retired, and founded the Native American Artifacts Recovery Foundation. NAARF's mission is to purchase Native American artifacts and return them to their tribe of origin. At his death Dr. Guelph was chair of NAARF's board of directors. He traveled throughout the United States attending auctions of Native American antiquities.

According to the Seattle Post-Intelligencer, Dr. Guelph left his vast estate to NAARF. He never married.

Dr. Guelph had flown into Atlanta from Seattle on Tuesday, December 13. He rented a car, drove to Witherston Wednesday afternoon, and spent Wednesday night in the Witherston Inn. At Hempton Fairfield's auction he acquired several Cherokee artifacts.

A memorial service honoring Dr. Guelph will be held in late January at the University of Washington, where he was a generous benefactor.

Edward (Waya) Gunter

Edward Gunter of Witherston, age twenty, died on December sixteenth in a fire in the Tayanita Village Council House. He was the only son of Ned Gunter and the late Martha Beylor Gunter of Witherston.

Eddie Gunter, as he was known then, played soccer at Witherston High School where he was elected co-captain of his team in his senior year. He also showed an avid interest in Cherokee history, according to his history teacher Miss Myra Whitbred. Miss Whitbred said, "Alt-

hough Eddie Gunter was full of mischief, he was single-minded in his search for his Cherokee ancestors. His death is a tragedy."

After graduation in May of 2015, Eddie took the name Waya and moved into Tayanita Village in honor of his eighteenth-century Cherokee ancestor Chief Bushyhead. Waya attended the University of North Georgia in Dahlonega where he was majoring in biology.

IN THIS MONTH IN HISTORY
By Charlotte Byrd

On December 17, 1881, Withers Francis (Witty) Withers, age twenty-three, married Obedience Olmstead, age twenty, in a ceremony in the Dahlonega United Methodist Church. Witty Withers was the son of Harold Francis (Harry) Withers and Patience Gray Withers. Witty and Obedience were the grandparents of the late Francis Hearty Withers of Witherston.

One hundred and thirty-four years later, at Hempton Fairfield's auction on December 14, 2015, I bought Witty and Obedience's marriage certificate. You might say that, for $60, I got a souvenir of the union of two families, and their experiences together, and the legal and social system of which their marriage was a part in in the 1880s in Lumpkin County, Georgia. I will use the document to get some knowledge of our region's history.

I also bought a parrot, but that's a story for another day.

My friend Carolyn Foster bought a Cherokee quiver made of rabbit skin for $925. She got a souvenir of a hunt—or possibly a battle—in which a Cherokee man used arrows for killing. She will put the quiver in the new

Cherokee-Witherston Museum with other Cherokee mementos to help us imagine the Native American civilization our White forefathers destroyed.

David Guelph, who came all the way from Seattle for the auction, bought for $6,400 a page of the Cherokee Phoenix, which was the first Native American newspaper. The Cherokee Phoenix was published in New Echota, Georgia, in both Cherokee, the first written Native American language, and English. Mr. Guelph got a souvenir of the public opinion of events the Cherokees considered important in 1830.

Time changes everything—ecosystems, civilizations, societies, and families. We look back at the remnants of the past and salvage what we can to remind us of what has gone. We turn whatever we find into souvenirs, which we use to imagine the whole from which they came.

With these souvenirs, we got little pieces of our past—fragments, scraps, debris.

What did we not get? An understanding of the whole ecosystem in which the people interacted with each other and with the animals, plants, rocks, and rivers. What these people saw, what they heard and smelled and tasted. What they thought about when they looked at the stars, when they fished in the streams, when they prepared for battle, when they warmed themselves by the fire, when they cared for their young, when they awaited the return of friends and relatives dear to them. The stories they told. The dreams they had. The love they felt for each other. The pain they suffered over love lost. Their hopes, their fears.

But beyond that: We did not get any understanding of the persons who left us these souvenirs of their existence. Of Witty Withers and Obedience Olmstead. Of the Cherokee hunter. Of Elias Boudinot, the first editor of the Cherokee Phoenix. Even if their names get recorded, their personhood—their soul—is lost in time, like the arrangement of molecules that once constituted their body and now constitute the bodies of other living things. The persons of the past are invisible to us.

But the persons of the present are visible to us, at least partially, if we try to imagine the depths of their feelings, if we imagine walking in their moccasins or flying on their wings. If we don't, they remain as invisible to us as their dead ancestors.

I like to contemplate a universe replete with persons, all of them thinking—human persons, as well as avian persons, canine persons, and the like—with whom we humans have empathy.

MENU SPECIALS

Founding Father's Creek Café: Chicken in red wine sauce with mushrooms, new potatoes, brussel sprouts, mixed greens, chocolate pudding.

Gretchen Green's Green Grocery (Lunch only): Rainbow trout, collard greens with pine nuts and raisins, parsnips, whole-wheat rolls, lemon sorbet.

Witherston Inn Café: Roasted chicken with tarragon over white rice, sauteed carrots, spinach salad, bread sticks, chocolate marble sheet cake.

CHAPTER 9

Saturday morning, December 17:

Saturday dawned cold and rainy. Mev rose before the others, poured herself a cup of coffee, and checked her email. She found the message from Jorge. "I love my team," she said to herself as she printed it out. She still preferred hard copy to electronic text when making notes, and she wanted to add a few things to the categories Jorge had created.

Beside "Facts" Mev wrote:

Guelph's clothing showed contact with feathers.

Doolittle made same sound as Thom's ring-tone, suggesting he was in Thom's possession when Thom received a call on his cellphone.

Thom is in custody. (Alpha doesn't know that.)

Thom says he "has killed."

Alpha was paying Thom to do "jobs."

Waya called Thom at 1:14 am. Therefore they were not together then.

NOTE: Check Thom's jacket for white

broiler feathers. Feathers on his jacket would indicate contact with both Guelph and chickens (in chicken truck). Run microscopic check to make sure all of the feathers come from same source.

Thom was sleeping in the Council House of Tayanita Village on Friday.

Thom brought out Waya's dead body from burning yurt.

Beside "Questions" she wrote:

What is connection between auction and deaths of Plains and Guelph?

Is Al Haash relevant to investigation?

What does Peg Marble know?

Were Plains' death and Guelph's death accidental homicide or murder?

What's connection between eBay and Amazon?

Did Thom go to Tayanita Village after killing Guelph? What did he do on Thursday?

Why did Thom leave after fire?

Why did John Hicks leave Tayanita Village Friday morning?

NOTE: Check John Hicks's alibi.

Beside "Theory" she wrote:

Thom and Waya kidnapped Doolittle.

One of them killed Gifford, either accidentally or on purpose—or unknowingly.

Thom and Waya separated. Thom got on Witherston Highway to go south to apartment in Dahlonega—with Doolittle.

> *Thom was right behind Dan's eighteen-wheeler.*
>
> *When eighteen-wheeler wrecked, Thom hid Doolittle among chickens.*
>
> *Thom left highway. He must have had all-wheel drive.*
>
> *NOTE: See whether Thom's truck has all-wheel drive.*
>
> *!!! Waya was only witness to Gifford's killing. Did Thom kill his best friend Waya to keep him from talking???*

Mev folded the paper and put it in her purse. She'd show it to Jake.

ᘓᘐᘓᘐ

"We're here," Jorge called

"We're here, Aunt Lottie," Jaime echoed.

Aunt Lottie opened her back door to Jorge, Jaime, and Mighty. Jorge and Jaime stood dry under their father's big black umbrella, but Mighty raced ahead into the house, all wet.

"Come in, boys. I thought the rain would bring you over. Lucky me."

Doolittle was already out of his cage. He scurried into the kitchen and looked at Mighty.

Mighty barked. Doolittle barked back and approached Mighty with his wings akimbo. Mighty fled into the laundry room.

Jaime leaned down and let Doolittle hop on his hand. "Hello, Doolittle. Good bird."

"Doolittle is fucking bird. OO EE AW AW."

"Doolittle is lucky bird," Lottie corrected him gently.

"Doolittle is lucky bird," Doolittle repeated.

"Boys, shall we do some more research on the blowgun and the Cherokee newspaper? I can make you all some hot chocolate."

"That's what came here for, Aunt Lottie," Jaime said.

"He meant we came here to do research with you, Aunt Lottie," Jorge corrected. "And we'd like hot chocolate, too."

"Neel is fixing my leaking shower. Let's ask him to help. Since he's an Oklahoma Cherokee, he may know some of the names on the certificate for the *Cherokee Phoenix*."

"Good idea."

Jaime gave Doolittle a dry-roasted unsalted peanut and carried him to the rope handle of his little cage. Doolittle clung to his hand and would not get off.

"Doolittle," Jaime said in his sweetest voice. "Step up. Up, up, up. Step up, please."

"I wanna divorce!" Doolittle screamed in a woman's voice. He clung to Jaime's hand.

"Hey." Neel came out of the bathroom. "Who said that?"

"Doolittle."

"So Doolittle comes from a broken home," Neel said.

"Doolittle is a witness to whatever he's heard," Lottie said. "He just let us know that Petal Fairfield was not happy in her marriage."

"She must have used the word 'fuck' a lot, Aunt Lottie," Jorge said.

"Maybe her husband was not a saint," Neel said.

Jaime gave into Doolittle's wishes. "Okay, Doolittle, be a good bird."

"Doolittle be a good bird," Doolittle repeated softly. "Up, up, up."

Lottie poured hot chocolate into four cups and set the cups on a teak tray. Neel placed the tray on the dining room table.

"Let's drink our chocolate before handling the certificates," Lottie said.

Jaime held Doolittle on his left hand and drank his chocolate with his right.

"Doolittle be a lucky good bird."

"I think we've learned a lot from Doolittle," Neel said. "Doolittle came to us feather-plucked. He said 'ugly bird' and 'shut the fuck up.' That's what he must have heard at home. He was afraid to leave his cage. He'd been yelled at."

"Doolittle's people didn't love him and didn't love each other," Lottie said.

"Doolittle told us their secrets," Jaime said.

"Doolittle should work for the FBI," Jorge said.

"As an undercover bird," Jaime added,

"But he might repeat what he hears from us," Jorge protested.

"Doolittle's people were the Fairfields," Neel said. "They sell Cherokee artifacts to the highest bidder, which doesn't endear them to me. So I may not be an impartial investigator. But I think we need to learn more about Mr. Hempton Fairfield."

ଓଓ

Mev entered Jake's office at nine-fifteen.

"I apologize for getting here late," she said. "Paco makes huge breakfasts on Saturday mornings—bacon, grits, scrambled eggs, and big biscuits—and I couldn't pass it up. I brought you bacon and a biscuit."

She set a paper bag on his desk.

"Thanks."

Mev gave him the cell phone. "Look at this, Jake."

Jake looked at the short string of email messages. "Thom was not much of an email correspondent," he said. "Maybe young people use text-messaging more than email."

Mev shook her head. "But notice the ones from Amazon. Thom has three email gift cards from Amazon. The first on Monday, November 30, at eleven p.m. for five hundred dollars. The second on Thursday, December 15, at nine fifteen a.m. for one thousand dollars. Right after Doolittle's kidnapping. The third on Friday—last night—at eight-oh-seven p.m. for one thousand. For his next job."

"Another pet snatching?"

"Alpha must have been paying Thom to snatch the bird—and possibly other pets."

"Why?"

"For money. The ransom was two thousand dollars," Mev said, "which Aunt Lottie paid into an eBay account."

"So how did the money get from eBay to Amazon?"

"Maybe Alpha gets his ransom money from distraught pet lovers on eBay and buys gift cards for the pet kidnappers who work for him on Amazon. Alpha is using Amazon to hide his illegal payments."

"Thom sure got a big cut of the two thousand dollars."

"He's now getting another ten thousand dollars. Alpha needs to silence Thom, Jake."

Mev pulled out the notes her sons and she had made. "Here's what I think," she said. "Thom and Waya each had his own truck at Rosa's Cantina, at least according to Smitty's source. They went to Lottie's house together and grabbed Doolittle. They were surprised by Gifford, and one of them knocked him out. Maybe whoever did it didn't mean to kill him. Then Waya must have headed back to Tayanita Village."

"And called Thom for some reason."

Mev nodded. "And Thom headed back to Dahlonega, but then got stuck behind the eighteen-wheeler chicken truck in the blizzard. The eighteen-wheeler skidded on the ice at approximately one thirty a.m."

"Thom hid Doolittle among the chickens and drove off the highway in his truck."

"Let's see. We have a witness to Thom and Waya being together right before the kidnapping."

"At Rosa's Cantina."

"And a witness to Thom's red pick-up being immediately behind the eighteen-wheeler."

"Buck Heller. I wonder if Buck Heller saw Thom get out of his truck," Jake said.

"Did Thom then go to Witherston Inn? If so, why?"

"Maybe he needed somewhere to spend the night."

"And ran into David Guelph there."

"And killed him."

"That's the way it looks, Jake. But why?"

"Guelph must have recognized him from the auction. Maybe he wanted to silence Guelph."

"How could a young man who was such a good guy in high school turn into a killer?" she mused.

"Remember he'd been drinking. And he may have been high on drugs, too."

"That would explain why somebody who'd inherited two hundred and fifty thousand dollars just last summer would be doing jobs for a thousand. He had a habit to support. So sad."

"Catherine will be here soon. I'm going to ask her again not to report that we have Thom in custody."

"She doesn't need to know we have Thom's cell phone."

When Catherine arrived, they told her only that Thom Rivers was a person of interest whom Witherston Police sought to interview. They gave her enough for a good story.

And they asked her not to report Jake's taking Thom into custody for another twenty-four hours.

ꕥꕥ

ZONGZINGZING.

When the next text-message came in Mev was in her office typing up a report on the case. She opened up Thom's cell phone and entered the conversation.

~ *Alpha, iMessage, Saturday, December 17, 10:05 a.m. Can you do the job tonight?*

~ Yes.

~ *Address is 1 Withers Hill Road, Witherston GA 30534.*

~ What pet do I grab?

~ *No pet. The pet was just a test.*

~ Oh.

~ *Take antique Cherokee pot on table in entrance hall. It is eight inches tall.*

~ OK.

~ *Nobody will be home. Find the front door key taped to the back of the porch lamp.*

~ Are you sure nobody will be home?

~ *Yes. Do it at midnight. Don't let the cat scare you.*

~ Do I leave a ransom note?

~ *No. Just text me a photo of it. Keep the pot in your truck until I give you further instructions. You will get paid $9,000 when I get the photo. Delete this message. Alpha.*

Mev did not delete the message. "Jake," she called out as she returned to his office. "Alpha wants Thom to burglarize the Fairfields' house tonight. I recognize the address. It's the old Withers house."

"Come downstairs with me to the jail. It's time for a visit with Thom."

They found Thom in bad shape, sweating and shaking. He'd been crying.

Jake asked Thom whether he wanted a lawyer present.

"No, Chief McCoy, Detective Arroyo. I just want to talk. I want to tell you everything."

"We're listening Thom," Mev said.

"I was hired to kidnap the bird."

"We know."

"How do you know?"

"We have your iPhone."

After a long pause Thom said only, "Oh."

"So who is Alpha?" Mev asked him.

"Alpha hired me. Alpha pays me. With Amazon gift cards. He's ruined my life."

"Talk to us, Thom."

Thom talked.

"Thom," Jake said, "you're saying Waya did not intentionally kill Dr. Plains?"

"No, of course not. I was carrying the cage with the bird. When Dr. Plains suddenly showed up in the storm, Waya knocked him out of the way. Dr. Plains fell down in the snow."

"Then what happened?"

"Waya went back to Tayanita Village. It was after one o'clock."

"Did Waya call you on his way home?"

"Yes. Is that important?

"Yes," Mev said. "But go on."

"I got on Witherston Highway to take the bird to my apartment in Dahlonega. I was supposed to keep it till

Alpha told me I could let it go. I was behind the eighteen-wheeler chicken truck when it skidded and went sideways. I almost hit it. Anyway, I didn't want to get caught with the bird, so I stuck it in the middle of the chickens. I had to move a few chicken crates, and I let a few chickens loose. Just for fun. I've always wanted to do that."

"Me, too," Mev said. "What did you do then?"

"I was high, so I didn't want the police to find me. I drove off the road and went to Witherston Inn. There's a bar there. I needed a drink."

"Does your truck have four-wheel drive?" Jake asked.

"Yes. Good thing, or I wouldn't have been able to cross the median and get off the highway."

"What happened at Witherston Inn?"

"I don't remember much. I ran into that old man from the auction. He was having a smoke outside. He recognized me. I panicked. I hit him in the head as hard as I could. I killed him. I dragged his body under a bush."

"Did you feel bad about that?" Mev asked.

"I can't remember. I was not in my right mind."

"What did you do next?"

"I drove to Tayanita Village. Crashed in the big yurt. I've crashed there before."

"What did you do on Thursday?"

"Slept. Mostly all day. Galilahi and Waya brought me some dinner. Then I went back to sleep. I was coming off the high."

"What did you tell them?"

"Just that I put the bird in with the chickens."

"Now I have to ask you, Thom," Jake said, "did you kill Waya?"

"No. Of course not. He was my best friend."

"Did you start the fire?"

"No. No, I didn't. Please believe me. I want you to

know the truth. That's why I'm talking. I want to help you catch the person who started all this."

ଓଓ

After conferring with each other, Mev and Jake re-entered Thom's jail cell.

"Do you really want to help us, Thom?"

"Yes, Chief McCoy. I do."

Mev showed Thom the morning's text message from Alpha. "Thom," she said, "would you be willing to do this job? Steal the Cherokee pot?"

"Yes, Detective Arroyo. What should I do with it?"

"Keep it in the cab of your truck. Go to your apartment in Dahlonega and leave the pot in the truck under a blanket. We'll give you a blanket."

"Okay."

"We're going to release you at eleven o'clock tonight. With a full gas tank and a new prepaid tracphone. Don't lose it. As soon as you get the pot, email me a photo of it. To your iPhone, not mine. I'll send Alpha the photo from your phone. When you're on the road call Jake and me." Mev gave Thom her cell phone number and Jake's.

"You will be followed," Jake said, "all the way to 1 Withers Hill Road, and all the way to your apartment—and then detained again," Jake said, "on suspicion of the murder of David Guelph."

"But I'm confident a judge will appreciate your helping us find Alpha," Mev added.

"Thanks."

"You'll have a deputy in your cell to keep you company," Jake said.

"Okay. May I have Pete Junior?"

"Sure."

"Thom, how did Alpha contact you in the first place?" Mev asked.

"By text message. I don't know why he chose me. Maybe because I've gotten into *Police Blotter* a few times."

"Did you delete all those messages?"

"Alpha asked me to, so I did."

"Are they gone forever?"

"I don't think so. A geek could probably retrieve them for you. Do you need my Apple ID?"

"Yes, please."

Thom gave it to her.

ꕥ

Mev sat with John Hicks in her office at the police station. "Thanks for coming in, John."

"No problem. If I can help Thom, I will."

She handed him Thom's phone. "Do you know how to recover text messages that have been deleted?"

"Sure. It's easy."

"Thom used his cell phone number as his password." She read it to John.

"What about his Apple ID?"

"Thomasrivers2014." John logged in to https://icloud with Thom's Apple ID and password, clicked on Text Messages, and proceeded to return Alpha's text conversations to Thom's iPhone. "That helps a lot," Mev said.

"Would you have a job for me? I could be a computer geek, or a deputy, or whatever you need."

"Let me talk to Jake."

"Be sure to tell him I'm part Cherokee. I come from a distinguished Cherokee family. I am a descendant of Elijah Hicks."

ꕥ

Jorge, with his iPad open, sat on one side of Lottie's dining room table with Neel. Jaime, with his iPad open, sat across from him with Lottie. Doolittle perched atop his cage by Lottie. Mighty lay asleep on the sofa. The hickory logs burning in the fireplace kept the house warm.

Periodically Doolittle said softly, "Doolittle is a fucking good bird" and automatically Lottie corrected him softly with "Doolittle is a lucky good bird."

"Let's look at Guelph's certificate of provenance."

"I recognize all the names on Guelph's certificate till we get to Al Haash," Neel said. "They are Cherokee names, including Bozeman."

"I wonder whether Ada Rogers Bozeman and Ellen Bozeman Carver are kin to Gregory Bozeman."

"At least distant kin, I'd suspect. I think I knew Ellen Bozeman Carver's younger sister in Tahlequah. Her name was Sarah. She married somebody named Duckwell, Ross Duckwell, as I recall."

"So she's your age?"

"She's probably a year younger."

"I've found a Ross Duckwell," Jaime said. "He sells insurance in Oklahoma City. Duckwell Insurance Agency. Here's his website, and his email address. It's ross.duckwell@duckwellinsurance.com."

"I'll email him," Neel said, pulling out his cell phone.

Dear Mr. Duckwell. I am Neel Kingfisher, formerly of Tahlequah and now of Witherston, Georgia. Are you married to a high school classmate of mine named Sarah? She may remember me. I would like to locate Sarah's older sister, Ellen Bozeman Carver, in order to track down a Cherokee artifact. I would be grateful if

> *you could email me her contact information if you are at liberty to do so. Thank you very much. Neel Kingfisher, MD.*

"I'll call you all if I hear back from him," Neel said. "Now I've got to be going. Gretchen and I are making Christmas presents today. For you all. Goodbye, Lottie, Jorge, Jaime. Goodbye, Mighty. Goodbye Doolittle."

"Cluck, cluck," Doolittle said.

Before Neel had zipped up his jacket his cell phone beeped.

"That was quick," Neel said looking at the screen. "Ross Duckwell has just sent me Ellen Bozeman Carver's email address and phone number. I'll call her." He took off his jacket and dialed the number. "Is this Ellen Bozeman Carver?" he asked. "My name is Neel Kingfisher. I went to school with your sister Sarah." Neel waited a moment. "Well, it's so nice to talk with you, Ellen. Let me tell you why I'm calling."

Neel told Ellen about the auction, the framed page of the *Cherokee Phoenix*, the certificate of provenance, and the death of David Guelph. He listened to her for some five minutes, asked her a few questions, thanked her profusely, gave her his email address and phone number, and disconnected.

He turned to Lottie and the boys, who'd been listening to his side of the conversation. "Ellen Bozeman Carver is a retired librarian. When she lost her husband in January of 2014, she moved into a small apartment in Alexandria, Virginia, and downsized. She donated her collection of nineteenth-century Cherokee books and papers to the Sunset Museum of Native American History, a small, newish museum in DC. Her collection included an intact issue of the *Cherokee Phoenix*—which could have been dated September 4, 1830, she said—which she'd inherited from her mother, Ada Rogers Bozeman. She was not aware that anything had happened to it. The other items were early documents pertaining to the removal of the Cherokees from the Southeast to Oklahoma."

"Here's the Sunset Museum's webpage," Jorge said. "Want to see it?"

"I'm there too," Jaime said. "Click on COLLECTIONS, Jorge."

Lottie and Neel looked over their shoulders.

"Okay. Looks like the museum categorizes its stuff by tribe: Apache, Blackfoot, Chippewa, Cherokee, Choctaw, Creek, Navajo, Pueblo, Iroquois, Sioux, and Other."

"Click on ADMINISTRATION," Lottie said.

"Okay."

"The director is Dr. Everett Mirkson. Good lord. Look who is associate director." Lottie touched Jaime's screen. "Dr. Albert Heche. Al Heche."

"Good lord," Doolittle said.

"Alhaash," Jaime said.

"Google Al Heche, museums," Lottie said.

The boys did.

"Albert Heche has an MA in museum studies and a PhD in Native American Studies," Jaime said.

"Here's an Alan Heche at a museum called Artifacts Americana in Denver," Jorge said. "He's the director. He too has an MA in museum studies and a PhD in Native American Studies."

"I wonder if they're twins," Jaime said. "Alan and Albert Heche. I'm Googling their images."

"Me, too." After a few seconds Jorge said, "They are. Look, Neel. Look, Aunt Lottie. Alan and Albert are identical."

"They shared a womb."

"They will share a cell if they've pilfered antiques for Alhaash Antiques Online," Lottie said. At that moment her phone rang. “Hello, Catherine,” she said. “Certainly. You and Dan come on over. I’ll tell you about Doolittle. And more…See you all soon.”

CHAPTER 10

Saturday afternoon, December 17:

The wood stove in the back of Gretchen Green's Green Grocery heated the establishment well. Gandhi, Swift, and Ama dozed on the floor beside it. Barack the cat dozed on the floor behind it.

Catherine and Dan sat with Gretchen and Neel at the table in front of it. Catherine had become a pescatarian the previous summer, and now she was converting Dan. They were eating rainbow trout, parsnips, collard greens with pine nuts and raisins, and whole wheat rolls.

Neel recounted the story of the morning's discoveries. "Ellen Bozeman Carver donated the issue of the *Cherokee Phoenix* to the Sunset Museum in Washington, DC, of which Albert Heche is associate director," he said. "And the certificate shows Al Haash—who is presumably Al Heche—to be the last owner before Hempton Fairfield. So we need to learn whether the last owner of the Cherokee blowgun before Al Haash also had a relationship with the Sunset Museum."

"I have photos of the certificates of provenance on my Android," Catherine said.

She found the photos and propped up her Android to

show the provenance of the Cherokee blowgun.

Dan jotted down the name of William Jackson Rumsay, III, on the paper tablecloth. "Now let's do some tracking."

"We need to follow the blowgun's tracks from Rumsay to Al Haash to Fairfield," Neel said.

"I'm going to look for Alhaash Antiques Online," Catherine said.

"They could be stealing antiques from their museums—pilfering is the word Lottie used—selling them on their eBay store, and signing the certificates of provenance with the name Al Haash," Neel said.

"Then dealers buy their stuff from Alhaash Antiques Online, get the certificates of provenance with the merchandise, and sell the stolen goods in their stores and at their auctions," Gretchen said.

"I'm on the Alhaash Antiques eBay website, folks," Catherine announced. "There's not much for sale there in ANTIQUES. A watch. Three etchings or engravings, whatever. I can't tell the difference. Looks like they came out of books or magazines. They're framed."

"May I see?" Neel asked. He took Catherine's phone and enlarged one of the images.

"What are you thinking?"

"This is a Winslow Homer wood engraving that I recognize. *The Expulsion of Negroes and Abolitionists from Tremont Temple on December 3, 1860*. Published in *Harper's Weekly*, I'm sure. *Harper's* employed Homer as an illustrator. It must have been torn out of the magazine and then framed. It's selling for three hundred dollars. Let me look at the others."

Gretchen turned to Catherine and Dan. "I had to make room for Neel's collection of nineteenth-century American art books when Neel moved in with me. He's read every one of them."

"Here's another Winslow Homer engraving selling for three hundred," Neel said. "*The Georgia Delegation in Congress.* I recognize it from a *Harper's Weekly* cover. Probably early 1861. But the *Harper's* banner head has been cut off, maybe by the framer. Now what's the third image?"

"I'll bet it's another Winslow Homer engraving," Gretchen said.

Neel scrutinized it. "Right you are, Gretchen. Another one from *Harper's Weekly.* This one is *The Inauguration of Abraham Lincoln.* From March of 1861. Selling for three hundred."

"May I check something, Neel?" Catherine asked. She took her phone back and clicked the button NATIVE AMERICAN ARTIFACTS. "There's nothing here. That's funny."

"Why would there be a category in an online store with no items for sale in it?" Dan asked.

Catherine's cell phone chimed. "Hi, Smitty," she said. "Really? How sad…Thanks for letting me know." She reported to the others. "That was my boss. Ned Gunter is selling his farm. He just sent Smitty a classified ad for it. Smitty's already posted the ad on *Webby Witherston.*"

"What kind of farm?" Dan asked.

"Mostly apple orchard. Up the valley. Thirty acres. Five hundred thousand dollars." Catherine smiled at Dan. "Interested?"

"If I had the money."

"The farm has a chicken coop but no chickens and two barns but no barn animals. I've been there."

"And now a house but no humans."

"That could be fixed. Here's the ad." Catherine had gone to the classifieds on *Webby Witherston.*

Placed on 12/17/2015

Property Type: Land

Street Address: 8500 Valley Road, Witherston, Georgia 30597

Thirty acres of apple orchard w/furnished farm house, well, two large barns, chicken coop, pond. Property enclosed by post and rail fence.

$500,000

Email: ralphbankley@bankleysrealty.com

Gretchen's cell phone rang. The ringtone was chirping crickets. "Hi, Lottie. What's up?" Gretchen listened. "That's interesting…Of course. I will be happy to join you and Michelle, and I'll invite Neel. Thanks. See you at six thirty. Or so."

"What did Lottie say?" Neel asked.

"Peg Marble is gone. Michelle Plains Palacio is here. She arrived this morning to scatter her father's ashes. Lottie is having her to dinner tonight." She glanced at Neel. "Lottie wants us to join them. She's also invited Jon and Gregory. Do you want to go?"

"Of course," Neel said.

"I want to look at the engravings again," Catherine said. "Maybe the description tells who framed them." She clicked the AMERICAN ANTIQUES button on the Alhaash Antiques Online website. "What? Now the engravings are gone. There's nothing here anymore."

"Holy smoke," Gretchen said.

Dan looked up from his lunch. "I'll bet the Heche brothers contact their buyers before they put their merchandise on eBay. They're not selling to you and me, or to anybody else browsing the web. They're selling to dealers."

"So the stuff spends only minutes on eBay," Neel said. "We just happened to see the Winslow Homer engravings before they were bought by someone."

"Like Doolittle. Doolittle spent only a couple of hours on eBay before Lottie bought him," Gretchen said. "And Lottie was told where to go."

Dan scooted his chair close to Catherine's. "Let's check the previous owners."

"I'm looking up William Jackson Rumsay, III. We need to find out whether he gave a blowgun to the Sunset Museum," Catherine said. "Oh. He's dead. Here's an obituary from the *Washington Post*, dated July 7, 2014." She read it aloud.

> "William Jackson Rumsay, III, MD, pediatric endocrinologist, died on July 3, 2014, in Washington, D.C., at the age of 81. He was preceded in death by his wife Eileen Mayfield Rumsay and their only child Mayfield Rumsay. Dr. Rumsay, an amateur archaeologist, devoted the last twenty years of his life to his family's collection of 18th- and 19th-century Cherokee and Creek artifacts. According to the executor of his will, pediatric endocrinologist Dr. Pablo Arena, Dr. Rumsay's collection will be donated to the Sunset Museum of Native American History."

"Call Dr. Arena," Gretchen said.

Catherine looked for Pablo Arena's contact information. "I'll have to call Dr. Arena on Monday," she said. "His office is open Monday through Thursday from eight thirty to four thirty. No home phone number."

"Ask him whether Dr. Rumsay had a Cherokee blowgun in his collection," Gretchen said.

"And call Everett Mirkson. Dr. Everett Mirkson. He's the Sunset Museum's director," Neel said. "Find out whether the museum has a record of having received a blowgun in the collection."

"And find out who was responsible for accepting the collection and accounting for the objects in it," Dan said. "My bet's on Albert Heche."

"Okay, okay, okay." Catherine smiled. "I will do all of that on Monday. Right now I'm calling Mev. I give her what I know, and she gives me what she knows."

"Everything?" Dan asked.

Catherine ignored the question and went on, "And after I talk to Mev, I'm writing a story about Doolittle."

ɕ೨ɕ೨

Jaime showed Annie the photo of the page from the *Cherokee Phoenix* on his iPad. "Mom forwarded this to me. It's a long, long letter to the editor. I'll make it larger for you."

Jorge, Jaime, Beau, and Annie were sitting around the Arroyos' kitchen table. Paco was putting their lunch dishes into the dishwasher.

"Let me read it," Annie said. It took her five minutes to read the document.

"What does it say?" Paco asked.

"The Cherokee authors of the letter, Elijah Hicks, Johnson Rogers, and B.F. Thompson, tell about being arrested for digging for gold on land that belonged to the Cherokee Nation. For three days they were marched by gun-carrying guards to Wadkinsville—spelled W-A-D-K-I-N-S-V-I-L-L-E."

"Maybe Aunt Lottie can write a story about that on *Webby Witherston*," Jorge said.

"This letter tells something even more interesting," Annie said. "Some Cherokees in Habersham County had to leave their homes to avoid persecution by Georgia officers. They locked up their few possessions and fled into the mountains. The officers broke the lock of a house and took—guess what?—a blowgun. And, according to this letter, the constable was a man named Crow."

"Was it the blowgun that Dr. Plains bought at the auction? Paco asked.

"According to the blowgun's certificate of provenance the first owner was Travis Ironside Crow," Lottie said.

"From Habersham County," Beau said.

"Maybe Travis was a brother of Constable Crow. Or a son. Or a cousin."

"Or a daughter," Jorge said.

"Travis is a man's name, bro," Jaime said.

"I thought Travis was like Mavis," Jorge said. "Mavis is a woman's name."

"Mavis is pronounced MAY-VIS, bro."

"Oh."

Annie continued. "You all, this is a sad, sad letter. And I'll bet Mr. Fairfield never even read it."

"Mr. Fairfield auctioned it off as a souvenir," Jaime said.

"I'm texting Mom to tell her that we found the origin of Dr. Plains's blowgun," Jorge said.

ꕥ

Paco had driven almost two hours that morning to north Atlanta in search of a parrot stand for Doolittle. He found a green one in HealthyPets in Sandy Springs. As he paid for the stand he spoke with HealthyPets owner Timothy Raider.

"You have a very nice store here, Mr. Raider, with lots of bird supplies, but no birds."

"Right. No birds. And no dogs or cats either. When I

bought this shop last April I discontinued the sale of live animals, except for fish. My wife and I adopted the one African Grey who was left, and I found good homes for the Military Macaw, the Double Yellow-Headed Amazon, and the budgies. Parrots are too intelligent, too sensitive, and too deserving of respect to be traded as merchandise in a store. So are dogs and cats."

"You have an African Grey? How old is he?"

"She is eighteen months old. Her name is Cosmo. I thought she was a he when I named him, or rather her. Then last month a DNA test showed that Cosmo was a she. She was already calling herself Cosmo, saying 'Cosmo is a good bird' and 'Cosmo has feathers,' so I couldn't change her name. She's a delight."

"Cosmo is eighteen months old? Did this shop sell other African Grey parrots?"

"Yes. The shop usually kept one or two for sale. You know African Greys are among the most intelligent birds on the planet and the most talkative. They attract lots of visitors to the store, though not necessarily buyers. They are expensive. Cosmo's sibling sold last December. Cosmo was still looking for a permanent home in April."

"Mr. Raider, I am buying this stand for my wife's aunt, who bought an eighteen-month-old African Grey at an auction. Do you have any records of the sales of the other African Greys?"

"Sure. They're in the computer. What should I search for?"

"Search for Hempton Fairfield."

Timothy searched.

"No Hempton Fairfield. But here's a Petal Fairfield. She bought a six-month-old African Grey chick on December 24, 2014. Probably Cosmo's clutchmate."

"That's the bird my wife's aunt got in Fairfield's auction. He's named Doolittle. Hempton and Petal Fairfield said they traveled too much to keep him. *Pobrecito*. He has no feathers on his chest."

"Another abused parrot. Does Doolittle talk?"

"Yes. He says 'fuck' a lot."

"That speaks volumes."

ဗ၁ဗ၁

"I would like to make a phone call," Thom said to Pete Junior.

He and Pete Junior, who was a year older, had played basketball together in high school. They'd been friends. They'd stayed friends despite the numerous occasions when Pete Junior had had to arrest him. Till now, all the offenses were minor: traffic violations, practical jokes, political activism that did not appeal to the authorities. Today Pete had brought him a cheeseburger and a coke and had taken a seat on the other bench in his jail cell. "Do you want to call a lawyer?"

"No. I want to call Mr. Gunter, Waya's father."

"I'm supposed to stay with you."

"That's fine. I understand."

"Use my cell, Thom."

Thom punched in Ned Gunter's home number.

"Mr. Gunter? This is Thom." Thom began to cry. "I am so sorry for everything I did." Thom listened. "No, no, Mr. Gunter. That's not what happened. I tried to save Waya…I loved him. I love you." He listened another minute. "So I may never see you again, Mr. Gunter." He let out a sob. "I want to thank you for taking care of me when I needed a father. I am sorry I turned out this way." He disconnected and held his head in his hands. "Mr. Gunter hates me. He blames me for Waya's death. And now he's selling his farm and moving to northern Alabama."

Pete Junior moved over beside Thom and put his arm around Thom's shoulders.

"What went wrong, Thom? You seemed to have everything going for you in high school. You were smart and popular and funny. How did you end up here?"

"I don't know. Drugs, gambling. I don't know. I used up my inheritance from old Withers, and I needed money."

"Jesus, Thom."

"Do you want more? Okay. I had a hole in my heart so I filled it with alcohol. Now my cup runneth over."

"Jesus, Thom. You had so many friends."

"Not close friends. Only Waya."

ꕥꕥ

Mev told Jake what she'd learned from Catherine about the provenance of the *Cherokee Phoenix* page and the blowgun.

"We started out with two mysteries to solve, Jake. Doolittle's kidnapping and the murder of David Guelph."

"And possibly Gifford Plains."

"Right. Anyway, we've solved those mysteries. Thom Rivers kidnapped Doolittle and killed Guelph, and possibly Plains too. But now it looks like we have two other mysteries to solve. The identity of Alpha and the relationship of Hempton Fairfield to Al Haash. You and I may soon solve the first, and my team is working to solve the second."

"Mev, you have a great team. I'm lucky to have you—and yours."

"And I you, Jake."

"Josephine and Billy went to her folks in Athens for the weekend, so I plan to catch up on work here," he said.

"I'm heading home while it's still Saturday. The

boys have rented a movie called *Naqoyqatsi* which they want us all to watch together."

"I'll monitor Thom tonight."

"As will I, from home," she said. "Let's talk after Thom gets the pot. It's strange that Alpha has changed the object of his affections from pets to pots."

"And that Alpha doesn't care that Thom is the subject of a manhunt. Maybe he, or she, doesn't know."

"She? Do you think Alpha could be a woman? Peg Marble?"

"We'll find out when we see who takes the pot from Thom's truck."

CHAPTER 11

Saturday night, September 17:

The wind had picked up and the temperature had dropped into the twenties by the time Neel, Gretchen, and Gandhi arrived at Lottie's.

"At least the rain has stopped," Gretchen said as she pulled her green wool poncho over her head, hung it on the coat stand, and followed Lottie into the kitchen. She saw the bowl of cleaned shrimp, the garlic, the dried peppers, the extra virgin olive oil, and the sherry. "Terrific. I love shrimp *pil pil*."

Neel went over to stoke the fire. Gandhi stretched out in front of the fire and fell asleep.

"Hello," Doolittle said.

Gretchen jumped. Tonight Doolittle was using Lottie's soft voice. The bare-chested parrot looked up at Gretchen from the kitchen floor.

"Hello," he repeated. "Doolittle wanna peanut."

Lottie leaned over and placed a plate with five dry roasted unsalted peanuts in front of Doolittle. "Be careful not to step on Doolittle," she warned Gretchen.

"Is Doolittle free to roam the house now?" Gretchen asked Lottie.

"Of course," Lottie said. "Isn't Gandhi free to roam the house?"

"Yes, but Gandhi is a dog."

"Would Gandhi like to be in a cage? Doolittle is as much a person as Gandhi."

"You're right. Here. I brought us a fresh cheddar from Elberton. The maple cheeseboard is your Christmas present." Gretchen handed Lottie the Georgia cheese on the cheeseboard wrapped in green cellophane.

"How about a glass of *vino tinto*, dear?" Lottie had already uncorked a couple of bottles of 2009 Tinto Pesquera, a tempranillo from the Ribera del Duero in northern Spain. She poured the red wine into three of the six goblets she'd set out on the counter, gave one to Gretchen and took one for herself.

"Neel," Gretchen called. "Come and get it before I throw it out."

"Neel!" Doolittle called.

"To Doolittle," Gretchen said, raising her goblet as Neel entered the kitchen.

The doorbell rang. *DINGDONG*. Lottie ushered in Dr. Michelle Plains Palacio. A beautiful woman in her early forties with short, curly brown hair, Dr. Palacio wore a black cashmere brimmed hat, a white pashmina scarf, and a black leather coat over a teal wool pantsuit, dangling silver earrings that resembled tree branches, silver bangles, and a silver anklet.

She carried a purple University of Washington canvas tote bag.

"Come in, Dr. Palacio. We're so happy you could join us this evening. Let me hang up your coat."

"Call me Michelle, and I'll call you Lottie. My father spoke fondly of you. She pulled a heavy object wrapped in white tissue paper out of her bag. "I brought you a present from Seattle."

It was an owl carved out of white steatite, seven inches tall. "How beautiful," Lottie exclaimed.

"The owl was carved by an Inuit artist outside Fairbanks who signs his name Akycha. You were my father's closest friend in Witherston. I want you to know that I appreciate your kindness to him. I collect Inuit sculpture."

"Thank you so very much, Michelle."

The doorbell rang again: *DINGDONG.*

"Dingdong dingdong dingdong." Doolittle mimicked the doorbell perfectly.

Jon and Gregory walked in with Renoir. Lottie introduced all three of them to Michelle. Renoir bounded to the hearth to greet Gandhi.

"Hello, sweet baby," Jon said to Lottie, giving her a bear hug. "We brought Doolittle a jar of our favorite dry roasted unsalted cashews—"

"And you a bottle of our favorite port," Gregory said, finishing Jon's sentence.

"We'll have it for dessert. Thanks so much. You all know I love port."

"Dingdong." This time the doorbell sounded from under the dining room table.

"Time to go back in your cage, Doolittle," Lottie told him.

Neel, always the gentleman, got down on his knees and persuaded Doolittle to hop on his hand. He returned the parrot to his cage on the coffee table.

Suddenly the lights went out.

"Woof."

"Woof."

"Good lord."

Prepared for the loss of electricity, which occurred fairly frequently in Witherston, Lottie quickly produced matches to light candles.

"No problem," Lottie said. "We have plenty of wine and cheese to hold us over till I can cook the shrimp."

"And plenty of logs for the fire," Neel said. "Who cares if the lights stay off?"

The lights stayed off. By candlelight and firelight and with plenty of wine and cheese Jon and Gregory told Michelle about Giff's last night on Earth and his phone call to them after midnight. Lottie told Michelle about the circumstances of Giff's death. Neel told Michelle, Jon, and Gregory about the provenance of the Cherokee blow-gun. Gretchen told Michelle, Jon, and Gregory about the identity of Al Haash. Lottie told Michelle, Jon, and Greg-ory about the provenance of the page from the *Cherokee Phoenix.* Gretchen told Michelle about the circumstances of David Guelph's death.

"I knew Dave Guelph," Michelle said. "I knew him well. And so did my father."

"How?"

"I'm on the board of the Native American Artifacts Recovery Foundation, which Dave chairs. Chaired. The foundation buys outstanding relics of Native American tribal culture that go on the market and gives them to mu-seums. That's what Dave was doing here. Dave traveled all over the country searching for bits and pieces of the civilizations our White ancestors extinguished. He was an idealist. He thought that if we could assemble enough parts of the whole civilizations we'd understand what we had lost."

"We'll never understand. A living whole is greater than the sum of its parts," Neel said. "Once the whole is broken—"

"All the king's horses and all the king's men can't put the whole together again," Jon said.

"Because the whole is a system," Neel said. "A civi-lization is a system."

"Like an ecosystem," Gregory said.

"I should tell you that I am Cherokee," Neel said to Michelle. "I grew up in Oklahoma, and I came back here…well, for a number of reasons, one of which was to learn about my grandparents. So I've spent a lot of time thinking about what our continent's White immigrants eradicated. They did more than decimate a population. They did more than steal our people's land and gold. They did more than relocate our people to Indian Territory. They destroyed the relationships between things that constitute a civilization. They destroyed the Cherokees' relationships to their land, to their ancestors, to their gods, to their past, to each other. It's these relationships that make a culture, not the things that are its parts, like the blowguns, the pots, the baskets, the newspapers. The relationships are gone forever."

"All we have are souvenirs, like newspapers, baskets, pots, and blowguns," Lottie said as she uncorked another bottle of wine.

Neel got up and stoked the fire. For a few minutes Lottie's guests listened to the wind whistle through the pines.

Suddenly a big branch dropped onto Lottie's tin roof and noisily rolled off.

The dogs woke up and started barking.

"Stop it, stop it," Doolittle screamed. "Stop it, stop it, stop it!"

"Here we have another souvenir of the past," Lottie said. "A souvenir from Doolittle's life with the Fairfields."

"Did Doolittle come with a certificate of provenance?" Jon asked as he opened Doolittle's cage door.

"No, he didn't. But Paco discovered his provenance. A pet store in north Atlanta."

Doolittle climbed up to the rope perch.

"I'm thinking," Michelle said slowly. "The name Al Haash is slightly familiar to me. But I don't remember where I've heard it before."

"Check the certificates of provenance you've gotten for the Native American relics that your foundation has bought," Gregory said.

"I will. Now tell me about Tayanita Village."

Gregory looked at the others. "I'll tell her," he said, looking around the room. "I'm the only one of us who's been there."

"Go, ahead, Gregory."

"Tayanita Village is a community of fifteen—now fourteen—young people, ages thirty and under, who want to find their Cherokee roots. Their parents and grandparents did their best to be assimilated into the White society that developed on top of their ancestral society. They believed that assimilation, along with education, was the best way into the American middle class. And they abandoned the Cherokee language."

"Language is the vehicle for culture," Lottie said. "If a people lose their language, they lose the vision of the world that was embedded in the language."

"And they lose their roots, their connection to their parents and grandparents and great grandparents," Neel added.

"Right," Gregory said. "Ten years ago, Witherston High School hired a teacher named Myra Whitbred who taught the history of the Southeast beginning long before the first European explorers arrived. Miss Whitbred got her students interested in the Cherokee and Creek cultures and allowed them to do genealogical research if they wanted. In fact, she guided them. Eddie Gunter, who took the Cherokee name Waya, was a student of hers. Probably most of the residents of Tayanita Village were her students."

"May I go up to Tayanita Village?" Michelle asked.

"I'll take you up there tomorrow, and I'll introduce you to John Hicks, a descendant of Elijah Hicks."

"My father left me his collection of Cherokee artifacts," Michelle said. "I will give most of the collection to the Native American Artifacts Recovery Foundation, but I'd like to leave some things here. I plan to give some pottery and basketry to the Cherokee-Witherston Museum, and anything else Carolyn Foster can use. But now I want to give something to Tayanita Village too."

"How about a peace pipe?" Neel asked.

"Good idea," Jon said. "I'll bet they do a bit of smoking up there."

"I was thinking of the blow-gun," Michelle said.

"I'll pick you up at ten thirty tomorrow morning, Michelle," Gregory said.

ꕥꕥ

Mev, Paco, Jaime, and Jorge were ten minutes into *Naqoyqatsi* when the electricity went off. *Naqoyqatsi* was an experimental film of 2002 directed by Godfrey Reggio with music by Philip Glass and no dialogue. None. The Hopi word *naqoyqatsi* means "life as war."

"Oh, no," Jaime and Jorge exclaimed in unison.

"Oh, yes," Paco exclaimed. He gave Mev a wink and a thumbs up, moved Mighty off his lap, and went over to the hearth to poke the fire.

"*Hijos*, you can watch the movie on your iPads."

Mev took a call from Jake.

"Hi," he said. "Did your power go out, too."

"Yes, we're in the dark too," she said.

"Do you think we should go ahead with the plan?"

She considered his question for a moment. "Let's proceed. Alpha may not know that Witherston's lights are out. Give Thom a flashlight, and send him up to the Fairfields at eleven forty-five. If we catch the person who takes the pot from Thom's truck, then we have Alpha—Or a link to Alpha."

"That was my thinking, too. Let's do it."

"Okay, Jake. We'll talk later."

ꕥ

Dan and Catherine sat side by side on Catherine's sofa with Muddy at their feet. Catherine was reading her story about Doolittle aloud to Dan when the lights went out. Dan grinned. "How nice."

Muddy barked once and went back to sleep.

Catherine continued reading. She'd bought her backlit Android to be able to work in the dark.

Her cell phone rang. It was Smitty. She took the call. "I'll tell him," she said. "And Rhonda can talk with him directly." She gave Smitty Dan's cell phone number and disconnected.

"Rhonda has put in an offer for Ned Gunter's farm. But she wants to work out a deal with you."

Dan's cell phone rang. He put it on speaker phone. "Hello, Rhonda. How are you tonight?"

"I'm in the dark, Dan, but I'm excited to tell you something. I have a deal for you."

"I'm listening."

"I just put in an offer of four hundred and seventy-five thousand dollars in cash for the Gunter farm, and Ned accepted it. We close on Wednesday, the sixth of January."

"Congratulations."

"Here's the deal. I lease the farm to you for a dollar a month if you use part of the farm, not the orchard part but the barn part, as a sanctuary for barnyard animals in need of a good home. That's one dollar a month. I will get you started, and I will bring you some animals. Probably not many. A donkey or two, a few old horses, maybe a mule."

"Sounds wonderful, Rhonda."

"And some chickens. Many chickens."

"Perfect."

"You will take care of the animals, give them food, love, and medical attention, do normal repairs on the property, and live in the house. Let the chickens range freely. Next December you and I will reassess the situation. If you are a good keeper of the animals, and if the animals are happy, and if you are happy, then I will give you the farm. I will put it in your name. All you will owe me is a promise to take care of unwanted farm animals for as long as you own the property."

"Thanks, Rhonda. Thank you, thank you. It's a deal."

"There is another condition. You may not sell the property, though you may pass it on to your heirs if you should have any. If you decide you don't want to live on the farm any more, or if you decide you don't want to keep up the sanctuary, then you give the farm back to me, or to my estate."

"It's a deal, Rhonda."

"Would you like to ride out there with me tomorrow, Dan? Ned has already left."

"May I bring Catherine?"

"Of course. And Muddy too. I'll pick you all up at Catherine's at noon. After church."

"All I can say is thank you, Rhonda. Thank you! What good fortune I had to be your cellmate. I'll be happy to go to jail with you any time."

"Just go to jail for justice."

ᏡᏡ

"Hi, Jake." Mev looked at the clock as she took the call. "It's eleven thirty. Is Thom ready to go?"

"He's ready. A little nervous, but he seems eager to help."

"My intuition is telling me there's something strange going on here, Jake. Be sure to have your deputies follow Thom, but at a distance. Fairfield's mansion is at the top of Withers Hill. You might have them wait at the bottom of Withers Hill Road where Thom can see them as he leaves the property to get on Witherston Highway."

"That's a good idea. I'll be with them."

Mev nodded as she listened. "Okay. Sounds good. I'm glad you'll be there too."

ᏋᏋ

As he settled into bed trying not to disturb Mighty, Jaime said to his brother, "I feel awful for Thom. He was a great athlete. Remember? How could he have gone bad?"

"Dad said he was a good student, real funny in class."

"Dad likes funny."

"He made more points than anybody who's ever played for Witherston High."

"Now when I go to basketball games I'll wonder what will happen to those players after they graduate."

"What will happen to us?"

"We've got plans, bro."

"Yeah. You're going to be an ecologist, and I'm going to be a journalist."

"I wonder if Thom had plans."

"Thom had bad luck."

"Thom didn't have an *hermano*."

"True. I can't imagine not having an *hermano*.

Mighty woke up and made his way to Jaime's pillow, where he found a comfortable spot by Jaime's head and promptly fell asleep.

"*Buenas noches, hermano.*"

"*Buenas noches.*"

After five minutes, Jorge spoke. "Are you awake?

"Yes."

"Do you love Annie?"

"I guess so. She likes me. And I like to be close to her. I mean, I like to be near her. She smells good."

"Oh. Do you tell her what we talk about?"

"No, bro. I wouldn't do that."

"Do you kiss her?"

"Yes."

"Do you touch her? You know…like have you touched her breasts?

"No, bro. But we hug each other."

"Would you tell me if you had touched her breasts?"

"Of course. Would you tell me if you had a girlfriend and touched her breasts?"

"Yes. I tell you everything, Jaime."

"*Buenas noches, hermano.*"

"*Buenas noches.*"

CHAPTER 12

Saturday, December 17, 11:55 p.m.:

Thom drove up the steep, narrow, half-mile Withers Hill Road slowly. Good thing his pick-up had all-wheel drive. Or was it a good thing? *I'm being set up*, he said to himself. *Either by Alpha, who wants to kill me so I can't kill him, or by Chief McCoy, who wants to use me to trap Alpha. Whichever it is, I'm expendable. If I complete this mission, I'm expendable. If I don't complete this mission, I'm expendable. I'm already worthless. I just want to die. When I get the pot, I'll turn around, go back down the road, and take off as soon as I see my tail. I'll make the cops shoot me. Death by cop. That's what I want. Death by cop.*

At the top of the hill, Thom parked his car, got out, and turned on the flashlight Chief McCoy had given him. The wind was blowing hard. Thom zipped up his jacket.

Hempton Fairfield's house was totally dark. Totally. *How convenient*, Thom thought, illuminating the front door and then the open garage with the flashlight. *Lights out and no vehicle in the garage. So Alpha was right. Nobody's home.* He walked up the steps onto the front porch, retrieved the key taped to the back of the porch lamp and quietly unlocked the massive front door. *The electricity must be off. Now why would a wealthy man not have an alarm system on a generator? Does he have an alarm system that works only when the electricity is on? Weird.*

Thom opened the door and shone his flashlight inside. He saw no evidence of anybody at home. The house was silent. *Of course. No electricity for the fridge or the heater or the lights. A house with electricity makes noise even when no one's home.*

Thom stepped inside and shone his flashlight all around. He saw the Cherokee pot on the marble table in the entryway in front of a ten-foot high mirror framed ornately in brass. *This is too easy, but I'll go ahead with the job. Even though the nine thousand dollars won't do me any good if I'm in jail. Or in the ground.*

Thom set his flashlight on the table to illuminate the pot, took a picture of it, emailed the picture to Detective Arroyo, and pocketed the phone. As he lifted the pot he heard the snarl of a cat. He turned around. He saw a flash and felt the bullet enter his chest. He crumpled to the floor and lost consciousness.

ꝏꝏ

Jake and Pete Junior arrived in two vehicles less than a minute after Hempton Fairfield's 9-1-1 call. They found the front door open. With the aid of an LED flashlight, similar to the one they'd given Thom, they saw Thom face up on the slate floor with blood flowing from his mouth. Hempton Fairfield knelt beside him. The shards of a shattered black pot were scattered across the entrance hall.

"Move," Jake shouted to Fairfield. "Get out of my way."

Fairfield backed off.

Jake unzipped Thom's jacket to expose Thom's bloody shirt. The bullet seemed to have hit his heart. He felt for a pulse and didn't find it. Thom was dead.

He heard the ambulance siren.

While Pete Junior set up LED lanterns in the entrance hall and the living room for picture taking and the ambulance personnel put Thom's body in the ambulance to be taken to Chestatee Regional, Jake sat down with Fairfield. "Do you mind if I record this conversation, Mr. Fairfield?"

"No, of course not."

Jake set up a small recorder and moved a lantern onto the coffee table. He saw that Fairfield wore a navy silk bathrobe over navy striped pajamas.

"What happened, Mr. Fairfield?"

"I was asleep. I heard an intruder, got my gun, came downstairs, and shot him. Once."

"Where's the gun?"

"Here." Fairfield pulled a semi-automatic pistol out of his bathrobe pocket. Jake bagged it.

"Why did your alarm system not work?"

"The generator needs to be replaced. I'm going to have somebody look at it next week."

"Do you know the person you shot?"

"No. Who was he? I couldn't see him in the dark."

"Thom Rivers. You don't know him?"

"No, I don't. I know who Thom Rivers is, but I don't know him. I saw him at the auction. He was one of the troublemakers."

"How could you see to shoot him?"

"He had a flashlight. The mirror reflected the light. I saw his body. And the front door was open."

"So the moonlight helped."

"Yes. The moonlight and the mirror."

"What did you think the intruder was stealing?"

"An Ewi Katalsta pot. Cherokee. Worth at least fifteen hundred dollars. From the mid-nineteenth century."

"That's a lot of money for a clay pot. Where did you get it?"

"I don't recall. I've had it for a while. Maybe I got it from a dealer in North Carolina."

"How could the intruder have known about the pot?"

"It was in the auction. And it was mentioned in *Witherston on the Web*."

"How could the intruder have known where to find it?"

"How would I know? Look, I heard an intruder and shot him inside my house. That's legal. The Castle Law allows me to shoot an intruder."

"An intruder who is threatening you."

"Yes. And I felt threatened. I thought he might have had a gun. Remember, it was dark."

"How do you know about the Castle Law?"

"I live in an expensive house filled with expensive antiques. I bought a gun to protect myself and my property. Why would I not know about the Castle Law?"

"Where is Mrs. Fairfield?"

"She went to Atlanta for the weekend. We keep a small apartment there near the High Museum."

"Where is your car?"

"I parked it behind the house. I want to clean out the garage tomorrow, or rather later today, Sunday, while Petal is gone."

"Thank you for talking with me, Mr. Fairfield. Let me ask you to keep me informed of your whereabouts until we process this case. Under the circumstances you should not leave the country."

"I understand, Chief McCoy." Hempton Fairfield stood up.

Pete Junior called out from the entrance hall. "I've finished taking pictures, boss. May I go now?"

"Yes, Pete Junior. It's five of one. Go home, go to sleep, and then enjoy Sunday with your wife.

"Thanks. Will do."

Jake shone his flashlight around the lavishly furnished living room, thanked Fairfield again, and carefully made his way past the pool of blood.

"I will send a clean-up crew first thing in the morning, Mr. Fairfield," Jake said in parting.

"No need. But thanks. In the morning I'll be able to do it myself."

As Jake shut the front door behind him, he got a call from Mev. "Hi, Mev. Thom's dead." He got into his vehicle, turned on the engine, and told her what he knew.

"I think we should go ahead with the plan. I got the picture of the pot."

"I think you're right, Mev. Go ahead and text the photo to Alpha. Alpha won't know that Thom's dead till the news breaks tomorrow morning."

"Okay, sending it now. I will talk to you in the morning."

Yes, let's talk in the morning."

"Next Jake got a call from Catherine Perry.

"Hi, Catherine."

"Hi, Jake. I heard on my police scanner that there was an incident at the Fairfield's house. Can you tell me what happened?"

"Yes, I'm happy to give you the facts." He spoke to her on his Bluetooth while driving home.

ꟹꟹ

After talking with Jake Mev opened Thom's iPhone and texted the photo to Alpha.

~ *Six, iMessage, Sunday, December 18, 1:20 a.m. I have the pot. Here's the picture. When may I have my $9,000?*

Then she joined Paco in bed.

"Honey, Thom is dead."

"*¡Caramba! ¿Qué pasó?*"

"I'm responsible. I sent him on a mission to steal a pot—from Hempton Fairfield. I was trying to smoke out the person who was paying Thom to do jobs. And Thom got shot by Fairfield." Mev told Paco what she'd learned from Jake.

"*Señor* Fairfield must have been expecting a visitor. You say he was wearing a bathrobe over his pajamas when Jake got there? He would put on a bathrobe to go downstairs to shoot a burglar, when he was already wearing pajamas?"

"That's what Jake said he was wearing when Jake got there. And Jake got there in less than a minute from the time of the 9-1-1 call. Jake was parked at the foot of Withers Hill Road."

"*Mevita*, if I heard a burglar come into our house, I'd go downstairs in my birthday suit to protect us."

"But you don't have a gun, honey."

"I'd shoot him with an arrow. I'd get the bow from the boys' room, find some arrows in their closet, and shoot our visitor with an arrow."

"And I'd take pictures. Of sweet naked you, slightly paunchy, pulling the bow string back to strike down an intruder with a rubber-tipped arrow."

"I'd be proud."

"Paco, let's be serious."

"Okay."

"Do you really think it's strange that Fairfield was wearing a bathrobe when he shot Thom?"

"Yes. Didn't Fairfield tell Jake he'd been asleep?"

"Yes."

"Nobody sleeps in a bathrobe."

"Nobody I know," Mev said with a smile. "So I think we should investigate Fairfield. But Fairfield could have heard Thom drive up Withers Hill Road."

"If he had, why didn't he call 9-1-1 then? Instead, he put on his bathrobe, got his gun, and shot Thom dead. I'd say he wanted to be dressed for the police, who would be taking pictures."

"Paco, you're so suspicious."

"*Sí. Es verdad.*"

"Okay. You've got a point. I'll talk to Jake in the morning."

"*Buenas noches, Mevita.*"

"*Buenas noches, Paco.*"

Five minutes later, Mev heard *ZONGZINGZING.* Paco was already asleep, so she slipped out of bed quietly, walked into the bathroom, and opened Thom's iPhone. Thom had gotten a message from Alpha.

~ Alpha, iMessage, Sunday, December 18, 1:41 a.m. I will send you amazon gift cards of $2,000 now and the other $7,000 as soon as I get the pot. Delete this message. Alpha

Mev read the message from Alpha and went back to bed.

WWW.ONLINEWITHERSTON.COM

WITHERSTON ON THE WEB
Sunday, December 18, 2015
8:00 a.m.

BREAKING NEWS

Thom Rivers Shot Dead

Thomas Rivers, age nineteen, was killed at approximately 12:00 a.m. this morning during a burglary attempt at the home of Hempton and Petal Fairfield, 1 Withers Hill Road.

According to Police Chief Jake McCoy, Hempton Fairfield shot Thom in the heart with a Glock semi-automatic pistol. Mr. Fairfield said he woke up, heard the front door open, grabbed his gun, went downstairs, and fired at the intruder in the dark. Mr. Fairfield said that he did not recognize the intruder.

Chief McCoy and Deputy Pete Junior Koslowsky arrived within minutes of Fairfield's 9-1-1 call and found Thom dead in the entrance hall. A valuable Cherokee pot, made by Ewi Katalsta in the nineteenth century, was in pieces on the floor.

Rivers graduated from Witherston High School last June. Known locally as a prankster, Rivers had acquired an arrest record for minor offenses. However, on Friday, December sixteenth, Rivers, who was already considered a person of interest in the kidnapping of the parrot Doolittle, was arrested in connection with the death of Dr. David Guelph. He was released last night for undisclosed reasons.

Rivers has no known family. After autopsy, his body will be cremated. Chief Atohi Pace of Tayanita Village will take responsibility for scattering the ashes along Tayanita Creek.

~ Catherine Perry, Reporter

LETTERS TO THE EDITOR

To the Editor:

My friend Grant Griggs divides the world between people and food for people. Mr. Griggs must believe that God told humans to have dominion over the fish of the sea, and the birds of the air, and the cattle, and over all the wild animals of the earth, and every creeping thing that creeps upon the earth.

Lucky humans. Poor God-forsaken chickens. Imagine being born to be food.

Gretchen Green, Witherston

WEATHER

High winds last night brought a power outage to 4,000 Witherstonians from approximately 7:05 p.m. last night to 2:25 a.m. this morning. There is some disagreement as to the cause of the electrical outage. According to Mayor Rich Rather, "a damned squirrel" got into the transformer. His wife, Rhonda Rather, disputes that theory. According to Georgia Power officials, the 60 mile-an-hour winds caused a huge dead oak to fall on a transformer.

Today will be sunny, with temperatures rising into the 50s. Lows tonight will be in the high 30s.

Here comes the sun, here comes the sun, and I say it's all right.

~ Tony Lima, Weatherologist

Doolittle Byrd, an African Grey Parrot
Photo by Catherine Perry

Last Wednesday, December fourteenth, Witherston on the Web columnist Dr. Charlotte Byrd purchased an unhappy, feather-plucked, young African Grey parrot named Doolittle at Hempton Fairfield's auction. She bid and paid $2,000 for him. That night Doolittle was kidnapped. On Thursday morning, Dr. Byrd paid the $2,000 ransom in hopes she would get Doolittle back. She did. As you know, Rhonda Rather, the mayor's wife, discovered Doolittle in Dan Soto's eighteen-wheeler chicken truck. Go, Rhonda.

Doolittle talks. First he listens, and then he talks. People in his presence should realize that he is listening to their conversations and may make them public at a later date. Doolittle listened to the clucking of the chickens in the chicken truck and now he clucks. Doolittle is revealing that he has spent time with chickens.

Doolittle mimicked Thom Rivers's unusual ringtone and enabled Detective Mev Arroyo to identify Thom Rivers as his kidnapper. By reporting what he had heard, Doolittle served the cause of justice. Go, Doolittle.

According to Dr. Byrd, Doolittle has uttered these phrases: "Ugly bird," "Doolittle is a bad, bad bird," "F—k you," and "I wanna divorce." Uh, oh. Somebody has used bad language in front of this juvenile bird. Somebody wants a divorce. What more will Doolittle tell us about his past? Dr. Byrd expects to hear lots.

In the last few days, Dr. Byrd has done some research on African Grey parrots. African Greys in the Congo, where Doolittle's wild ancestors flew freely in large flocks, spend the first year of their life with their parents. They learn their calls from their parents. When African Grey chicks born in captivity are separated from their parents at three to six months, they learn the calls—the language—of their human adoptive parents. Doolittle speaks English because that is what he heard in his formative months.

But think how Doolittle must have felt being taken away from his parents before he had even learned to peep like a Grey parrot. Now if he met his biological parents or his biological siblings, he wouldn't be able to communicate with them. That's sad.

But the story has a good ending. Doolittle seems to have finally found happiness. He is now a free-range parrot in Dr. Byrd's home. And he's talking!

~ Catherine Perry, Reporter

IN THIS MONTH IN HISTORY
By Charlotte Byrd

On December 18, 1960, the reputedly humorless Hearty Harold Withers, born in 1889, died. HaHa, as the millionaire was called, left his vast fortune to his only offspring, the humorless Francis Hearty Withers. HaHa's wife, Maud Olive McGillicuddy, had died in 1939.

HaHa Withers passed down to his son not only his vast financial holdings in the Lawrence Company but also a fierce prejudice against those of Cherokee descent. HaHa's sister, Penance Louise Withers, had eloped with a Cherokee named Mohe Kingfisher. Now Penance Louise and Mohe Kingfisher's grandson, Neel Kingfisher, who identifies himself as Cherokee, lives with Gretchen Green, who identifies herself as White. The marriage of Mohe and Penance Louise and the union of Neel and Gretchen attest to the effectiveness of intermingling—whether in marriage or in friendship—in overcoming prejudice.

MENU SPECIALS

Founding Father's Creek Café: Southern fried chicken, green beans with bacon, grits, rolls, pecan pie with vanilla ice cream.

Gretchen Green's Green Grocery (Lunch only): Saffron shrimp, pasta, roasted fennel, apple slices and Manchego cheese.

Witherston Inn Café: Chicken and sausage stew, broccoli, corn bread, wedge of iceberg lettuce with blue cheese dressing, peanut butter cookies.

CHAPTER 13

Sunday, December 18:

Mev checked Thom's email as soon as she got up. Yes, Thom had received a gift certificate from Amazon.com. She'd open it later. Now for Sunday breakfast. She showered and joined her family downstairs.

Paco was already cracking eggs for his special fluffy omelettes with grape jelly filling. Jorge and Jaime were drinking orange juice, eating sausages, and reading *WITHERSTON ON THE WEB* on Jorge's iPad. Mighty was eating his own breakfast in the corner of the kitchen.

Paco poured Mev a cup of coffee and moved a platter of sausages near her.

"According to Mizz Perry, Thom had no family," Jorge said. "So who gets his stuff?"

"What kind of stuff do you think he had, bro?"

"The usual. You know, truck, clothes, smart phone, tablet, TV."

"Boom box."

"Money in the bank."

"Yacht."

"If Thom made a will, the will will specify," Mev said.

"The will will?" Jorge said.

"Yes, the will will." Jaime said. "You heard Mom. She said the will will."

"Willy nilly?"

"Thom's last will and testament," Mev said. "If he made one. We can find out from Lauren. He may have filed it in Probate Court in Dalonega."

"*Oye, Mevita*, what happens to the tracphone you gave him?"

"The tracphone. I hadn't thought about it, Paco. I'll call Jake to see if he got it."

"Wow. Look at Doolittle's picture," Jorge said, scrolling down. "Doolittle is destroying Aunt Lottie's phone book."

"What a lucky good bird!"

"Mizz Perry's telling the world that Doolittle reports what he hears."

"Not the world, Jorge, just the residents of Witherston."

"All four thousand of them, Jaime. And all four thousand saw my drawing of the chickens."

"And your photo of me and Doolittle."

"We are famous, Jaime."

ꕥ

In Chapel Hill, a cell phone rang with an incoming message. A young man read the text in silence.

~ Alpha, iMessage, Sunday, December 18, 8:21 a.m. Four, are you still available to work for me?

~ Yes. Talk to me

~ Where are you now?

~ Chapel Hill

~ *How soon can you get to Witherston, GA?*

~ Eight tonight. What's the job

~ *No antiques this time. You are to kill a parrot in the home of an older woman who lives alone. Address is 301 N Witherston Hwy.*

~ How much will you pay

~ *$2,000*

~ I want $3000 total, $1000 now and $2000 when I kill parrot. OK?

~ *OK.*

~ When do you want me to do the job?

~ *Tonight. Wear a ski mask. And arm yourself just in case.*

~ All I have is a shotgun. Is job dangerous?

~ *No. But you may have to show her your gun. When I get your photo of the dead parrot I will send you two gift cards of $1,000 each.*

~ OK

~ *Now delete this message thread. Alpha.*

The young man did as he was told and deleted the text message.

ꟹ

Mev called Jake at home. "Jake, did you find the tracphone on Thom's body?"

"Yes, I did. I had to look for it. I found it in his jeans pocket."

"It's interesting that Thom had time to take a picture of the pot before he was shot."

"That must have been the first thing he did."

"And put the phone back in his jeans pocket."

"Are you thinking that Thom didn't put the phone back in his pocket himself?"

"I don't know."

"How about if I have it dusted for fingerprints?"

"Good idea. Do you have Fairfield's fingerprints?"

"No, I don't. Or rather, not yet."

"Jake, I told Paco the story you told me about Thom's getting shot. Paco wondered why Fairfield took time to put on his bathrobe over his pajamas before coming downstairs to see who was breaking and entering."

"Maybe that's how Thom had so much time."

"Alpha said that Fairfield would not be home."

"Fairfield said his wife went to Atlanta for the weekend."

"Fairfield's got some secrets, Jake. My team, as you call it, suspects him of receiving stolen property from museums, falsifying their provenance, and selling them to private collectors at auctions."

"If you can make a good case for that, then we can get a search warrant from the Lumpkin County Magistrate Court in Dahlonega."

"I'd have to figure out what I'd be looking for."

"Mev, are you thinking that Fairfield may have known Thom was coming to rob him?"

"I'm just thinking that Fairfield is hiding more than he's disclosing."

"I'll call him and tell him that you and I'd like a follow-up visit with him tomorrow."

"And I'll make a list of what we'd search for with a warrant. I'll send it to you this afternoon. Maybe Ricky can search his house while we have our visit with him. I will probably put his computer on the list, and his cell phone, and any other electronic devices he may use in his antique business."

"You deserve a day free of detective work, Mev. What are you going to do in this nice weather?"

"I'm having a birthday party tonight for Lottie and the boys. Jaime and Jorge, who are turning fifteen, have gone for a hike and a picnic with Beau and the dogs. I told them to stay out all day. Paco, Neel, and Jim are building a chicken coop back in the woods as a birthday surprise. Would you like to join us?"

"Thanks, Mev. But Josephine and Billy will be back. I'll get a search warrant for tomorrow morning."

ꕥꕥ

At noon Rhonda arrived at Catherine's apartment with Giuliani. After Giuliani and Muddy had gleefully become acquainted, Giuliani reclaimed her front seat in the Escalade, and Catherine, Dan, and Muddy climbed into the back. They drove up Valley Road and entered the Gunter farm through a twelve-foot-high log arch that announced in faded green letters *WELCOME TO GUNTERLAND*. They followed the gravel driveway past two barns that had once been painted red up to an old two-story farmhouse that had once been painted white.

There they got out, dogs first. Rhonda replaced her high heels with tennis shoes, put on her pink parka, and led Catherine and Dan up the steps of the wrap-around porch.

"We can't go in the house, but we can look in the windows," Rhonda said.

They did.

"I like it a whole, whole lot," Dan said. "What do you think Catherine?"

"I like it."

"A lot?"

"A whole, whole lot."

"And the cat?" A little calico had just come around the corner on the porch. She was obviously nursing.

"I like her too, and I'll like her kittens."

The cat headed toward a food station with a large

plastic water dispenser and bowl. Ned had left enough dry cat food and water to last a week.

"Ned abandoned everything. Even his cat," Rhonda said. "Poor man."

"We'll take care of her," Dan said, "and your chickens, horses, mules, donkeys, pigs, goats, and sheep, Rhonda."

"Llamas, alpacas, zebus, water buffalos, and camels," Catherine added.

"Whatever. You bring them, we'll love them."

ഗ്ദ

Gregory, Jon, and Michelle arrived at Tayanita Village to be greeted by a large flock of white and brown chickens. No segregation here. They climbed down from the cab of Gregory's pickup and shook hands with John Hicks and Galilahi.

"Dr. Palacio, meet our Cherokee friends John Hicks and Galilahi Sellers. John and Galilahi, meet Dr. Palacio. Dr. Michelle Plains Palacio is the daughter of Dr. Gifford Plains, who collected Cherokee artifacts," Jon said.

"I know who he is," John said.

"Dr. Palacio is also on the board of the Native American Artifacts Recovery Foundation," Jon added.

"Thanks for calling this morning, Gregory," John said. "Occasionally on sunny Sundays some of us go hiking in the mountains. You all come into our Council House."

As they entered the big yurt and felt the warmth of the wood stove, Gregory turned to Michelle. "John Hicks is a descendant of Elijah Hicks, the second editor of the *Cherokee Phoenix.* Elijah Hicks took over after Elias Boudinot, who was ousted in 1832 for supporting the relocation of the Cherokees to Indian Territory."

"Elijah Hicks was anti-removal," John said. "He wanted the Cherokees to keep their homeland. I've studied the injustices the Whites did to my ancestors, and I want justice."

"What would constitute justice?" Michelle asked him.

"I wish we could just undo history," John said. "You know Woodie Guthrie's song 'This Land is Your Land'?"

"Yes."

"Well, Woodie Guthrie was not singing about the people who lived on this continent from ten thousand BC to the arrival of Europeans in the fifteen hundreds. He was singing about his own people, White people, who came here and didn't consider the Cherokees and other Indians to be rightful owners of this land. They didn't consider them real people. Woodie Guthrie wasn't singing about the deer and the antelope either. It was their land too," he said.

"The Indians didn't think they owned the land. They just lived on it and shared it. They didn't think of land as something to possess," Galilahi said.

"Right. The Whites taught the Indians about ownership. The Whites turned the Indian land into parcels of property and took it for themselves," John said. "You've heard of the Georgia Land Lottery?"

"Yes."

"That was an injustice that was never rectified."

Galilahi took John's arm. "We can't change that now, John."

Michelle studied him. "Since you can't undo history, what else might rectify that injustice, John?"

"Tell her about the auction, John," Galilahi said.

"You must know about the auction, Dr. Palacio. Your father bought a two-hundred-year-old Cherokee blowgun there."

"And that is what I would like to give to Tayanita Village, John and Galilahi," Michelle said, "as soon as my father's estate is probated."

"You would do that?"

"Of course. Could you keep it safe—for future generations of young people trying to preserve the Cherokee culture?"

"Where would we put it, John?" Galilahi asked.

"In the Council House. I could build a cabinet for it. A very heavy, very safe cabinet. Out of hickory."

"The Native American Artifacts Recovery Foundation buys up cultural artifacts and returns them to the tribes for their safekeeping. Usually we donate them to museums, but occasionally we give them to groups of Native American people trying to preserve their heritage, like Tayanita Village."

"Thank you."

"I don't need thanks. The blowgun belonged—and belongs—to the Cherokee people. The foundation is trying to rectify the injustice you're talking about. We can't undo history, but we can try to save cultures that the powerful have almost destroyed. My father was working with us. In his will, he gave a hundred thousand dollars for this purpose."

"Would you have a job for me?"

"I can't offer you a position in Seattle, at least not all by myself. And Dr. Guelph is dead. But I can have the foundation send you to auctions from time to time to buy Native American artifacts. Would that suit you?"

"It would."

"I will also arrange for the framed page from the *Cherokee Phoenix* to go to the Cherokee-Witherston Museum."

"What can we give you in return, Dr. Palacio," Galilahi asked. "Would you like some chickens?"

"Not for me, Galilahi. But I know of some folks who would."

ഗ്ദ

Mev had just carried lunch out to Paco, Neel, and Jim when she got Jake's phone call.

"Hi, Mev. Sorry to interrupt your afternoon, but I have some interesting news for you. I've gotten three autopsy reports from Dirk Wales. Both Gifford Plains and David Guelph died of hypothermia—after a blow to the right side of the head. Apparently, Thom knocked them unconscious and left them in the snow, but didn't actually kill them. The weather did."

"And the third report? It's about Waya?"

"Waya's skull shows a potentially fatal crack on his left side. But Waya died of smoke inhalation."

"So Waya tripped on a rug, hit his head on a bench, fell to the floor, and died of smoke inhalation."

"Or Waya went into the yurt to confront Thom about the deaths of Plains and Guelph and Thom hit him and knocked him out."

"And then Waya died of smoke inhalation."

"Remember, Waya was the only witness to the kidnapping and the encounter with Plains. Thom benefitted from Waya's death."

"I can't believe that Thom meant to kill his best friend."

"Do we know whether Waya was outside the yurt when the fire started?"

"No, Jake, we don't. And we may never find out."

"So we may never find out whether Thom meant to kill anybody."

ഗ്ദ

After their picnic of peanut butter sandwiches, Jaime, Jorge, and Beau trudged up muddy Old Dirt Road toward Tayanita Village. Mighty and Sequoyah led.

"So Thom was robbing Fairfield's house when he was shot," Beau said after hearing the twins' account of Thom's death. "That shows a connection between the two mysteries we're trying to solve. Maybe there's just one mystery."

"You mean the mystery of Al Haash and the mystery of Doolittle's kidnapping are the same mystery?" Jaime asked.

"You think Fairfield is involved in Doolittle's kidnapping?" Jorge asked.

"Could be," Beau said. "Here's what you all are telling me. Mr. Fairfield got his merchandise from Al Haash—or A-L-H-A-A-S-H—who probably got it illegally from collections given to museums. Al Haash used eBay to disguise his sale of stolen property. Mr. Fairfield used eBay to disguise his purchase of stolen property."

"And Thom Rivers?"

Beau puffed out his chest, proud of his theory. "Thom Rivers worked for Alpha to kidnap pets for ransom—or at least one pet—and he got paid in gift certificates from Amazon."

"Anonymous gift certificates."

"Alpha called Thom 'Six,'" Beau said. "I'll bet there were others working for Alpha called One, Two, Three, Four, and Five."

"And Alpha hired Thom to steal a pot in Fairfield's house," Jorge said.

"And Fairfield killed him," Jaime said.

"Convenient for Alpha, isn't it," Beau said. "And for Fairfield. Now Thom can't talk. Alpha had told Thom that nobody would be home, and Fairfield was home after all, but without his car in the garage."

"So Alpha set up Thom to be killed."

"By Fairfield."

"Either Alpha and Fairfield are close associates or Alpha is Fairfield," Beau said. "I think Alpha is Fairfield. Fairfield has a gang of thieves. He communicates with them by text messages. He hired members of his gang to steal pets or jewelry or antiques, and he put the items on eBay for sale. Then he used the profits to buy merchandise through eBay from the Alhaash online store."

"Wow. That's neat," Jaime said.

"He paid the thieves by Amazon gift cards so the gang couldn't trace their money."

"That's ingenious," Jorge added.

"So how do we catch Fairfield?"

"I think Mom has to catch him," Jorge said.

"Let's go advise Mom," Jaime said.

"First, let's go look at the chickens," Jorge said.

The three boys and the two dogs sprinted the rest of the way to Tayanita Village. There they ran into Galilahi and about thirty chickens.

"You boys need any chickens?" Galilahi asked them. "We have chickens galore."

"We'll ask our parents if we can have some Galore Chickens," Jorge said.

"Would you like to help John and me clean out a co-op?"

"Sure."

ꕥ

Jorge, Jaime, and Beau got back at five thirty, too late to help their parents set out the plates and glasses, put the pork roast on the grill, put the potatoes in the oven, or cut up the purple cabbage for the microwave, but in time to watch Mev make Hollandaise sauce and Paco build a fire. Sitting at the kitchen table, the boys explained their theory that Fairfield was Alpha.

"Uh, oh," Mev said. "If you're right, Fairfield knows that someone has Thom's cell phone and is pretending to be Thom. I answered Alpha's text message after Thom was killed."

"*Mevita*, do you think Fairfield will suspect you?"

"Probably, love."

"Are you in danger?"

"Probably not. Anyway, I'm going to be surrounded by a whole bunch of folks tonight. Fairfield won't crash the party."

"What about One or Two or Three or Four or Five? He could have hired one of them."

"I'll talk to Jake. He can send Pete Junior or Pete Senior to watch our house."

"*Buena idea*."

"And I'll tell Jake he needs to deputize the boys."

"Wow, thanks, Mom," Jorge said.

"Boys, you all smell ripe. How about going upstairs and taking showers—you too, Beau—before our guests arrive? And put on clean clothes."

"We have some Keep Nature Natural sweatshirts, Beau. Do you want to wear one?"

"Sure. Then will I look like you guys?"

"We'll be triplets."

After the boys had gone upstairs, Mev called Jake. "Jake, we need to put Fairfield's cell phone on the search warrant."

"For sure. Meet me at the office at seven thirty tomorrow morning. We'll surprise Mr. Hempton Fairfield when he's still in his silk bathrobe."

Then Paco called Galilahi.

ଓଡଓ

~ *Alpha, iMessage, Sunday, December 18, 5:55 p.m. Hello, Four. Where are you?*

~ I just got to Witherston. Am at Rosa's Cantina.

~ *Do your work before midnight.*

~ OK. Then I am going back home

~ *Text me photo of dead bird. I will pay you when I get it.*

~ OK.

~ *Delete this message. Alpha.*

ଓଓ

One of the wonderful aspects of their life in this small Georgia mountain town, Mev thought, was the Witherstonians' tradition of eating together, often. At every opportunity, usually on weekends, Mev and her friends dined in each other's homes, cooked together, barbecued together, picnicked together, drank wine together. They never tired of each other, for they formed an extended family. In fact, they spent so much time with each other that they never needed to begin a new discussion. They simply continued the one they'd started before they'd parted previously. Friendships forged over meals could last a lifetime. Mev knew people in Witherston who had dined weekly in each other's home for thirty years.

Paco had gone upstairs to shower and change. Jim had gone home to shower, change, and get Lauren. Neel had gone home to shower, change, and get Gretchen.

The party began at six thirty.

Lottie arrived first, holding her cane with her right hand and carrying Doolittle's cage in the other. "There are four bottles of Rioja and two small wrapped presents on my back porch," she told Paco. "Could you go get them for me?"

Paco did. Five minutes later, Jon and Gregory arrived with Renoir, a six-foot Christmas tree, and two presents. Next, Gretchen and Neel arrived with Gandhi, Swift, and Ama, a huge tossed salad, and two presents. Jim and Lauren arrived with freshly baked whole wheat bread, a big Manchego cheese, and two presents.

Annie Jerden arrived with a rectangular chocolate birthday cake and two presents. The cake was adorned with a frog made of green icing and the words "Happy Birthday, Lovers of Nature."

Jaime let Doolittle out of his cage and picked him up.

"Doolittle is a lucky good bird," Doolittle said. "OO EE AW AW." Then he bit Jaime's finger.

"That hurt." Jaime parked him on his rope perch.

"That hurt," Doolittle said. He bit Jaime again.

"Ow!"

Mighty, Sequoyah, Ama, Gandhi, and Swift settled into their favorite spots on the living room carpet. The twelve humans sat together around Mev and Paco's long dining room table, enjoyed the dinner and the wine, consumed the birthday cake, and speculated about Fairfield's activities.

About eight thirty the doorbell rang. Jorge answered it. Galilahi Sellers and John Hicks stood on the porch with six chickens. That is, three crates, each holding two clucking chickens.

"Happy birthday," Galilahi and John sang in unison.

"Wow! Galore chickens," Jorge exclaimed. "White galore chickens."

"For our birthday, bro."

"Thank you, Galilahi and John. We can keep the chickens in our room," Jorge said. "Bring them upstairs."

"*¡Hijos!* The chickens will go in your new chicken coop. Jim, Neel, and I built you all a chicken coop out back in the woods today. For your birthday."

"Really?"

"Thanks, Dad, Mom, Neel, Dr. Lodge."

"Thank you so, so, so much."

"We want to introduce your chickens to you," John said. "In this crate, we have Moonshine and Sunshine. In that crate, we have Feather Jo and Feather Jean. And in the crate over there we have Mother Hen and Henny Penny."

Suddenly a shot rang out in the direction of Lottie's house. Somebody had blown open Lottie's front door. Through the picture window, Mev could see a man in a ski mask holding a shotgun enter Lottie's house.

The dogs barked. Doolittle screamed.

Mev pulled out her cell phone to call 9-1-1. But before she could punch in the three numbers, Pete Junior and Pete Senior ran up Lottie's sidewalk with their guns drawn and entered her house. Mev and her guests waited, but they heard nothing more.

A minute later, the Petes exited Lottie's house with the intruder in handcuffs.

Mev grabbed her jacket and joined them. "I'm following you all to the police station," she told the Petes. She got in her car and called Jake.

ꕥ

Mev conducted the interview, while Jake observed from behind the two-way mirror. "What is your name?"

"Harlan Dannon."

"What is your address?"

"It's 215 Crocker Creek Road, Chapel Hill, North Carolina."

"How old are you?"

"Twenty-four."

"Why are you in Witherston?"

"To kill a bird. I was hired to kill a bird at 301 North Witherston Highway."

"Who hired you?"

"I don't know. He goes by the name of Alpha."

Mev gasped. "And what does Alpha call you?"

"Four."

"The number four?"

"Yes."

"How do you communicate with Alpha?"

"By text messages."

"What were Alpha's instructions?"

"To kill the bird and text him or her a picture of the dead bird."

"Have you committed any other act of violence for Alpha?"

"No, this is the first time Alpha has asked me to kill anything."

"What else have you done?"

"Burglaries. I've stolen antiques for Alpha."

"Such as?"

"Small things. A silver mirror, a pocket watch, jewelry, paintings. Alpha would tell me what to take."

"How does Alpha pay you?"

"With gift cards from Amazon."

"How much were you getting for this job?"

"Three thousand dollars. In three gift cards."

"What do you do with the gift cards?"

"I buy computer parts. I have a computer repair shop in Chapel Hill, called Dannon's Computer Help."

"Harlan, I'm going to ask you the next question as a mother of teenage boys, not as a detective. Help me understand why you are involved in this petty crime. Why did you become a burglar?"

Harlan rubbed his eyes. "I don't know. I majored in computer science at NC State. Got mostly A's. After graduation I opened up the computer repair shop. Two months later I got busted for selling marijuana—less than five pounds—and had to spend half a year in prison. So I closed the shop for those six months. When I got out, on November 7, 2014, I had a criminal record and no money. I couldn't get a bank loan to get back my business. Then I got a text message from Alpha offering me money."

"When was that? Do you remember?"

"Yes. It was January 19, my birthday."

"What did Alpha say?"

"That he or she would pay me well to steal small items from homes when the owners were out of town. That there'd be no violence."

"How did Alpha get the items from you?"

"I put them in a small public storage locker in Durham which I'd leave unlocked when Alpha told me to. Alpha picked them up on the first of the month."

"Did you delete the text messages?"

"Yes. Alpha always asked me to delete them."

"Thank you, Harlan, for cooperating with us."

"How much prison time do you think I'll get?"

"Some, maybe not too much. Depends on the number of burglaries. You were lucky to be caught before you killed the bird."

"May I have my cell phone back?"

"No, Harlan. We need it to catch Alpha. Could you please tell us your password and Apple ID."

Harlan did.

ശശ

"Hello, Catherine."

Jake was fond of Catherine, although she always called him just a little bit before he was quite ready to talk to the press. Always. On every single occasion, it seemed. She must have the police scanner in her ear twenty-four hours a day.

"Hi, Jake. I understand you have the intruder at Lottie's in custody."

"Yes, Catherine, we do have the intruder in custody. Here are the facts."

While Jake and Catherine talked Mev called John Hicks.

"Hello, John. We've got another cell phone job for you. Can you come in tomorrow morning?"

"Sure. What time?"

"Nine o'clock. Thanks. We'll pay you this time."

ᘓᘔᘓᘔ

By the time Mev got home, the party had broken up.

"You missed all the excitement, Mev," Lottie said. "Doolittle said to me, 'I love you.' In front of God and everybody."

"I also missed the presents, Aunt Lottie. What did everybody get?"

"Let me tell you what I got. First, lots of hugs and kisses. Then, as you know, I got from you, Paco, and the boys a T-stand for Doolittle, so that he can be out of his cage whenever I'm home. Thanks so much, dear."

Lottie got up and gave Mev a hug.

"And I got toys for Doolittle, some parrot treats, and two perches for the big cage that Jorge ordered for him."

"What did the boys get, besides our chicken coop and six chickens?"

"Shaving gear from me. I've noticed that they are starting to grow little mustaches. A turntable from Neel and Gretchen, so that they can listen to my vinyl records. You know that Jaime likes to play sixties songs on his guitar. A pair of binoculars from Beau, Lauren, and Jim. And two books from Annie, Darwin's *Voyage of the Beagle* for Jaime and *Dangerously Funny*, about the Smothers Brothers, for Jorge. Remember the Smothers Brothers, Mev?"

"I think they were of your generation, Aunt Lottie."

"Oh yes. Also six chickens from our Tayanita Village friends."

"I'll bet the boys like the chickens best."

ꕥꕥ

Jaime turned the lights out and climbed into bed with Mighty.

"Are you still awake, bro?"

"Yes," Jorge mumbled. "I'm thinking about Henny Penny and Mother Hen, Feather Jo and Feather Jean, and Moonshine and Sunshine. Do you think they'll like the chicken coop?"

"I think they will."

"I'm afraid they'll get cold."

"They'll snuggle together in the straw."

"We can feed them and let them out tomorrow morning," Jorge said.

"That's right. No school."

"I'm going to treat each chicken the way Aunt Lottie treats Doolittle, like a feathery little person."

"The way we treat Mighty, like a furry little person," Jaime agreed.

"You know what the difference is between a chicken and a dog?"

"Feathers and fur?"

"No. It's the way we treat them."

"Okay. What's the difference between a Cherokee and a White person?"

"Skin color?"
"No. It's the way we treat them."
"*Buenas noches, hermano.*"
"*Buenas noches.*"
"Do you like our razors, bro?"
"Yes. Aunt Lottie has noticed that we're manly."
"We're very manly."
"*Buenas noches, hermano.*"
"*Buenas noches.*"

CHAPTER 14

Monday, December 19, 2015, 7:45 a.m.:

Mev and Jake knocked at Hempton Fairfield's door at seven forty-five in the morning.

Fairfield answered wearing a suit and tie and holding a black cashmere coat. Mev could see two black Louis Vuitton suitcases at the foot of the stairs. She figured he was expecting to travel. He would be disappointed.

"Hello, Mr. Fairfield," Jake greeted him. "My colleague Detective Arroyo and I would like to ask you a few questions about events that have transpired since our last meeting."

Mev extended her hand. Fairfield shook it politely. "I'm afraid that I am in a bit of a rush today, Chief McCoy," he said. "I have a plane to catch at eleven thirty, and I would like to leave the house in fifteen minutes."

"This may take a bit longer than fifteen minutes, Mr. Fairfield."

"Okay. Come on in, both of you. Let's sit down." He hung his coat on the coat rack and led the way into the living room.

"Where are you going, Mr. Fairfield?"

"Denver."

"I'm afraid you'll have to postpone your trip, Mr. Fairfield," Jake said. "Your shooting of Thom Rivers is still under investigation. You are the only witness to the event, you know."

"I don't know that you have the right to block my traveling, Chief."

"We have some questions for you, Mr. Fairfield," Mev said. "And we have a search-and-seizure warrant issued by Judge Henry Fohrster in Dahlonega." She showed Fairfield the warrant.

"What is the reason for this?"

Jake extended his hand, palm up. "May we have your cell phone?"

"Why?"

"Your phone may provide evidence in the prosecution of Harlan Dannon. Mr. Dannon was arrested last night for breaking into the home of Dr. Charlotte Byrd."

"What?" Fairfield looked stunned. "What does that have to do with me?"

"And your phone may provide evidence in the kidnapping of Doolittle from Dr. Byrd Wednesday night."

"What does that have to do with me?" Fairfield repeated.

"Again, let me ask you for your cell phone, Mr. Fairfield," Jake said.

Fairfield extracted his cell phone from his trouser pocket and handed it to Jake.

"What's your password? And your Apple ID?"

"Password is Hash!@#."

"Apple ID?"

"Antiquarian123."

"You're making it easy for us, Mr. Fairfield," Mev said.

"We would also like to impound your computer and

any other electronic communication devices you may have, such as a tablet," Jake said.

"Help yourself. May I ask why you are interested in my computer?"

"We are interested in the source of your merchandise," Mev replied.

Jake answered a call on his own cell phone. "Yes, Ricky. We've served the warrant. Please come in."

Deputy Hefner entered the front door, with a large burlap bag.

"Ricky, please collect all the computers, tablets, cell phones, and guns you can find in Mr. Fairfield's house. Follow standard policy regarding search-and-seizure. Thanks. And let's trade cars for today."

Jake and Ricky exchanged keys.

"You already took my gun, Chief McCoy. I don't have another," Fairfield said.

"Fine."

"We would like for you to come with us to the police station, Mr. Fairfield," Mev said. "You are officially a person of interest in the kidnapping of Doolittle, the shooting of Thom Rivers, and the receipt of stolen goods in your antique business."

"If you do not come with us willingly, I will put you under arrest," Jake said.

"I will come with you willingly, though I have no idea what you're talking about."

Jake frisked Fairfield and helped him into the back seat of Ricky's patrol car.

WWW.ONLINEWITHERSTON.COM

WITHERSTON ON THE WEB
Monday, December 19, 2015
8:00 a.m.

BREAKING NEWS

An intruder carrying a shotgun was arrested at 8:50 p.m. yesterday in the home of Dr. Charlotte Byrd, 301 North Witherston Highway.

Harlan Dannon, age twenty-four, from Chapel Hill, North Carolina, told police he had been hired to kill Dr. Byrd's parrot Doolittle.

Doolittle was not home at the time. Neither was Dr. Byrd.

Mr. Dannon is the owner and operator of Dannon's Computer Help in Chapel Hill. He is helping Witherston police identify the person who hired him.

WEATHER

Blue skies smiling at me. Nothing but blue skies do I see.

~ Tony Lima, Witherston's Webbyweatherman

OBITUARY

Thom Rivers

Thomas Robert Rivers, age nineteen, died on Sunday, December eighteenth, of a gunshot wound.

Thom was the son of Robert Rivers, whereabouts unknown, and Martha Evans Rivers, late of Lumpkin County, who died of cirrhosis of the liver in January of 2015. In his senior year Thom lived with Ned Gunter and Ned's son Eddie (Waya) on their farm.

At Witherston High, Thom held the respect of his fellow students. He was president of the senior class, captain of the basketball team, co-captain of the baseball team, and member of Keep Nature Natural, the school's environmental organization.

"He was smart, but he was also a heap of fun," said Christopher Zurich, who is now KNN's vice-president. "He wasn't afraid to get arrested to save the environment. I admired him."

Miss Myra Whitbred, Thom's history teacher, said, "I can't believe that Thom killed anybody. At least not intentionally. I'll never believe it. What happened was just a pile of accidents."

When told of Thom's death, Ned Gunter wept. "Now I have lost two sons," he said.

IN THIS MONTH IN HISTORY
By Charlotte Byrd

This weekend my young friend Annie Jerden, age fifteen, may have cracked a 185-year-old cold case.

Annie, Beau Lodge, and my great nephews Jaime

and Jorge Arroyo have been studying the certificates of provenance that accompanied two items in Hempton Fairfield's auction. They are about to solve the mystery of Fairfield's source of the Cherokee blowgun that the late Gifford Plains bought and the framed Cherokee Phoenix newspaper clipping that the late David Guelph bought.

Beau, Jaime, Jorge, and I have focused on the provenance of the items. We noticed that the first "owner" of the blowgun was Travis Ironside Crow of Habersham County.

Annie was more interested in the newspaper than the blowgun. And she didn't just want to study its provenance. She wanted to read the story.

She did, and this is what she found.

In a long letter to the editor of the Cherokee Phoenix of September 4, 1830, authors Elijah Hicks, Johnson Rogers, and B. F. Thompson reported that Constable Crow of Habersham County was involved in a raid on some Cherokee families that resulted in a forced entry into one of their vacated homes and the confiscation of a blowgun.

Was Travis Ironside Crow that constable? Or that constable's brother or son? We don't know, but if we dig into county records, we may find out.

We will probably never know whether the blowgun Dr. Plains bought at Fairfield's auction is the same blowgun that Constable Crow's officers took into their possession in 1830.

We do know that Elijah Hicks, Johnson Rogers, and B. F. Thompson, speaking for the Cherokees, viewed Constable Crow's actions as unjust.

Figuring out what happened 185 years ago is not easy.

Nevertheless, we may speculate that the original

Cherokee owners of the blowgun did not give their weapon as a gift to the Crow family out of generosity.

Dr. Michelle Plains Palacio, visiting Witherston to scatter her father's ashes, has returned the blowgun her father bought at Fairfield's auction to the Cherokee people, or at least to their local descendants, the residents of Tayanita Village.

MENU SPECIALS

Founding Father's Creek Café: Chicken noodle soup, carrots, cabbage, rolls, apple cobbler.

Gretchen Green's Green Grocery (Lunch only): Oven roasted cauliflower, carrots, and broccoli, wild rice, deviled eggs, lemon sorbet.

Witherston Inn Café: Coq au vin, new potatoes, tossed salad with thousand-island dressing, eggnog cake.

CHAPTER 15

Monday, December 19:

At nine o'clock, John Hicks appeared at the police station.

"Hi, John," Jake said. "Mev and I've been talking. If you do a good job helping us today, we will hire you as a technology consultant."

"Would you be willing to work for the Witherston Police Department?" Mev asked.

"I guess I wouldn't be too embarrassed. Would I have to wear a uniform?"

"No," Jake said. "You wouldn't be a cop. You'd be a consultant."

"So what do you have for me to do today?"

Jake handed him the two cell phones, one from Harlan Dannon and the other from Hempton Fairfield.

"Can you retrieve the text messages that have been exchanged between Hempton Fairfield and a man named Harlan Dannon?" Mev asked him.

"Sure. I can recover everything they've ever deleted."

"Mev will give you their passwords and Apple IDs," Jake said.

"I'm ready to start."

"Fairfield used the name 'Alpha' when he wrote Dannon. And he called Dannon 'Four.'"

"The number four?"

"Yes, spelled out." Jake said.

"Specifically," Mev said, "we want all the text messages going back to November 26, 2014."

"Gotcha," John said.

John went to work.

ᏒᏒ

"Am I speaking to Dr. Pablo Arena," Catherine asked, "the executor of William Jackson Rumsay's will?"

"Yes," Dr. Arena said.

"My name is Catherine Perry. I am a reporter in Witherston, Georgia, investigating the sale of stolen goods, and I'd like to ask you some questions."

"About stolen goods? I'm a physician."

"Oh, I know, sir. But you are familiar with the collection of Cherokee artifacts that Dr. Rumsay willed to the Sunset Museum of Native American History, aren't you?"

"I am indeed, Miss Perry. Dr. Rumsay was my close friend. How can I help you?"

"You turned the entire collection over to the Sunset Museum?"

"Yes, I did. Two people from the museum came over and packed it up. But I supervised."

"Was a four-foot-long Cherokee blowgun made out of river cane in the collection?"

"Why, yes. It was one of Bill's prizes. It had been in his family for almost two hundred years."

"Who was your contact at the Sunset Museum, Dr. Arena?"

"A Dr. Heche. I think his first name was Bert."

"Could it have been Albert?"

"Yes."

"Have you been back to the museum to see what they've done with the collection?"

"No, I haven't. Why? What's up?"

Catherine told him.

"Do you want me to go to the museum and ask about the blowgun?"

"Better not," Catherine said. "But thanks, anyway. Detective Mev Arroyo of the Witherston Police Department is on the case. She'll contact you."

After disconnecting, Catherine called Mev. "Detective Arroyo, I have a story, and this time it's for you."

Then Catherine turned to Dan. "Do you want to go with me to the police station?"

"Why, not? I know where it is."

ೲೲ

"I hate to disappoint you, Detective Arroyo, but the earliest text message on Mr. Fairfield's cell phone was sent on November 30, 2015." John Hicks sat in the old leather arm chair in her office at the police station with Hempton Fairfield's cell phone in his hand.

"Do you think this is a new phone?" Mev asked him.

"Must be."

"Maybe he uses this phone only for business."

"Who is Peg Marble?"

"She's Gifford Plains's wife, or rather widow," Mev replied. "Why?"

"She and Fairfield have spoken a lot on the phone in the past month."

"Really? I had no idea they knew each other."

"Let's see. Since the first of December, I count twenty-seven calls, most of them from Fairfield to her, but some from her to Fairfield."

"Any emails?"

"No. No emails at all."

"Maybe Fairfield doesn't use his cell phone for emails."

"He doesn't."

"What about text messages?"

"The only text threads here are between Fairfield—calling himself Alpha—and Thom Rivers, and between Fairfield-slash-Alpha and Harlan Dannon. All of them between November thirtieth and December eighteenth of this year."

"Anything else interesting, John?"

"One call to an Alan Heche on December second and two calls to an Albert Heche, one on December third and another on December seventeenth."

"The Heches?"

"Do you want me to send the text messages to your computer?"

"Yes, please."

Mev printed out the text messages to show Jake. "Now could you check Dannon's phone?"

"I'm on it."

Jake read Fairfield's text messages in his office. Mev waited for him to finish.

"These messages will convict Hempton Fairfield of premeditated murder," he said. "Fairfield sent Thom Rivers to his own house, told him where to find the key to the front door, and told him where to find the pot. So he knew that Thom was the intruder, he knew where Thom would be standing, and he used deadly force to kill him."

"Now what do you suppose Hemp Fairfield and Peg Marble were planning?"

"Maybe they were just having an affair," Jake said.

"An affair. Maybe. I wonder."

"Detective Arroyo?" John called out. "I'm into Dannon's phone."

"What have you found?"

Mev hurried back across the hall. Jake followed.

"Dannon and Fairfield communicated frequently. Two text conversations on December eighteenth between Dannon and Fairfield, about killing the parrot. And then maybe twenty-five or thirty earlier conversations starting on January 19, 2015. Look at this first one."

Mev leaned over John's shoulder:

~ *Alpha, iMessage, January 19, 2:14 p.m. Hello, Harlan Dannon. Would you like to earn some money?*

~ Who are you?

~ *Call me Alpha. I have work for you.*

~ Computer work?

~ *No. But it will help you buy computer equipment for your business.*

~ Explain.

~ *It involves burglary when owners of house are gone. Antiques, small items. Would that bother you?*

~ How much can I earn?

~ *$1,000 for easy jobs. $2,000 for hard jobs. I know you need the money.*

~ Explain.

~ *I send you a text with a street address and a description of the item I want. When I tell you to, break into the house and take that item. No violence.*

~ What do I do with it?

~ *I will mail you a key to a storage locker in Durham. Put it there. OK?*

~ OK. How do I get my money?

~ *I will buy Amazon gift cards for you. You use them to buy whatever you like on Amazon.*

~ OK.

~ *I will call you Four.*

~ The number 4?

~ *Yes. I will be in touch soon. Don't try to find me or you will be hurt. Now delete this message. Alpha*

"We've got him," Mev said to Jake. "We can lock up Fairfield for a long time."

"I've already put in a call to the district attorney in Dahlonega."

John knocked on the door of Jake's office. "Would you like me to send this message thread to your computer, Detective Arroyo?"

"Yes, John. Please send all of the text messages between Fairfield-slash-Alpha and Dannon. Thanks."

"There's more on Dannon's phone. Hundreds of emails starting back on November 11, 2014, when, I think, he got the phone."

"Who are they from, and to?"

"Banks, mostly, in November and December of 2014. Appears he was trying to get a loan. There are some rejection letters here."

"What else?"

"Some emails from Amazon.com. Fourteen of them. They are gift cards. Hmmm. This recent one is for a thousand dollars. He got it on December eighteenth at nine-fifteen in the morning. Yesterday. But he didn't open it."

"It would be for killing the parrot," Jake said.

"Could you please forward to me all his emails from Amazon?" Mev gave John her email address.

"I'm on it, Detective Arroyo."

Mev turned to Jake. "Now we have to correlate the gift certificates with Fairfield's messages to Dannon regarding the burglaries."

"And with police reports of stolen antiques."

"Done," John said. "Detective Arroyo, you have the fourteen Amazon emails with the gift certificates. I imagine that all but the last certificate have been used.

"What else can you find out, John? What about Dannon's phone conversations?" Mev asked.

"There are lots of them. Lots and lots and lots. That's what he used his cell phone for. Do you need to know who called him and whom he called?"

"Not now," Mev said. "Maybe later."

"Do you need me for anything else, Detective Arroyo, Chief McCoy?"

"No, John. I don't think so. Not today."

"My office will send you a check for a hundred dollars, John," Jake said.

"Thank you, sir. It's been a pleasure." John gave the two cell phones back to Mev.

"Thank you. Now will you accept an appointment as a technology consultant to the Witherston Police Department?"

"Yes. Yes. Thank you. Thanks so much."

"Congratulations, John."

"I have one question, Detective Arroyo. Why did Fairfield want to kill the parrot?"

"Parrots talk."

ઌઌ

As John exited Mev's office Muddy, Catherine, and Dan entered it, in that order. Muddy took the chair. Mev, Catherine, and Dan stood.

Catherine reported what she'd learned from Dr. Arena.

"Excellent work, Catherine," Mev said. "Now we have the real provenance of both the blowgun and the *Cherokee Phoenix* page."

"We should correct the certificates, Detective Arroyo," Catherine suggested.

"We should," Dan said. "We need to add the thief Albert Heche to the list of owners. And the maker of the blowgun from whom Travis Ironside Crow stole it. And the Sunset Museum of Native American History."

"The museum may not have had actual custody of the blowgun and the *Cherokee Phoenix* page before Albert Heche sold them to Fairfield," Mev said.

"So an official certificate of provenance could carry names of thieves as well as names of legitimate heirs," Catherine said.

"Yes, if thieves had custody of the antique in the course of its history."

"Would you say that a certificate of provenance is like a chain of custody, Detective Arroyo?" Dan asked.

Catherine opened up her Android to take notes. "What's the definition of a chain of custody?"

"A chain of custody is a legal concept referring to the possession of evidence from the time it's seized to the time it's presented to the court," Mev said. "When officers of the law seize evidence they must keep a record of the persons or places that have custody of the evidence."

"So a certificate of provenance is proof that the record of custody or ownership was checked," Catherine said.

"It's like a title search," Mev said. "If we buy land, a lawyer has to do a title search to determine the chain of ownership of the property. The title letter certifies that the title is clear, and the property can be legally purchased."

"Purchased from whomever possesses it now and can prove he owns it. If we go far enough back, say, a century or two, we'll probably find that the land was stolen from somebody," Dan said.

"Like all of Witherston, Dan. It was stolen from the Cherokees," Catherine said.

"What if historians could construct a chain of custody for every piece of land on Earth? Or even one piece of land? What if historians could construct a ten-thousand-year chain of custody for the twenty-five square miles that Witherston is built upon?"

"Aunt Lottie would like that project."

"So would Neel."

"They would be developing a chain of occupancy, rather than ownership, since for more than ten thousand years the Native Americans considered land not as property to be owned but as space to be occupied, and shared. When the British arrived the Crown took large pieces of land with the assumption that it belonged to nobody and granted it to the colonies as property to be owned," Dan said. "And the colonies, or states, turned the land into lots to be owned."

"You do know your history, Dan," Catherine said.

"This piece of land was originally stolen, as you said, Catherine, from people who hadn't thought of it as property. But maybe all the land we know was originally stolen, or taken by force, or confiscated in war."

"We can't return land to the original owner, Dan, even if we were able to identify him, or her," Catherine said. "We can't return it to the dead."

"You're right, Catherine. We can't return anything to the dead. We can't undo the thefts of times long gone for the simple reason that we've built our present upon the past. And the past is replete with injustice."

❧

"Why do you collect Cherokee knives, Neel?" Jaime asked.

On this sunny afternoon, Jaime, Jorge, Neel, and Gretchen were hiking down Founding Father's Creek trail toward Founding Father's Bridge. Their dogs—Mighty, Ama, Swift, and Gandhi—chased each other in and out of the water.

"Because the knives connect me with my ancestors, Jaime. I like knowing where I came from. When I grasp the handle of one of my bone knives, I imagine being a Cherokee man in the year 1830 skinning a rabbit for my family's dinner."

"But some knives were used for killing people, Neel," Jaime said. "Can you imagine using this knife to slit the throat of a White settler who was taking Cherokee land?"

"And gold?" Jorge added.

"Yes, boys. I can."

"Red Wilker bought an antique rifle that someone used to kill Indians," Gretchen said.

"If we go back in time two hundred years," Neel said, "we go back to the attitudes our own community had toward other communities. The knives of the Indians and the rifles of the Whites were not souvenirs to your ancestors and mine, Gretchen. They were household tools. They were their means of self-defense. Your ancestors and mine, dear, did not get along."

"They killed each other," Gretchen said.

"They weren't totally successful or you all wouldn't have been born," Jorge said.

Neel resumed his lesson. "We like antiques, I think, for their stories. Every item in Fairfield's auction was part of a story we want to know. The bone knife I bought holds a mystery. Who used it? How? Where was it kept? Did it belong to a great, great, great grandfather of mine? I'd like to know all that. Same with the rifle Mr. Wilker bought. Did it belong to a great, great, great grandfather of his? Mr. Wilker and I may have bought the knife and the rifle for the same reason, to connect ourselves to our people's past."

"I think Red Wilker just likes guns," Gretchen said.

"And Mr. Wilker thinks I just like knives," Neel replied. "Boys, does Beau just like arrowheads?"

"Beau likes Cherokee arrowheads because he likes history," Jaime said.

"Cherokee history," Jorge said.

"That's my point, boys. Lots of people like history. Lots of people, like me, want to know how their great, great, great grandparents lived. We want to know our ethnic and cultural roots."

"And our genetic roots," Jaime said.

"I have Neanderthal genes," Gretchen said.

"Maybe that's why you're lactose intolerant, Gretchen," Neel said. "Anyway I think that our desire to know what our genome says about us is related to our desire to know what our past says about us. We want to know who we are and where we came from."

As they approached the bridge a flock of white chickens rushed out of the woods.

"Where did these come from?" Gretchen exclaimed.

"They came from Dan's truck," Jorge said.

"They look a lot like Henny Penny and Mother Hen, Feather Jo and Feather Jean, and Moonshine and Sunshine."

"There they go."

The chickens scurried back into the woods as soon as they noticed Swift, Mighty, Ama, and Gandhi frolicking in the creek.

"Boys, why do you think keeping backyard chickens has become popular?" Neel asked.

"Fresh eggs?"

"That's one reason, Jorge. But I think chicken keepers feel nostalgia for a time when people knew where their food came from. Why do you want to keep chickens?"

"I want to do something our grandparents did," Jaime said. "Actually, our great grandparents."

"On our mother's side. They had a farm near Gainesville. They kept chickens and goats and cows."

"So you want to know what their world was like?"

"Yes, Neel," the boys said in unison.

"Could your interest in chickens be similar to my interest in Cherokee knives?"

"Yes, Neel." Jorge said. "Galore chickens are our antiques."

❧❧

At eight o'clock, a hundred Witherstonians gathered in Reception Hall of the Witherston Baptist Church to hear a tribute to the holidays by Tony Lima's Mountain Band featuring Rhonda on the piano. Rhonda, wearing a red velvet pant suit, black patent leather high heels, and earrings that flashed red and green, took the mic for the encore.

Accompanied by Tony Lima on the guitar, she sang "Grandma Got Run Over by a Reindeer."

The whole band joined in the final verse.

As Tony Lima thanked the audience, Chief McCoy stood up in the back row and said, "I have an announcement. Mr. Hempton Fairfield has been arrested for receipt of stolen property, fraud, and first degree murder. He is in jail now."

The audience emitted a collective gasp.

"Petal's husband?"

"The wealthy Mr. Fairfield?"

"Whom did he murder?"

"Hempton Fairfield is accused of murdering Thom Rivers," Jake replied.

"Do we get to keep what we bought at the auction?" Griggs asked.

"Maybe, maybe not. We've called in the FBI to trace your purchases. Some of the items were stolen from museums and will have to be returned," Jake said. "Mrs. Fairfield has agreed to reimburse you from the auction proceeds if you bought one of those items."

"My tomahawk wasn't stolen from a museum," Griggs said. "It has a certificate of provenance that doesn't mention a museum."

"Your tomahawk was stolen from an Indian, Grant," Gretchen said. "Where do you think your tomahawk came from?"

"We Indians want our tomahawk back, Mr. Griggs," John Hicks shouted from the back of the hall.

"According to the certificate of provenance my tomahawk was first owned by a man named Terrance McGraw."

"Mr. Terrance McGraw stole it from an Indian," Gretchen said.

"Well, the land your grocery store occupies originally belonged to the Cherokees, Ms. Green. So it's stolen property, too," Griggs said. "Do you want to return it to the Cherokees? Or rather, the descendants of those Cherokees?"

"May I have a moment to think about it?" Gretchen asked.

"Great idea." John said. "Return it to the Cherokees' descendants."

"I guess I'll have to return my gold fillings to the Cherokees' descendants," Alvin Autry said. "Would you like to extract them, Mr. Hicks?"

"You may keep them, Mr. Autry, as my gift to you,"

John said. "You'd lose your looks without them."

"Let me put it this way, Gretchen," Griggs said. "Do you propose to undo everything that's happened since the early nineteenth century? And why would you choose the early nineteenth century to restore? Why not the fifteenth century? Or the century the first native Americans crossed the Bering Straits and invaded this continent?"

"Maybe our forefathers stole stuff from the Indians, but we shouldn't suffer because of what they did," Red Wilker said.

"We are wealthy because of what they did," Gretchen said.

"I've got a proposal," Jon said. "All of us Witherstonians will return our two hundred and fifty thousand dollar inheritance from the late Francis Hearty Withers because Francis Hearty Withers's great, great grandfather, Hearty Withers, became rich from Cherokee gold and land and passed his money down through four generations. That's how those of us in this room got rich."

"Whoa, Jon."

"Let's not get carried away."

"I've already spent mine."

"Yes, yes, yes. Give the billion to Tayanita Village," John said.

"We can give our billion dollars to the Cherokee Nation, headquartered in Oklahoma," Jon said.

"I've changed my mind," John Hicks said.

"What about Doolittle, Chief McCoy?" Jorge asked. "Does Doolittle have to go back to anyone?"

"Doolittle stays."

"Woohoo!"

Lottie spoke for the first time. "Doolittle can't go back to the Congo where his relatives live because he doesn't speak their language and he doesn't fit into their culture. Doolittle is not the bird his grandfather was."

EPILOGUE

WWW.ONLINEWITHERSTON.COM

WITHERSTON ON THE WEB
Saturday, December 31, 2016

THE YEAR IN REVIEW
By Catherine Perry Soto, Reporter

Hempton Fairfield is serving a life sentence without parole in Georgia State Prison in Reidsville for the premeditated murder of Thom Rivers.

Petal Fairfield has filed for divorce. She lives in their home on Withers Hill.

Albert Heche is serving a fifteen-year sentence in the Federal Correctional Institution in Petersburg, Virginia, for theft of Native American artifacts from the Sunset Museum of Native American History in Washington, DC. His twin brother Alan Heche is serving a fourteen-year sentence in the Federal Correctional Institution in Englewood, Colorado, for theft of American antiques from Artifacts Americana in Denver.

Harlan Dannon is serving a three-year sentence at Carroll County Prison in Carrollton, Georgia, for burglary.

Chief Jake McCoy hired John Hicks as IT Security Officer for the Witherston Police Department.

Peg Marble published a new mystery titled Online Crime and moved to Witherston.

Dr. Michelle Plains Palacio succeeded Dr. David Guelph as chair of the Native American Artifacts Recovery Foundation's board of directors.

Carolyn Foster, director of the Cherokee-Witherston Museum, accepted a $100,000 grant from the Native American Artifacts Recovery Foundation for the acquisition of Cherokee artifacts.

In November, Rich Rather was re-elected mayor of Witherston, defeating Gretchen Green. Trevor Bennington, Jr., Smitty Green, Ruth Griggs, and Atsadi Moon were elected to the Town Council. Mr. Moon at age twenty-four is the youngest person ever elected to the Town Council.

Smitty Green retired from the editorship of Witherston on the Web. Reporter Catherine Perry Soto succeeded Smitty Green as editor. She hired Amadahy Henderson as reporter.

Doolittle Byrd, who lives with Dr. Charlotte Byrd, told his first joke: "Telephone for Doolittle."

Tayanita Village has a human population of twenty-one as of December 1, 2016. It is now on the Lumpkin County map. Witherston has a human population of 4,011. No telling what the burgeoning population of chickens is.

On Saturday, May 21, at 5:00 p.m., Catherine Perry and Dan Soto were married by Probate Judge Lauren Lodge in an outdoor ceremony at the home of Jon Finley and Gregory Bozeman. Catherine wore her grandmother Perry's wedding dress from 1950.

In attendance were Catherine's parents Wyatt and Margaret Perry, her paternal grandparents Branch and Helen Perry, her maternal grandparents Gary and Joan Beer, her aunt and uncle Adam and Eleanor Beer, her cousin Susan Riverbend, Dan's parents Diego and Elena Soto, his grandmother María Josefina Soto, his uncle and aunt Hugo and Patricia Soto, and their friends Charlotte Byrd, Paco and Mev Zapata, Jaime Zapata and Annie Jerden, Jorge Zapata and Mona Pattison, Gretchen Green and Neel Kingfisher, Jim and Lauren Lodge, Beau Lodge, Smitty and Jane Green, Rich and Rhonda Rather, Jake, Josephine, and Billy McCoy, Pete Senior and Bonnie Koslowsky, Pete Junior and Irene Koslowsky, Ricky and Angie Hefner, Scorch and Abby Ridge, Galilahi Sellers and John Hicks, Atohi and Ayita Pace, Moki Pace, Tony Lima, and Trevor Bennington, III.

Also at the wedding were Doolittle, Muddy, Renoir, Swift, Ama, Gandhi, Mighty, Sequoyah, Giuliani, Sassyass, Vincent Van Goat, Felicia, Felix, nine hens named Anna Ruby, Marilyn, Cher, Paddycakes, Rachel Madow, Ronda, Madeline Allbright, Bette, and Dixie Darling, a rooster named President Clinton, and a rescued horse named Arnold.

Tony Lima's Mountain Band performed the Herman's Hermits song, "There's a Kind of Hush All Over the World," before the wedding. Annie Jerden, accompanied by Jaime Arroyo on the guitar, sang Paul Stookey's "The Wedding Song" during the marriage ceremony and John Denver's "Annie's Song" after the vows.

The End

About the Author

Dr. Betty Jean Craige is Professor Emerita of Comparative Literature and Director Emerita of the Willson Center for Humanities and Arts at the University of Georgia. She has lived in Athens, Georgia, since 1973.

Craige is a teacher, scholar, translator, humorist, and writer. She has published eighteen books in the fields of literature, politics, art, history of ideas, and animal behavior, including *Conversations with Cosmo: At Home with an African Grey Parrot.*

Fairfield's Auction is the second novel in her Witherston Murder Mystery series published by Black Opal Books. Her first was *Downstream,* released by Black Opal Books in 2014.

CPSIA information can be obtained
at www.ICGtesting.com
Printed in the USA
LVOW04s1510040216
473701LV00020B/776/P